MW00942661

A Respite from Storms

Ashes of Luukessia, Volume Two

Robert J. Crane
with Michael Winstone

A Respite from Storms
Ashes of Luukessia, Volume Two
Robert J. Crane
with Michael Winstone
Copyright © 2018 Ostiagard Press
All Rights Reserved.

1st Edition

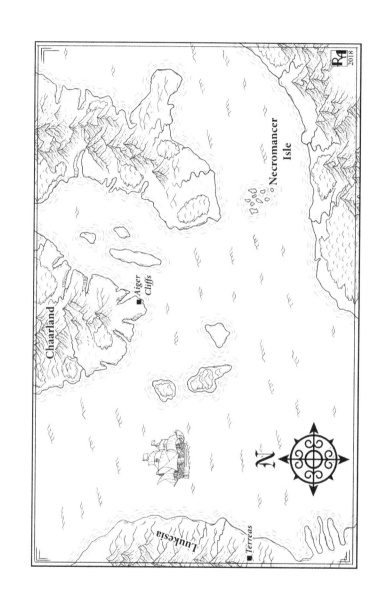

1

Luukessia burned.

Smoke and flame tarred the twilit sky. Winds had dragged the uppermost parts of the smoke tower sideways in an unholy streak, smearing it out like paint under a thumb.

The mountains that had once cradled Terreas drew the land to a gradual peak, off-center. They oughtn't to have been visible in the falling night, at least not as anything more than a dark, diagonal mark against a velvet blue sky. Yet a fire burned within that crescent range, a churning, molten flame that belched smog into the approaching darkness, illuminating the landscape in hellish shades of red and orange.

The land descended in a long slope that led to sandy white beaches, which in turn gave way to water, a liquid reflection of the sky, the ocean gently rising and falling with waves as if it breathed.

Upon that ocean rested a boat.

And upon its deck, shivering and sopping, Jasen crouched. He cradled Alixa, one-armed.

Dark-skinned men surrounded them in a rough half circle, looking down at them. Upper halves of their bodies swaddled in a cloth wrap that had been fashioned into tunics, their clothes were patterned, but dark: deep blues, twilight purple speckles, diamonds and lines and curlicues in midnight black. Their sleeves came only partway down their biceps, the muscle there corded and thick. Black leggings clung tight to calves and thighs that were powerfully strong.

Jasen's jaw chattered. He should be spent; a night without proper sleep had preceded them to here. A day on the run, his collision with hard, compacted earth at the beach as the cart broke, then treading water to keep himself afloat ... All of it had sucked every bit of energy it could from him. Not to mention everything they had lost ...

Now, a new threat—?

"Who are you?" he wheezed.

The dark-skinned men replied, or perhaps talked among themselves. A rising lilt to their voices sounded like questions, but Jasen could not understand the language they spoke. The consonant were harder and the vowels more guttural than the softer sounds of the Luukessian language.

He tried again, raising his voice. "Who are you? Where have you come from?" Only this, too, came out as a croak, lifting barely higher than his last call. A child could have drowned him out.

The men continued to speak. A handful eyed him, but their conversation was not directed to them any longer; they spoke back and forth between each other, their words and questions alien to Jasen's ears.

"What do we do?" Jasen muttered to Alixa.

She was shivering too. Bent low on knees, her hair stuck to her face, braids glued to the fabric of her dress. The ocean had washed away some but by no means all of the mud and grime that coated her skin and clothing, and grains of sand flecked her face where the sea hadn't touched.

She shook her head. "I don't know."

Scourgey whined, to Alixa's right. The hairless beast cowered as low as it would go against the wooden decking.

The men arrayed on the deck conversed—and then they parted, talk stifling. To both sides, Jasen saw, were decks raised above this one, to the front and rear of the ship. Though obscured by tall masts and by the men who'd pulled them from the sea, Jasen glimpsed lights through windows built into the deck. A door had opened, and through it came a man whose presence was imposing, strong—yet as he strode across the deck, he did not tower over any of his men. Indeed, several of the largest were a half head taller than him, built more powerfully than he, frames larger. They deferred to him nevertheless, quieting in his wake.

Dressed in a snugly tightened tunic fashioned of the same square of swaddling, patterned cloth, and trousers of banded crimson, his steps through the crowd were calm, measured, and strong. Cords of muscle stood out on his neck and forearms. Hair shorn short drew to a widow's peak above dark eyes flecked with light spots, like white pebbles embedded in earth.

He asked a question, or perhaps gave an order, to someone he passed, a shorter man with a thin strip of fabric tied around his forehead. Whatever he had said, the man responded, and the crimson-dressed man's eyes found their way to Jasen, Alixa, and Scourgey.

Jasen drew a suffocated breath.

These men were not friendly.

The crowd parted, and the man in crimson approached until he was maybe four feet shy of where Jasen and Alixa cowered.

"*Tanok-to?*" he said.

Jasen stared. Any words once in his throat had evaporated.

"*Cebrahna?*"

A man with a short beard fashioned into three braids with single beads at the end rattled off a quick flurry of incomprehensible syllables.

Jasen swallowed against the lump in his throat. His eyes cast about spastically, for—what? A weapon, was his first thought ... but he and Alixa were vastly outnumbered, and exhausted, so what hope did they have against new foes? Scourgey was their best chance, if these men grabbed out for him and Alixa. Yet Scourgey was whimpering like a kicked dog.

Jasen glanced rearward. Another five, six feet between him and Alixa, and the edge of the ship.

If it came to it ...

"Do you speak?" the man asked.

Jasen's heart skipped. Eyes bugging, he stared, mouth open.

Those were words he recognized, his language. Not perfectly formed; they were a little heavy on the consonants, and gravelly speech made it sound almost harsh. But they could communicate.

"Who are you?" Alixa asked, for Jasen still had not summoned back his voice.

The crimson-dressed man peered at her with stony, assessing eyes for a long time.

Then he said, "I am Shipmaster Burund."

Someone behind him said something, or asked; Burund answered in their language without looking away from Alixa. He spoke quicker in that one. Then he asked, "And what do you call yourself?"

"A-Alixa," she stammered.

"Alixa," he repeated: *Ah-lix-ah.*

His gaze turned back to Jasen.

Had he blinked yet? Even once?

"And you?" he asked.

A lump settled in Jasen's throat. He swallowed against it—*click.* "Jasen," he whispered; Burund's stare permitted no further volume.

"Jasen," Burund repeated.

Jasen nodded. And then, suddenly, he added, "Rabinn. My name is Jasen Rabinn." It was deathly important that Burund know, that all these men knew, whoever they were: Jasen was a Rabinn, still, and always.

"Jasen Rabinn," Burund said slowly. His lips rolled over the name. A little too much tooth showed as he spoke, like he drew back his mouth as if it would free the words more cleanly from his throat. "Alixa."

"Weltan," she put in.

"Alixa Weltan," Burund said.

More chatter from the men on deck, a few at once this time. Burund answered in staccato bursts, nary taking his eyes from Jasen and Alixa. Not one glance was spared for Scourgey. For that, Jasen was perhaps glad: the crippling effect of Burund's look would surely extract a more noisome, frightened clamor than her present mewling.

Jasen tugged Alixa's sodden sleeve.

"What do we do?" he mouthed.

Alixa shook her head: *I don't know.* Dark bags hung beneath her eyes. Though the night was dark, lit torches upon the deck, and that orange glow from the windows farther up, threw her pallor into stark relief. Wide eyes, a yellowish-white in this light, compounded the contrast. She looked ill, terrified, or perhaps both.

Burund snapped something—and Jasen and Alixa jerked back around to him.

He brought his attention to the children.

Forward a step.

Another.

Jasen's chest seized. He inched backward, fingers twisting into claws against the wood under his knees—

Burund knelt, down right to eye level.

Their gazes held—this dark-skinned man from across the sea, whose face was a mask of angles, whose body was thick with hard muscle, and whose eyes could bore a hole into the hardest stone; and Jasen Rabinn, whose body had given all it could give and still he asked more of it, whose home had been razed from the earth, and who, here, perhaps mere hours after escaping a shoreline of scourge, needed to fight for an empty survival again, survival he only wished for because that was what the living did: they fought to keep on living.

He prepared a clawed fist, to scratch and gouge.

Burund's lips parted.

"Hello," he said quietly, "Jasen Rabinn and Alixa Weltan. Welcome to my ship. We are friends."

Friends?

The word did not parse, getting stuck in the barely turning cogs of Jasen's mind.

"Who are you?" Alixa asked again.

He looked at her plainly. "Shipmaster Burund. And these are my crew."

"Where do you come from?"

"Many places."

"I hear we've visitors."

The voice came from behind. Burund turned to see, between another parting, a more elaborately dressed man, whose pea green tunic was fashioned into overlapping layers. The undersides were lined in dark, opposing colors; flashes of purple, orange, red.

His skin was a shade lighter than his comrades. He was longer-haired. Curly, it was arranged into what looked like tresses, one coming down each side of his head at the back. Beads held them together, wooden and gaudily painted, wider than Jasen's wrists. Middle age had crept in to him: the frail light-licked hairs starting their turn to grey in a few places. Crow's feet radiated from the corners of his eyes.

"Interesting piece of flotsam you've pulled out of the sea, Shipmaster," he said. He came to the fore. He stepped quicker than Burund had, his bootsteps clipped.

Reaching Burund's elbow, he fixed Alixa and Jasen with a smile that was miles too wide. "G'd evening, little ones." He bowed. "My, my. Did you want for a nighttime dip?" And then he threw his head back and laughed heartily, a great, heaving belly laugh, like it was the funniest joke he had ever heard in his life.

Jasen stared.

Alixa, on his right, stared too.

Shipmaster Burund's expression was difficult to read. Momentarily, he watched this new man sidelong, before resuming his intense stare at Jasen and Alixa.

"Are you thirsty?" he asked.

"Thirsty?" the other man hooted. "You just pulled them out of all the water they could ever dream of, Shipmaster!" And once more his head went back, and he bellowed a laugh to the darkening skies.

The ship rocked.

"Who—" Alixa began.

"Kuura," Burund introduced, looking up at the laughing man rather than pointing. "He is a mad man."

ROBERT J. CRANE

"Aye, well, now that is true." Kuura calmed immediately, looking somber and nodding.

Jasen stared.

All cognitive ability had left him now. All he could do was exist as a shell, watching through eyes a thousand miles away, as the evening grew steadily more …

"Unhinged," Kuura put in, as if reading Jasen's thoughts, and it jarred him into a jerky lurch that went ignored by Kuura and Burund both. "Deranged. A *loon*. What other words are there for it in Luukessian?" He pondered for only a second. "Not enough. Ah, but in Coricuanthian—we have a wonderful word," he said to Jasen earnestly. "*Bannock-tahhi*." He seemed not to speak the word with his mouth, but his entire face. "It means …"

Burund held up a hand. Kuura's lips stilled.

"Aye, well, I s'pose you've not the interest in hearing it at the moment."

"Forgive my first mate," said Burund to Jasen and Alixa. He added not what they should forgive Kuura for, precisely, and in his rundown and befuddled state, Jasen could not comprehend what Burund meant. So he settled for only a wide-eyed nod in reply.

Burund pivoted on his heel. It was the slightest of motions, yet simultaneously enough to swing him around from Jasen, allowing those deep, dark eyes to settle upon Alixa.

The intensity of his gaze had much the same effect on her as it did on Jasen, apparently, for Kuura tipped his chin at her and said, "You c'n stop shaking, girl. You're safe here."

"Wh-who are you?" The stammer quaked her body for a short moment. Then, as if remembering herself—or perhaps some reprimand from Shilara for her fear at some point in the days prior—she took a steadying breath, and inflated her little chest. Still little, but her shoulders squared. She could not oppose even the weakest of these men, yet the set of her frame dared them to think otherwise.

"Where have you come from?" she asked.

"Many places," Burund answered.

"You've said so before. Where exactly—"

"We sail from Arkaria."

Arkaria. The name rung a distant bell in Jasen's mind.

A full second later, he realized: that was what he'd heard people call the continent to the west. And these men hailed from its lands?

The mental fog that had slowed Jasen's comprehension had also removed him from the exchange occurring upon the deck right and in front of him. He tuned back in to the tail end of another question from Alixa: "… boat doing here?"

"Investigating," said Burund plainly.

Alixa's eyebrows twitched down. "Investigating what?"

Kuura squawked a laugh, distinctly birdlike this time. He clapped a hand over his mouth.

Someone asked him something in a consonant-heavy lilt. He answered it quickly, then said, "So sorry. What a mad question. Is your head fully connected to those shoulders?"

"Kuura," Burund said over his shoulder. And though his voice had barely changed from the somewhat simple tone he adopted, Jasen believed he could detect the slightest hint of warning.

If Jasen could pick it out already, Kuura's ears must be attuned to it, for he fell silent.

Burund swiveled carefully back toward Jasen and Alixa. Quiet, for long moments … only it was broken by the whimper of Scourgey, her claws scratching against the deck as they rattled back and forth with her fearful vibrating.

A wave broke against the ship's edge. The mainsail puffed out, filled with a breath of salty air. It tilted the ship sideways, carrying it farther out to sea.

Someone murmured. A few voices joined—agreeing, perhaps, or mumbling some assent to whatever had been said.

"We witnessed a cataclysm many miles from here," said Burund. His eyes moved between Jasen and Alixa in turn, smooth, slow. "The mountains glowed with fire, and the sky was streaked with smoke. You know this, yes?"

Alixa swallowed hard. She glanced to Jasen—and then back, behind and over the ship's edge, where Luukessia continued to shrink. The sky had faded down almost to black now, and much of the sea rendered invisible. That faint line of sandy white had faded out of sight … or maybe it had just receded so far as to be pressed invisibly thin, as the winds had picked up and already, in this short time, pulled the ship even farther out to sea. Why, Jasen could reach out and blot out the lands he had called home his whole life with one palm.

However dark the night grew, though, Jasen and Alixa would not lose sight of Luukessia. The cratered mountain—or the remainder of it, cleaved open—glowed with hot fire, a beacon that was impossible to miss.

Laying eyes on it hollowed Jasen's stomach, filled his mouth with bitter taste.

"We know it," said Alixa. "We just came from there."

Quiet.

When Jasen turned back, Burund was looking at them with wide eyes under low eyebrows, and a forehead full of lines.

Kuura's expression was not much different.

Someone on the deck asked a question.

When there was no answer, a volley of others followed.

Burund snapped a quick, two-syllable response.

The chatter ceased.

Burund shifted on his feet. Leaning forward, past Jasen—the boy was forgotten now, all but background—he brought himself to within some eight, ten inches of Alixa.

She swallowed again, the movement of her throat visible in the glow from the decks. Yet she held her ground.

"What did you say?" Burund asked.

"We came from there," said Alixa, breathy and fighting to clamp down on her nerves. "Luukessia."

Burund looked past her, to the light aglow in the distance. "You cannot have."

Jasen followed his gaze.

A tumult of fire burned. From here, it was but a blot; but it had streaked down the mountainside, buried Terreas, and in the intervening day was surely consuming yet more of Luukessia as it poured inexorably on.

"Nothing lives there," said Burund. "Nothing."

"Well," Jasen shook his head, just slightly, "we used to."

2

"Come," Burund said, rising.

"Come where?" asked Alixa. She clambered to her feet with ease; but when Jasen tried to do the same, he struggled, and fell hard onto a knee. All the air blew out of his lungs as though he'd taken a punch to it. He keeled over, slapping out a palm just in time to stop from impacting face first into the deck.

Alixa scrabbled for him. "Jasen!"

"I'm okay," he breathed, feeling anything but.

She hoisted him by one wrist, hooking it around her shoulder.

"I can do it," he wheezed—but even saying it, he was sure he couldn't. The well of energy once fueling him had run truly dry. Not even the faintest heat from dying coals kept him moving anymore.

"I've got you," Alixa said. "Let me help."

He did, maybe because he was too tired to argue the point, or maybe because if he didn't he would remain on the deck until he died there.

Rising was difficult, even with Alixa's help. She was not particularly strong, much of her power residing in her fingers from long hours weaving with Aunt Sidyera. Her legs held, though, and she helped Jasen rise to full height. Almost, anyway; she was shorter, and in any case he hadn't the strength to straighten his neck.

When he looked up to Burund, the captain regarded the cousins through a veil of suspicion.

Alixa cleared her throat. "What?" The faintest tremor.

"Your comrade," said Burund, meeting her gaze head on. "Is he sick?"

"No," Alixa answered. "Just tired. Our village—"

Burund muttered something to Kuura, who nodded. He regarded the children with his own peculiar expression, perhaps not suspicion,

9

but certainly a wariness, mixed—maybe—with pity.

The men on deck began to murmur too.

Burund retorted. The murmurs did not still. New speakers joined, louder, addressing the captain directly. A handful of them stood and stepped forward. Most loudly vocal, they illustrated whatever they were saying with wild gestures. Whatever Burund answered only made their gesticulation more manic.

One thrust a finger at Scourgey, speaking hard and fast.

Language was not a barrier now. Jasen could not know specifically what he was saying, but his tone communicated his mood well enough.

Perhaps these ebon-skinned men had encountered scourge too.

Perhaps they knew to fear them.

Burund answered, nodding once. Then, to Alixa: "I will summon our doctor to assess your friend. If he is sick, he cannot remain aboard."

Alixa's eyes widened. "But—"

Then men were pushing past her. Sinewy muscle flexed as they approached Scourgey. One carried a rope—another unsheathed a sword, curving gently and polished to reflect a perfect bar of orange light from the windows into the other decks.

"What are you—*no!*" Alixa shunted Jasen along, sideways, throwing the pair of them in front of Scourgey—who, at the sight of the men moving threateningly toward her, whimpered louder than ever, and thrust herself backward.

The man with the rope barked something at Alixa.

She held out an arm, blocking the scourge, but did not move. Her eyes blazed.

He barked something again—an instruction.

"What's he saying?" Jasen asked.

"He orders you to step aside," Kuura answered. Then he spoke to the man holding the rope, a more thickset fellow than most on board, with a thick leather strap wound about his forearm.

An answer came.

"The beast is dangerous," said Kuura to Alixa. "You should stand clear so Hamisi can deal with it."

"Scourgey is not dangerous! Scourgey saved us."

An eyebrow drifted up Burund's forehead. "Scourgey," he repeated.

"Yeh named it?" asked Kuura.

"*Her*, and yes, I named *her*." Alixa directed a fiery stare at Hamisi and widened her arms yet farther to block any sight of the scourge. Jasen was wobbled along and teetered precariously.

The stink of rot assailed his nose. Fear seemed to make it worse, that pervasive odor that clung to the scourge like an immoveable mist. If these people had never once encountered scourge in their life, and the sight did not put them off, Jasen could not imagine the smell was doing Scourgey any favors.

"Scourgey saved us," said Alixa. "I forbid you from harming her."

It was a ridiculous thing to say, Jasen thought, even in his fractionally composed state. A girl of Alixa's stature could not forbid anything against such a collection of adult men, whose bodies were lean, sculpted with the muscle of constant physical exertion.

Yet there was a pause. Kuura exchanged a look with Burund.

Chatter on the deck. Raised voices. The collection of sailors who had approached to deal with Scourgey began to talk again, loud and fierce. Hamisi spoke over all of them. Though he stared down Alixa, he appeared to be speaking to Burund, for he interjected harshly, in short bursts, which Hamisi quickly answered with more hard-sounding language.

"What's happening?" Alixa asked Kuura.

Kuura appeared uneasy. He glanced to Burund. The captain paid him no heed. And so he answered, "They are discussing what to do with it."

"*Her*," said Alixa. "And they're not *doing* anything."

Kuura said something in the native language of the boat-dwellers. A few voices spoke hurriedly.

"Is it a pet?" he asked Alixa.

"*She*," she began, putting as much emphasis on the word as she possibly could, "is a friend. She saved us—plenty of times. None of them are touching her."

A fragmentary thought came to Jasen as he leaned there against her, the wall obscuring this beast, a hill that Alixa seemed to have chosen to die on. If Burund's men did wish to harm Scourgey, what did that mean for him and Alixa? She would not let them … so would they be cast out to sea again, lobbed overboard?

Then again, what had Burund said about an doctor? Something about assessing Jasen for illness. And if he were found to be diseased …

Kuura was speaking. "… believe it is a dead thing," he told Alixa. "They wish for it to be cast off the ship."

"Scourgey isn't dead."

Scourgey whined dramatically, as if to illustrate.

"Scourgey is alive, and just as deserving of remaining alive as …"

"To keep it here is to invite death upon us," said Kuura.

"Well, she has been keeping us company for days, and we're still alive! Surely you don't believe that."

Kuura shrugged. "It isn't about what I believe. It is what Burund believes."

Alixa turned her attention to the captain. "Please listen to me. This creature saved our lives. She is a friend."

Burund did not look round from addressing the men on deck. Nor did he stop to acknowledge Alixa.

She huffed, and turned to Kuura. "I'm not lying to you."

Kuura tugged his lips to the side. He spoke again, to the men arranged on the deck.

Hamisi's nostrils flared. He gripped the rope tighter. One threatening step forward, and—

Burund snapped again, a quick string of syllables. Whatever he said, it did not silence Hamisi, for he retorted and again resumed a back and forth with the captain. It did, however, still him; he approached no farther, even dropping back a step. After maybe the fifth interjection from the captain, his hard features began to soften into a look of disbelief. At the next, he turned to Burund, attention off Alixa—or, more likely, the scourge behind her.

"What's going on?" Jasen asked.

"Burund has listened," said Kuura slowly. He appeared to still be listening to the conversation happening alongside him, head cocked slightly to one side, the way a dog lifted an ear for its master with offal from the butcher. "He is … willing to allow this … Scourgey … to be housed below decks … in one of our cages."

"Cages?" Alixa asked, apparently bypassing the good news entirely. "Scourgey isn't some wild beast who can just be locked up—"

There was an outcry on the deck then, loud enough to silence Alixa. Then it, too, was silenced as a great gust of wind blew. The sails whipped, filling and then dragging the boat across the frigid, black waters. Waves broke against its prow.

No stars winked overhead; the scattering that Jasen had seen at the beginning of this night had vanished. Blotted out by the smoke dirtying the sky from Luukessia? Outshone by the lamps on deck?

Another gust shook the ship. Something rattled above, and Jasen squinted up and into the darkness. Posts crossed the mast at perpendicular angles. Rope and chain hung. A coil of silver whipped, clanking wood.

"A storm approaches," said Kuura warily. "We should rally ourselves inside, Captain." Why he didn't say it in their native language, Jasen did not know. Politeness, perhaps, keeping the children in the loop.

Burund nodded. Turning to Alixa, he said, "As you vouch for it, I will allow this creature upon my ship."

She loosed a breath she must have been holding. "Thank you."

"But you must lead it. I have compromised with my men. If it is unwilling to go, it will be killed and thrown overboard."

Alixa tensed. But she set her jaw, inclined her head. "She will follow."

"I will not have that thing wandering my ship," Burund said. Then he spoke to his crew, loud and firm, so that none would speak over the top of him. Thirty seconds, the diatribe lasted; then he spun on his heel and returned to the confines of the ship.

The crew began a process of disbanding. Awkwardly, some of them, and Hamisi most of all. He stared, halfway between morose and thunderstruck, at Alixa and Jasen. Rope hung limp between his fingers, apparently robbed of its own integrity too.

Kuura said something to him. Whatever it was caused Hamisi to stalk off, the other would-be killers of Scourgey in his wake. Into the ship they went, Hamisi slamming the door.

Kuura looked at Jasen and Alixa, momentarily awkward. Then he hooked a thumb in the overflowing material of his tunic, and bobbed on his tiptoes, up and down, midriff swaying back to front. "The captain called them a bunch of wet old women," he said cheerily.

Alixa bore an unreadable expression. "And what is wrong with being a woman?"

"Ask the ones the captain offended," said Kuura. "This way." He waved and led them toward the door into the rear upper deck—not the way Hamisi and friends had gone, fortunately.

Alixa didn't move. Her mouth tightened just a fraction. "Or ask the captain himself," she murmured to herself.

Not all of the men upon the top deck had disbanded. A couple were presently pulling at ropes affixed to the mainsail. It blustered in another forceful gust of wind. The men braced. They stayed put, somehow. Jasen was pushed though, and he had to clutch tight around Alixa's neck to keep himself from toppling over.

She grimaced, tamping down a choked cough.

"Come," Kuura called, when the wind's whistle had died down. He waited beside the deck's door, hands gripped in front of him. If the blast of air had dislodged him from his place, or even disturbed more than the hairs on his head and the loose fabric of his clothing, he did not show it.

"Let's go then," Alixa mumbled. Wheeling about, she extended her free hand to Scourgey—

Who looked positively depressed. Once such a fearsome, frightening beast, she was more and more the sad, sorry dog that Jasen increasingly came to see her as. A quivering, misshapen wreck, she shuddered with great, racking spasms. Those coal-lump eyes, usually empty, tonight seemed to be filled to brimming with pure sadness. Her sporadic clumps of wiry hair were plastered down where they'd allow it. A sheen of water still clung to her, intensifying the stink of rottenness coming off of her. Jasen felt sorry for anyone downwind of Scourgey when the approaching storm sent another gust across the ocean waves—which was him and Alixa, this moment.

Jasen leaned into the wind.

A spray of seawater and foam erupted against the side of the ship and rained down upon them. It was cold now. Night fallen, the day's warmth had been stripped away.

Alixa bowed toward Scourgey, stroking the side of her face gently. "I need you to come with us, okay? Just for now."

Scourgey made no move. Her capacity to understand was a constant question in Jasen's mind. Many moments on this trip, he had believed she understand what was said around her, but now she was just a terrified animal, cringing and witless.

Alixa wrapped a hand around Scourgey's front leg, just below the shoulder joint. She pulled.

Scourgey didn't move, except to whine even more loudly.

"Please move," Alixa said.

She tried again.

Scourgey wailed. She pulled backward, loosing herself from Alixa's hold.

"Come on!" Alixa snapped her fingers around again. She pulled—

Scourgey quaked. Her legs shook with great force. Claws rattled on the deck, their clacks muted by the puddled water soaking into the wood.

Someone on deck shouted something—one of the men pulling at ropes. Jasen turned back, expecting to see him calling to his shipmate; but he looked to Alixa, and Scourgey, pointed a finger.

Kuura piped up. "If it ain't movin', Captain Burund said—"

"She'll move," called Alixa. Then, to Jasen: "*Help me.*" Desperation turned her words into a vicious whisper.

"I don't think I—"

"*Please.*"

That same desperation had crept into her eyes too. Hers was the wild-eyed look of a cornered thing.

Jasen could do nothing but oblige her. "Okay," he said, reaching his own free hand for Scourgey's limb, "I'll try."

"Thank you."

"Sorry, Scourgey," Jasen whispered to her. "But you need to come with us."

They pulled. Scourgey held firm, but yowled.

Kuura: "If it's not tame enough—"

"*She'll move.*" Alixa, again. Hard, under her breath: "Would you just stop messing around?" She pulled and pulled—and then she let go of Jasen so she could wrap both hands about Scourgey's leg, tugging. Scourgey was stronger. Jasen thought for a moment that she might have slid a fraction of an inch on the wet deck, then decided that movement was an illusion and that she was simply leaning forward a bit more than she had.

Jasen gripped her, taking a deep breath.

Then he braced, the way the men adjusting the mainsail had, and pulled …

Only he had no strength. He couldn't move a child, let alone the hulking brute that was a scourge. His yank was feeble, barely a contribution.

Now both the men working the sail were shouting.

A glance backward.

Pointing, too.

Kuura began to step for Jasen and Alixa again—and Scourgey, Scourgey who had saved them but who Jasen and Alixa could not seem to save in return.

His mouth opened—

As if sensing it, Alixa's mounting frustration exploded—

"*Would you just MOVE?*"

And that did it. Scourgey's frantic noise built to a last crescendo and then slipped into a softer, constant wheezed squeal. She moved, though, coming unwillingly, but coming nevertheless. After the first few steps, Jasen was able to relinquish his hold; Alixa too, except for one palm she kept rested on Scourgey's ribs.

Her head twisted relentlessly as Alixa brought her across the deck, to Kuura.

More than a handful of sailors kept their own wary watch.

Jasen stumbled just a half-step behind.

Kuura had eyes on Scourgey, and Alixa. His mouth turned down at one side, and his eyebrows were crooked.

"Well then," he said after a moment, "follow me. Careful now."

He opened the door leading into the rear deck—there were terms for these, Jasen thought out of nowhere, but he couldn't grasp them; either the memory itself had been overwritten, only the memory of having had it remaining, or his fatigue was causing him to fail at finding it.

The entryway was initially wide. The overall space was small though, Jasen thought: like a squat loaf turned on its side, only a few steps in it ended in a wooden wall held erect by thick beams, almost the width of the masts. Two lanterns hung upon a post each. Liquid pooled in the bottom in a separate compartment to a lit wick, in the upper, wider chamber. This part was bulblike and round, and dirtied by smoke. A hole had been wiped clean in both, probably with a cloth. The cleaning was imprecise, and finger marks remained.

On the right was a door to what Jasen supposed must be crew quarters. It was closed.

"This way," said Kuura, gesturing left. A staircase stood there, descending a level.

Jasen peered at it. All dark wood, and thrown into crisscrossing shadows by the lanterns up here, another midway down the steps, and surely more in the level beneath. The steps were cramped—wide, offering enough room for two men side by side to walk, but only spacious enough for half of a foot to be placed upon them. Six steps down, where the lantern hung, was a little landing. There, the stairs twisted ninety degrees, leading toward the front of the ship.

There was no rail of any sort here, to protect someone from going over. Jasen wondered how many times the sea had caught a man unprepared, and sent him careening over the ledge.

"Bring your ... pet," Kuura finished. His voice lifted, angling for the answer to his half question. Then he commenced for the stairs, moving down the first two. On the third, after neither Jasen nor Alixa took a step, he looked back and said, "C'mon then?"

"Where are we going?" Alixa asked.

"To the hold."

The word "mizzenmast" popped suddenly into Jasen's head, unbidden. He frowned, then discarded it—certainly not the name he had been looking for.

"The hold," said Alixa. "Right." She took a breath. "Where your cages are?"

Scourgey whined, as if she understood.

Looked like everyone's cognition was just coming back to life now.

"Nothing to fear from 'em," said Kuura. "The people we keep in 'em won't mind a spot of c'mpany."

Alixa's eyes widened to great, pearly orbs. Her eyebrows shot so far up her forehead that they threatened to disappear into the matted remnants of her fringe, straggly and sticking out to either side of her face where she'd wiped it out of her eyes, and water had held it in position.

Kuura burst into a belly laugh again. He clutched his stomach, and leaned back.

"Hoo! You should've seen your face, girl." He slapped a knee, and grinned. "We've no people in our cages. Just animals. Come on, you'll see for yourself." And down he went, without waiting for them to follow.

Alixa exchanged a look with Jasen, eyes still as wide as they could go.

Her mouth moved to form words, but her throat would not offer any.

Jasen just nodded in understanding.

Burund had been right: this Kuura was mad.

"Keep up!" Kuura called from a floor below.

Alixa and Jasen followed, Jasen taking up the rear, behind Scourgey, who went unhappily. Alixa's feet fumbled on the steps, but she figured them out by the middle landing. Scourgey, on the other hand, never seemed to figure the things out. Possibly that came down in part to her nerves; probably, Jasen figured, it was her awkward body shape, not apparently designed to have finesse in any area at all, with that unnaturally curved spine.

Twelve steps in all led down to the next deck. The ceiling was low—but the space itself was wide open. Only beams carved it. Otherwise, the full floor could be walked. Metal contraptions, bulky things with long, cylindrical extrusions laid horizontal across the top, were placed at even intervals ahead of portholes to either side of the ship, presently closed. Racks were affixed to the walls in between the contraptions. Dark balls, also apparently metal, rested upon the lower shelves.

Jasen and Alixa peered at them curiously. But Kuura was already waving them for the next staircase down, descending it with scarcely a look at this open, almost cavernous chamber.

Jasen followed after Alixa and Scourgey. He paused for a moment before descending, eyeing the room one last time. Did it run the full length of the ship? And what was the burnt smell, just at the edges of his senses?

The next floor was fourteen steps down. The ceiling was higher here. Not open this time, the staircase terminated in a four-way junction: steps leading up and down, then a corridor moving straight ahead, and another, shorter one to the left. Quarters were a bit tighter here, after the steps; the hallways were just wider than a single person. Anyone passing in opposite directions would need to turn side on to slip by each other.

"Down again," said Kuura, and already his head was disappearing into the next hole. "Last flight, I promise."

Alixa shared an uneasy glance with Jasen. Yet she followed, gently coaxing Scourgey along. Softly whining, the scourge obeyed, claws skittering against the wooden steps.

Down Jasen went too.

The hold must be right at the bottom of the ship, because no further stairs led down at the bottom, at least as far as he could see. It was a dimly lit place; the lanterns were fewer, spread more widely.

A smell of manure and ammonia—piss—wafted to Jasen.

Outside of a clean halo, sodden straw was trodden throughout the walking space cut between cages. Most of them were small, and a full half empty. Farther back, though, Jasen glimpsed cages the size of a cow—estimated by the fact that he did, indeed, see a cow grazing upon a mound of dried grass in one, flicking its ears distractedly.

Alixa screwed up her face, plugged her nose. "This is awful."

"Be kind, now," said Kuura. "They might think the same of your stink, now you're down here." He threw his head back and hooted.

Jasen stared.

When he'd calmed sufficiently, Kuura said, "This way, please, this way." And he went off down a central aisle between the cages, not appearing to care remotely about the scat and urine that met the soles of his boots.

The animals in the cages were a mix of the mundane and the peculiar. Three short cages in a row housed pigs, the third a sow who lay on her side while piglets suckled. But then, separated by a single empty cage, Jasen locked eyes with a strange creature whose face and body were both decidedly humanlike. Covered in downy fur, it was a small thing, maybe eighteen inches tall. Its limbs appeared too long for it. It had been reaching through a gap in its cage toward the nursing pig, unsuccessfully—it would need a longer arm by a good twelve inches at least for that—but as Kuura walked by, it stopped, and stared. Its eyes were small, very dark. They shifted toward Alixa, and Jasen; then they landed on Scourgey. It cocked its head, then bared stubby little fangs and hissed ... and then decided there was no threat after all, and resumed trying to reach for the pig.

A pair of colorful birds occupied a cage hanging from a crossbeam. Kuura ducked underneath it. Alixa hesitated; the birds, asleep now, had covered the passageway in a half-crusted spatter of droppings.

Kuura looked back at her. His lips parted, showing that wide grin again, with too many teeth. "Yeh'll have worse'n that on your shoes before long. It won't harm you, so come on."

"It's disgusting," said Alixa. "Haven't you got any fresh straw? You're supposed to clean animals out every d—"

Kuura bellowed a chuckle. "And how d'you suppose we do that?" Turning serious: "We're at sea, Alixa. Everythin' we carry's gotta fit inside these walls. A month's supply of daily straw'd be a whole other vessel. Do you see?"

Alixa harrumphed.

Kuura waved a hand, turning and resuming. "It's just a bit farther. Step wide if yeh have to."

Begrudgingly, Alixa followed. She did as Kuura suggested, stretching her legs out as far as possible to avoid the birds' droppings. Scourgey minded less, traipsing through it. And Jasen, figuring that his boots were coated now with a film of urine and feces and decaying hay anyway, gave the pile only a slight berth as he passed.

"Here," said Kuura. He stopped right near the end of the aisle, where it turned a right angle and ran alongside more boxy cages. He patted one that came to chest height, separated from its occupied neighbors—a bull on the left, and what Jasen could only describe as a ball of spikes on short stubby legs on the right—by more empties.

Alixa turned her nose up at it. "There's barely enough room in there for Scourgey to turn. And there's no straw!"

"Never been on a ship before, have you? Space is a luxury, one we don't have a lot of. Anyway: a big wave hits us, you want your … thing there to have all the room in the world to walk about? Cages built to fit, the animal can travel a foot, two at the most, before it's stopped—no *splat.*" Kuura clapped his hands together for emphasis. "Now coax it in there, and I'll bolt the door."

Alixa looked sad. Bowing to Scourgey, she said, "I need you to go into this cage, okay? It's not for long …"

Scourgey whimpered.

A door was open at the front of the cage, with a bolting lock on. Alixa pointed into it, looking at Scourgey with her best kind face. It didn't quite hit the mark: Jasen thought she looked closer to heartbroken.

Scourgey obeyed. She walked inside slowly, claws clicking on wood. Fully inside, she turned around in a small circle—a very small one; she really *didn't* have a lot of room to move, at least to left and right—and then looked sadly back out at them. Her mouth hung open. Her black tongue lolled.

She whined one last little whine, and went silent.

Kuura snapped the cage door closed. He bolted it. Then he slipped a thicker lock around it, clicking it closed. A curved bar of metal prevented the bolt from being undone.

"Someone'll be by to refresh the straw in the morning," said Kuura. "Though, if you want that pet of yours to have any, you might want to do it yourself. Hold doesn't smell very fresh at the best of times, but that thing kicks up a real nasty stink. I dread to imagine the smell when it farts." And he hooted again. The birds jerked at the disturbance and rearranged their wings. "Say your goodbye, but be quick. I'll be waitin' on the stairs to take you to your room."

"Surprised they're not giving us a *cage* to sleep in," Alixa grumbled under her breath.

"Alixa," Jasen warned.

She glanced at him, then pursed her lips, shook her head. Then, leaning down to Scourgey—not onto her knees, for urine had soaked into these planks underfoot too—she reached through the bars. Fingers gripping each side of Scourgey's miserable face, she said sadly, "I'm sorry about this. We'll be back for you soon. I'm so sorry."

"Waitin'!" hollered Kuura.

Alixa swiped a hand across her eyes. They were dry, but going just the slightest bit pink. "I'm coming!" she growled in reply.

To Scourgey: "We're not going far, I promise."

"It'll be here tomorrow," Kuura called. "This ain't some final farewell you're giving it. Come on, now; my nose c'n only take this stench for so long."

"We'll be just upstairs …"

"Alixa," Jasen started.

"I promise, not far. And—and I'm s—"

"Really." Kuura again, and now he was beginning to sound annoyed. "If you think I *like* the smell of dung, yeh're sadly mistaken."

"*Coming!*" Alixa belted. Jasen flinched back—as did Scourgey.

"Sorry," she said.

"Alixa," Jasen whispered. He gently pulled at her wrist. "We should go."

She looked at him now like she might cry properly. A tremble had taken hold of her bottom lip. But then she clamped down on it and nodded, setting her mouth into a line. She said one last, "See you soon," to Scourgey, and then set off at a stride back the way they'd come. The downy thing with long arms tried to grab at her as she passed, but she barely looked back at it.

"Thank you," said Kuura, "for your swiftness." He hooted again, grinning like a maniac. "Up." And he led.

The floor above the hold was a maze of cabins, not very navigable at all. At least, that was how it seemed to Jasen. Now, he wondered how an outsider might make their way around Terreas. If you didn't know those pathways and the routes throughout the village, you'd loop back on yourself plenty, getting nowhere, or finding a destination only by chance.

He'd never thought of it before, because, well, he knew *only* those roads, same as everyone in the village.

The same was probably true of the people on this boat.

Kuura brought them to a small cabin, tucked away to one side. The door was not very wide. He opened it without a key, pushed it open—

A wave must have broken against the boat's edge, for the world canted suddenly to one side. Alixa and Kuura held firm, Kuura barely moving whereas Alixa needed to brace against the wall; but Jasen had no such luck. He staggered into the door, which mercifully yawned wide for him under the pull of gravity momentarily coming from the back wall. His shins banged a low bed with a hard frame, and he pitched forward, landing hard in a pile of folded—and terribly thin—bedding.

Kuura laughed. "Keen one."

Alixa was behind him, helping him up. "Are you okay?"

"Fine," he mumbled. But there would be bruises, big ones, tomorrow, and walking for the next week was not going to be pleasant.

Then again, there were no longer very many places to walk *to*.

"Yeh'll have to share, I'm afraid," said Kuura, nodding at the bed. "Cabin's only kitted out for the one … don't have many sharers, of course. Might be different when we pull into port; once or a twice a lady's wanted to see the inside of a ship, and a hopeful sailor's brought her back here." He leaned forward, adding in a conspiratorial tone that was no quieter than a moment ago, "Watch out for Odo. He'll bring aboard anything he can lay 'is hands on. Big or small … male, if it's a dry port." And he guffawed, showing plenty of teeth. "I'll see what the captain wants done with yeh. Food, probably, but cook's shut down for the night, so yeh might be waitin' a little, maybe till morning." Pointing to Jasen: "Doctor for you, when he pulls his fingers out." Another hearty laugh.

He clutched the door handle and pulled it to. Then he reached in and groped for the bolt running along its rear side.

"Close this, unless yeh want ol' Webster tryna mount yeh in the night."

Alixa looked frightened.

"I'm talkin' to him, not you."

He rumbled laughter again, and then pulled the door closed.

Barely before the sound of bootsteps took him far did Alixa slam the bolt into place.

"We are not opening this."

Jasen nodded. Fine by him.

Without Kuura here, he could take in the cabin.

There was not a lot of it to absorb. The bed was low to the ground, on a frame that was much thicker than the thin mattress laid atop it. A porthole looked out to blackness, a greasy film clinging to it.

A lamp hung on the wall, lit but low. A case sat at the foot of the bed. Jasen did not care to open it just yet. He expected, when he did, that he would find it empty anyway.

And that was all.

This musty-smelling room, with its claustrophobically close walls, and threadbare, too-small bed—

This was their home, now.

Jasen shook the thought loose. Not home. No place would be home again. That had been Terreas, in his house, with his father— and, for a long time, but a long time ago, his mother too.

Not this ship. Not even if he rode it till the end of his days.

Alixa settled on the bed, resting against the wall.

Jasen fell down beside her and leaned back against the opposite one.

She drew her knees to her chest, held them close. "It'll be a tight squeeze."

Jasen nodded. He hadn't the strength for words.

"We'll top and tail it," said Alixa, "one pillow each end. That okay?"

It was fine.

They were quiet. But the boat was not. People moved, ceaselessly. Snippets of conversation could be overheard, all of it in that foreign language. Waves broke against the hull, and now Jasen and Alixa were holding still, it was difficult to deny the somewhat nauseating sway of the vessel. If a storm was building outside, as Kuura had said, Jasen did not believe it would take long to break; the movements of the boat were growing stronger and increasingly more violent.

With no light, it was hard to tell how much time passed, but at some point, Alixa started to cry. She did not sob, and her eyes were barely wet, but every few minutes a solitary tear trickled down her cheeks. She rubbed it away with a knuckle.

"We're the last of our families."

She said it very quietly, her voice low. But it was enough to drag Jasen's attention to her, for him to meet her gaze head on.

She was sad—resigned.

"We are the last of our village. The last of the Syloreans. The last …" She stopped and steeled herself with a heavy breath. "The last of the Luukessians," she finished. Her voice was somber yet steady.

"The chain of all our ancestors," she said softly, "of the entire land … it ends with us."

She lapsed into silence then, staring at nothing.

Eventually, she lay down, silently bundling one of the blankets into the best possible approximation of a pillow.

The last thing Alixa murmured was, "I shouted at Scourgey." She shook her head very slightly, just once. Not long afterwards, she fell asleep.

For all his exhaustion, Jasen could not follow. Despite his fatigue, his brain kept whirring, whirring away at one thought, over and over.

Alixa was right. They *were* the last of their people.

Everything they had ever known, everyone they had ever loved—it had all been wiped out.

And the cause? The name echoed relentlessly.

Baraghosa.

With each reverberation, it grew louder. And the fires burning in Jasen's heart grew hotter, flames licking higher and higher.

His hands shook. He clasped his sodden trousers lest their movement wake Alixa, but still the fever consumed him, and grew stronger.

Baraghosa.

Jasen's lips were a pencil-thin line. Low eyebrows drew lines on his forehead above wild eyes, staring blankly into a far-off infinity.

Baraghosa.

He had destroyed everything.

There was only one thing for it, Jasen thought as he curled his hand into a tight fist.

Jasen would destroy *him*.

3

Jasen was woken by the sound of knocking.

He opened bleary eyes.

Alixa sat on the bed, knees tucked in close to her chin. She'd been awake for some time, maybe waiting for him; she looked at him as he lifted his head and raised a frail smile. "Hello."

Jasen made a grunting noise.

"It's morning," said Alixa.

True enough, the view from the porthole was two shades of blue: a deep blue, crested with bars of foam, and the pale color of sky. No cloud marred it, at least in the abridged view that Jasen could see; it appeared to be a nice day, just past dawn, last night's storm nothing but a memory.

Then he remembered that Terreas was gone, his father and aunt and uncle and cousins with it, and the possibility of any nice day ever again evaporated.

"And someone's at the door," Alixa added.

Three distinct knocks. The door rattled. It wasn't seated properly in the frame.

"Rise and *shine*," called Kuura, lengthening that last word. With his accent, it did not sound particularly natural. "Can't sleep in all day."

Jasen would have liked to try. Between the ship's lurching and rolling and his fevered dreams of revenge, he had gotten little rest.

Kuura thumped the door again. He said something in his native language, four or five words in quick succession. Irritation was creeping in now, it sounded like. He knocked again, harder. "How deep do you kids sleep? Anyone would think—"

Alixa had hopped off the bed. Now she pulled back the bolt, and threw the door open.

Kuura stopped mid-sentence. He looked down at her a peculiar

24

expression on his face—the faintest trace of amusement, maybe— then he let his arm drop and his fist uncurl. A over-wide smile spread across his face.

"Good morning," he said cheerily, all hints of annoyance gone. "So nice of you to answer the door. And so sorry if I woke you!" He cackled hard for a solid five seconds before cutting off abruptly and resuming speaking. "I've come to take you to breakfast, if you are hungry. And to the doctor."

He was unaccompanied, but he turned his head to the side and barked a word that sounded like "medley."

Another man appeared. He was short but bulky. His head was shaved. Perhaps he'd been joking with someone down the hall, for he waved someone off with a grin as he arrived in front of Jasen and Alixa's cabin.

When he looked at them, Jasen saw his eyes were different colors: left green, right brown.

"Medleigh will observe you for illness," Kuura said to Jasen. Then he spoke to Medleigh. A couple of sentences were exchanged between them, then Kuura said, "He will take good care of you. I will be back shortly."

Medleigh came into the room and pointed at the bed. He said a word Jasen did not understand, but which he took to mean "sit." He obliged, and Medleigh commenced a brief physical exam. It wasn't much like visiting the village doctor back in Terreas. The language barrier was a problem, for a start. Now and again, Medleigh would say something, and look at Jasen as if expecting an answer. Jasen's only answer was a blank look.

He wished Kuura were here.

Kuura did return some five minutes later. Medleigh was assessing Jasen's head—Jasen thought. Each side was clamped in a painful grip, and Medleigh rotated it back and forth with sharp motions. Each sent a jolt of pain through Jasen's neck.

"Stop," he said.

Kuura grinned. "He is quite the doctor."

"It hurts," Jasen grunted.

Kuura let Jasen's manhandling continue for a few long seconds more, then spoke to Medleigh. It must've been an instruction to cease, for Medleigh did, stepping away. He wiped his hands on his tunic and began conversing with Kuura in a mostly one-sided conversation, him the informer and Kuura the informee. Mostly he looked at Jasen while he talked, punctuating occasionally with a thrust of a finger at him.

When he was finished, Kuura said to Jasen, "Yeh're diseased, boy."

If he hadn't been fully awoken by Medleigh's assault, that did it. Wide-eyed, Jasen exchanged a frantic look with Alixa. "Wh-what?"

Then Kuura bellowed with laughter, so intensely he clutched his stomach with one hand and braced against the door frame with another.

When his rumbling had decreased to a low, but continuing, chuckle, Kuura wiped a tear from his eyes. "Oh, I got you good. You should have seen the look on your face."

"Uh …"

"You are not diseased, Jasen. Medleigh has given you a clean bill of health."

Jasen blinked in a daze. He glanced to Alixa.

"All that talk …" she began, "just to say that … Jasen is fine?"

"Oh, no. That did not take long. He was questioning your brains for sleeping in your wet clothes! Did neither of you look in your trunk?"

Another exchanged look between Jasen and Alixa. "Err …"

Kuura laughed and stepped through. He thrust open the lid of the crate at the foot of the bed—and there, in the bottom, were changes of clothes. Doubtful they were put in here specially—but they were *in* here. Which made Jasen feel stupid … as well as still damp.

"Um," said Alixa, peering into the chest, "thank you."

"Get dressed, and I will take you to eat," said Kuura. "I'll wait outside."

"Me too," said Jasen quickly, and he hurried out.

"Thanks," said Alixa. She closed the door behind him and bolted it.

Jasen waited. Kuura conversed with Medleigh, leaving Jasen out—though Jasen could hardly blame him; translating back and forth must get frustrating in short order. Jasen just leaned against the wall, hands in pockets, waiting for Alixa to open the door again. A couple of sailors went past, but none of them said anything, gracing him only with suspicious looks.

When Alixa unbolted the door, her old clothes were gone. In their place she wore the same garb as these sailors: a richly patterned, deep blue tunic, which was oversized on her small frame and so wrapped her much more thickly than any of the men under Burund's command, and black trousers. Those, too, came up very large on her, and had to be fastened with a belt.

Kuura laughed. "You really are—what do your people say? A fish out of water."

Alixa's lips were a thin line. "I gave you the bigger pair. Sorry if they're a bit wet …"

He went in and closed the door, locked it. As promised, another set of clothes lay out for Jasen. Slightly crumpled—and slightly damp inside—he found himself dwarfed in them. He assumed they had been cleaned prior to being left in this box, but whoever had done it had not done the best job; they smelled, a ghostly trace of animal clinging to the fibers.

His old clothes, he placed in a pile in the corner of the room, with Alixa's.

Medleigh had gone when Jasen opened the door again. Alixa was silent, hands gripped in front of her. Kuura whistled. He'd been watching her, at least when the door came open; then he turned to Jasen and beamed, with far too many teeth on show.

"Now then," he said, clipping the vowels in both words in that way he kept doing, "why don't you come to the mess hall and eat, and I will tell you about where you find yourselves."

The mess hall was maybe midway along this deck, corridors to either end depositing into it such that if you wanted to travel from a fore to aft cabin—more terms slowly coming back to Jasen from storybooks—you would need to pass through the mess hall.

There were six tables in all, with benches. Everything was affixed with thick steel screws—smart planning, if last night's storm was anything to go by. A strong enough wave could send the tables flying. And although *these* men, musclebound as they were, might not fare poorly under the impact, someone of Jasen's build would be smashed to a pulp.

Five of the six tables were empty. A lone man occupied the last, someone Jasen recognized from last night. He puzzled for a moment as he locked eyes with the sailor, scooping something hard and dry out of a bowl. Then he remembered: he was one of the two battling with the sail when Alixa had to goad Scourgey into following inside.

Kuura said something to him. The man with the bowl looked stony, answering with a single word, as he did to Kuura's next remark. Monosyllabic though his reply was, it elicited a laugh from Kuura.

There again, damn near everything elicited laughter from Kuura.

Kuura had Alixa and Jasen settle on one side of a table. He dropped himself heavily opposite. Hands on wood, fingers spread against its grain, he appraised them both with a cheery look.

"Right then. Yer breakfast."

He dug into a side pouch, apparently tucked beneath the ridiculous folds of his tunic. Deep green, almost black, the pouch was scaly and opened to a square of fabric. Kuura unwrapped it on the table.

Inside were sticks of something very dark in color, knobbly and uneven. Beside them:

"Crackers?" asked Jasen, peering.

"Never seen someone get excited over those before," said Kuura. "Daresay I won't again. Yeh're welcome to 'em, if Alixa don't want any."

Alixa pointed at the dark sticks. "What are those?"

"Biltong."

Blank looks.

"Cured meat. Dried. Yeh never had that where yeh came from?"

"Yes," Jasen said slowly, "but ..."

But it didn't look like that. Cured meat in Terreas had been delicious, cut into thin slices, a purplish-pink color if it came from pigs, reddish-brown if it were beef. Its seasoning was precise, mostly salt.

This biltong, on the other hand, could only have acquired its dark color from a dye of spices. The meat was practically dehydrated, by the look of it. And although Jasen would cede that this point was the least important, aesthetically biltong was not pleasant. Whoever cut it must've hacked it off without any care whatsoever.

"Eat," said Kuura, pushing the roll of fabric, with its biltong and crackers, toward them.

Jasen tentatively reached out a finger for the meat. Better to get that done with first. He knew crackers. If biltong tasted terrible—and he suspected it did—he could try to expunge its flavor with the biscuits.

Alixa joined him, taking her own piece.

They lifted it to their mouths, in sync.

Already wincing, Jasen bit—

Alixa spat hers out barely after it had connected with her tongue. She twisted sideways on the bench, as if to get away from it as she hacked.

Kuura laughed, hard.

"It's not funny," she coughed. "It's—*horrible.*"

"And how d'you find it?" he asked Jasen.

Jasen chewed slowly. The flavor was ... peculiar. Herbs and spices like these did not exist in Terreas. Maybe not anywhere on Luukessia. They were sharp, warming, like embers on the tongue. Like peppers, only stronger. It was also incredibly salty.

But it ... wasn't bad. Vinegary, some bites ... but not awful.

"It's okay," he said.

Kuura beamed. "Yeh have a fine palate."

"And me?" Alixa demanded.

Kuura laughed again. "You will be eatin' hardtack. None of the men here are fond of it, so we have plenty."

"Lucky me," Alixa said flatly, eyeing a cracker miserably. The crackers were the opposite of the biltong in flavor—utterly bland and tasteless—and they were even drier than the biltong was. Only halfway through, Jasen had to ask Kuura for water, or he would not have been able to swallow the crumbs absorbing every drop of saliva in his mouth. After giving them a cup of water each, Kuura began to fill them in.

"This boat is called the *Lady Vizola*. We are a cargo runner, bound for the Aiger Cliffs."

"For where?" Jasen asked.

"It is a port city," said Kuura, "to the east of your Luukessia. It is a very green place—like your lands, yes? The locals there, they call it the 'City of Lightning,' because it is also a very stormy place. Perhaps this is not like Luukessia."

He seemed to be fishing there. So Jasen confirmed simply, "Yes."

That was enough to satisfy Kuura, for he went on. "It is a prosperous place though, where many people meet to do business."

"What cargo do you run?" Jasen asked.

"You saw yesterday: the animals below us."

"People trade them?"

"Of course!" Kuura's face lifted in amusement. But then he saw that Jasen's question was serious, and he said, "Did your people not?"

"Our village trades, but not animals really," said Jasen.

Traded, he thought.

It hollowed his stomach. He dropped his piece of biltong.

"They … they can—could—rent an animal, but…"

He couldn't bring himself to finish. Just picturing them was like drawing from a well of sadness. The farmland he'd meandered alongside for every year of his life, watching people tilling, harvesting … watching Aunt Margaut as she tended to the crops that weren't quite enough to feed Terreas's population, which increased year after year as if to spite the scourge that had forced this last bastion of humanity into a wretched corner, to prove to them that they would live on, growing stronger even in the face of those creatures …

The memories hurt to look over. And so he pushed them down, aside, like closing a book.

If Jasen's mental anguish showed on his face, Kuura did not comment. He simply went on, oblivious even to the fact that both Alixa and Jasen now had stopped eating, letting their last half-chewed morsels fall.

"Well, plenty of folk trade 'em, and Aiger Cliffs is where we're goin' to trade."

"For other animals?" Jasen asked.

"No, nitwit! Keep up!" But there was no malice in this, for Kuura belted another great belly laugh, tilting back so far that Jasen thought for a moment he would topple off the bench. "Money's what we're after. The sailors on this boat want payin', and feedin'."

"Right."

"We'll maybe buy another pig while we're in port, or a cow, if time comes to slaughter our own. Stick around, and someone'll maybe show you how we cure that biltong you're making haste through."

Jasen looked down. He'd eaten half of it already. After the first few confusing bites, his taste buds adapting to this strange new heat and spices, it was as if his body remembered that it needed to eat, and for the past few days had not been doing very much of that whatsoever. The meat was chewy, kind of hard, even the thinner strips—but he made short work of them.

Alixa hadn't touched a bit more. A half-eaten cracker lay in front of her.

Now, Jasen realized: she had gone quiet, had been for some time without his noticing. He glanced to her face. She was staring into the table, past it, her share of the biltong and crackers ignored. She looked as if she might cry. Perhaps already was; pinkness tinged her eyes again, though they were dry, as was her face.

He touched her wrist. She looked up at him. He did his best to smile, but Alixa did not return it and cast her gaze down once more.

Kuura was still talking. "... course, not just livestock. Always a market for that, but—well, you saw some of the things we've g't down in the hold. That grabby little *drak*-flinger, he'll do someone as a pet, maybe a servant if they c'n train him up. I wouldn't bank on that personally—always with the hands. Obsessed with that bloody sow, he is."

Jasen looked blank.

Kuura shook his head. "Not going in at all, is it?"

"It is," he said.

"I suppose you're still muddled from your ..." Kuura waved a hand vaguely. "Well, what it is you said you been through. My, my. Luukessians. I'd never believe it." The expression on his face was suddenly serious. His wide eyes drifted back and forth between Jasen and Alixa.

Then he slammed an open palm against the bench.

Jasen jolted. Alixa flinched.

Kuura broke into a wide grin. "Why don't you come out on deck?"

Jasen was allowed to fish up the last of the biltong. Kuura offered him the dry biscuits, but Jasen took only one, and purely out of obligation. Alixa was offered some too, but she declined with a short shake of the head, her eyes downcast. Kuura shrugged and led them up. Jasen tried to keep an eye on Alixa, to try to draw her out of the dark hole she seemed to have slipped into, but with Kuura's relentless conversation, it was hard for him to focus on her.

Jasen had imagined the sea almost all his life in Terreas—or the beaches, more often, as they were more graspable. He couldn't quite picture the sand—only yesterday had he first experienced it—or the smell of the air, or the way the waters stretched endlessly on and on. There was one thing he *could* imagine though, and that was the sky. It was always endlessly blue in the stories he'd read or been told, a pure, soft sheet of it overlaying the horizon, unbroken except for the blinding white of the sun. But as Jasen stepped out on deck behind Kuura, the blue was streaked with cloud. It looked as if it had been painted over with a soft brush, or perhaps a glob of paint dabbed and then pulled across with fabric, till the paint was stretched thin and would go no farther.

Toward the horizon, it clumped, darker.

"Never been out to sea before, have you?" asked Kuura.

Jasen stepped away without thinking, feet carrying him almost to the edge of the deck. He looked out in wonder. So much water everywhere—Jasen had never seen so much of it. And it was so blue! Deeper in hue than the morning sky, it reminded Jasen of the sky at night.

Waves bobbed the *Lady Vizola* up and down. They were far apart and not very tall, so the ship's rise was gradual, its descent just as slow. These waves were unmarred, but farther out Jasen glimpsed larger ones, crested with a strip of foam—like a reflection of the clouds, he thought.

No spray this morning. But the tang of salt was strong in the cool air, and it filled Jasen's nose like nothing else had—save maybe the smog as his house burned in Terreas, or the even thicker smoke that turned the air noxious and heavy when the mountain exploded and rained molten fire upon his village.

That thought sapped the wonder from him. His face fell, his interest lost.

He turned, sweeping the horizon as far as he could see.

"What are you looking for?" asked Kuura.

"Luukessia."

31

"We are far from it now. Even the ash from your volcano has disappeared."

Oh. Jasen drooped.

But what did it matter, really? Whether Luukessia were a couple of miles distant, or the whole world away, Jasen and Alixa were not going back. Their homes were gone. The pathways they had walked all their lives were buried.

Their families were dead. Let the *Lady Vizola* carry them far, far from that place. Baraghosa was certainly not stalking its ashen lands any longer.

Luukessia held nothing for him now.

Kuura was talking again—he was always talking, Jasen was quickly learning—but a shirtless sailor with shaggy black hair and a mane of a beard meandered across the deck. Whether it was for instructions, gossip about the new blood boarding with them, or simply to chat, Jasen could not make out.

He did find the transition to their native language jarring, though.

He hesitated by Alixa. She'd not moved far. She grasped her left wrist, watching the sea morosely.

"Alixa—" he began.

"Jasen," said a voice.

He turned.

Burund approached, steps slow, but calmly measured and precise.

"Alixa," he greeted, nodding to her.

"Shipmaster," Jasen said.

Burund joined their side. His tunic was only half-buttoned. A layer of sweat greased his ebony chest and underarms, darkening patches in the crimson-banded fabric. Cords of muscle were more pronounced this morning.

He clasped his hands behind his back and stood very straight. Legs shoulder width apart, his poise was like a soldier's, disciplined and perfect.

He looked Jasen up and down, then Alixa.

"How are you finding it?" he said simply.

"Uhm." Jasen hesitated. He glanced to Alixa for support, but she was not forthcoming, so he took the reins of the conversation.

"Fine," he said. "Kuura fed us some, uh … this stuff." He held it out; two lonely pieces left. The biltong's spices had rubbed off slightly, turning his palm faintly reddish-brown. It looked as if he'd bled there.

"I like biltong."

"Yes," said Jasen.

When he said no more, Burund inquired, "And you?"

"I do too," Jasen confirmed quickly.

Burund nodded. His eyes roved to Alixa, but he did not ask, perhaps sensing the answer in her body language. He turned back to Jasen, then the sea.

They stood and watched for a while.

Jasen thought he should speak—because he should, really, at least something to this man who had taken them in from the sea and rescued them from drowning. Even just a "thank you."

But when he opened his mouth, Burund looked over, meeting his gaze head on—

And what came out instead was: "Why is your skin that color?"

He cursed himself almost immediately. Stupid, stupid! It was a burning question, yes, but to be so blatant in his asking, when they had not been here long—it was rude, the sort of thing Hanrey would've berated him over for an hour (half of which would be spent sparring with Euonice). But if Burund was offended, he did not show it.

Kuura could not have been offended, for he cut off the fellow he was talking to by exploding with laughter.

Burund waited patiently, the faintest crooked smile playing on one corner of his lips.

Jasen waited less patiently, feeling both embarrassed and defensive.

Kuura said through his chuckles, "You've not seen dark skin before?"

"Well … no," said Jasen. "We've never seen anyone outside our village before." He tacked on, as an unnecessary afterthought, "Until yesterday, anyway."

"My, my," said Kuura.

The man speaking to him asked a question—probably *What?* Kuura slipped back into his native tongue and answered, chuckling to himself as he (presumably) retold what had just happened.

Burund answered, "The place I am from is called Coricuanthi. All the people there have skin like the men on this boat."

"Everyone?" Jasen echoed. Suddenly he felt like a child, no more than maybe five or six years of age, listening to the tales spun by a parent or grandparent of days gone by, or places far-flung.

Burund nodded. "There are many of us. There are many of you: I have seen men and women with skin like yours, in the ports we visit. Firoba teems with lighter skin. As does Chaarland, and Arkaria."

Jasen marveled. These places—Jasen ran the names of them over his tongue, mouthing without allowing his lips to betray him. They were so strangely alien … but with them, the world beyond Luukessia grew more solid. Firoba was a place out there, a real place, touching the sea—the same sea that Luukessia was surrounded by—and its streets were trodden by people like Jasen and Alixa and Burund and Kuura, who were alive, still, when everything across the ocean had been so utterly extinguished.

There was a world out there.

And they were going to it.

In spite of the ache in his chest for the family he had lost, he could not help but feel a flare of excitement.

Then he saw Burund's expression. The shipmaster's lips quirked down. He watched the horizon warily, eyes fixed on something in the distance.

Jasen turned. "What is it?"

"A storm is coming."

There it was, building: the clump of cloud in the distance had grown noticeably darker even in the few minutes Jasen and Alixa had been on the deck. In another hour, those skies would be black.

"We'll avoid it," said Jasen, "won't we? It's alongside us."

Burund shook his head. "No." Without taking his gaze from the horizon, he said, "These are not storms we can avoid."

4

"Please talk to me."

Jasen and Alixa had retired below deck. He'd watched the storm for some time. At first, he questioned Burund. Maybe he even wondered just how good at captaining this vessel the man was, if in twenty-four hours he had run into one storm and was certain of barreling into another, even though the *Lady Vizola*, as far as Jasen could see, was sailing at a perpendicular angle to it.

Yet increasingly the shipmaster's assessment appeared correct. The waters grew rougher, waves higher and more frequent, breaking against the ship's hull and throwing a spray of foam into the sky. The dark cloud had spread, spilling across the horizon in each direction and approaching.

Jasen had rarely seen storms.

He did not know they behaved like this.

Burund may've been disturbed; it was difficult to tell, his expressions were so subtle. If this was not business as usual to any of the rest of the crew, though, Jasen would never know, unless relayed by Kuura—and he had dashed off at first sight of the storm, taking and distributing instructions from Burund in quick, hard syllables.

"You should return to your cabin," Burund told Jasen and Alixa at last.

They obeyed. And there they sat now. Alixa had her back to the wall, beside a porthole looking out at increasingly choppy waters. Dusk appeared to have fallen many hours early as the blanket overhead thickened.

Jasen sat against the door, on the floor. The bed was damp where they'd slept in their clothes. Unsightly and over-large though these were, he did not want to wet them too.

Alixa said nothing, just held her knees close.

Jasen tried again. "Please, Alixa. I know you're upset."

Nothing.

"I'm upset too."

She fiddled with a fold of her tunic. "Are you?" Sullen, not exactly questioning.

"Yes," said Jasen.

Quiet.

Then Alixa said, "So why've you still got an appetite? Why can you still question, and engage, and take everything in like it's some—some big adventure?"

She smacked her palms against her knees.

"This is not some big adventure," she told Jasen, looking at him for the first time since breakfast. "It's not. Our families are dead."

"I know."

It was quiet, for a time, or at least the approximation of quiet they were afforded on the *Lady Vizola*. The deck outside remained busy. Likewise above them, bootsteps sounded up and down once or twice, muted by the thick wood separating decks. Each wave hitting was its own sound, a forceful noise like a great buffeting hammer blow of wind—only it produced a weary groaning when the water broke against the ship. The spray rained down, also quieted by the size of the hull.

It continued, fading into the background.

"It's like …" Alixa said eventually. She paused, searching for words.

"It's like a great hole has been cut out of me," she said. "It's endless, and dark, and it hurts … and I know, completely, that it will never be filled again. It will never heal. It will just be an empty gash in my soul."

A tear trickled down one cheek. She thumbed it away. Another replaced its track. This one, she ignored.

"I'm looking down into the hole now," she said softly. "All I can do is stare into its depths." A sigh. "I don't think I'll ever be able to wrench my gaze from it again."

She closed her eyes.

Jasen sat, thought. He'd intended to cheer Alixa, to offer her his hand and to pull her out of the despair swallowing her. But to hear her say it now … he couldn't help but turn to his, too, looking into the great cleft that now split him. That was how he saw it: not a hole, exactly, but a canyon that had been scored out, like a claw or knife had been run through his heart. Where Alixa had one chasm, though, Jasen had two, crisscrossing. The older—that carved by the loss of his mother—had never healed. Some days, it seemed to bleed.

This new one—his father, and with him all of Terreas, although it was a fractional, secondary part of it—would be the same.

To keep from thinking of his father's last moments—if he had woken early at dawn and been there to see the mountain exploding, to hear it, maybe even turning to see it before a wave of fire washed over him—

To steer himself from these thoughts, Jasen instead turned to his last moments with Adem.

He'd gone to bed that night, in the Weltan living room, opposite his father. Their house had burned, all the memories of his mother, all her keepsakes, gone up in smoke … and Adem had held it together. He'd held strong for Jasen when another great piece of his life had been destroyed.

And Jasen had known all the while that he was leaving. He'd not said a word about his mission with Shilara and Alixa to save Terreas. Instead, he'd pretended to be a shocked-into-silence son, then awaited his father's snores and snuck out.

If the mission for grain had been successful, he reasoned, it was acceptable to leave his father—and for Alixa to leave her family—with the fear that they, too, had gone beyond the wall and been ravaged by scourge.

How cruel he'd been.

And so Adem had died, not knowing Jasen was alive and safe—was just on the other side of the wall, in fact, come home to save his people...

… and all of it was Jasen's fault.

Just as Alixa was confident the wound she bore would not heal, Jasen was certain that this was truth: he was the cause of Terreas's destruction. Not first-hand, exactly … but in allowing for his father to refuse Baraghosa, Baraghosa had in turn laid down a curse upon the village.

It had killed them.

And Jasen had had a hand in it.

If he were stronger, he would climb the steps to the top deck this moment and pitch himself into the sea.

He could not. His nerves were not enough.

Besides … Jasen's were not the only hands bloodied.

Baraghosa's were bloodier still. The sorcerer, with his strange lights and his promise that Terreas would come to regret their decision—he shouldered the blame for unleashing the magics that had caused the mountain to rupture and ruin Terreas.

And so Jasen had a reason to keep going: justice.

Vengeance.

He would murder Baraghosa, with his bare hands if he had to. He would strangle the breath out of the wizard, watch as the light left his eyes, as his face turned blue, then purple, and finally a waxy, pallid white.

This was why he kept moving. He *had* to keep moving.

And so did Alixa. If he could do anything for her now, it was to remind her of that.

He licked his lips. "Remember when my house burned down?"

Alixa's face flickered. "How could I not?" she asked quietly. "It was … barely days ago."

It was. It felt like a lifetime though. So much had happened between then and now. Alixa felt it too: Jasen could feel it in the way her words sighed out, reluctant yet resigned.

"If it had happened to you," Jasen said, "what would you have done?"

Alixa frowned. "What?"

He repeated himself, a touch more forceful.

Alixa's mouth twisted, pulling sideways. Her eyebrows drew down, pressing a line between them. "What would I …" She shook her head. "I don't know, Jasen. Probably cry."

"And after that?"

"I don't know." She sounded exasperated. "Why does it matter? My house *did* burn down, more or less, and I am here." Scowling, she added, "I didn't have much choice in it, but I am here. Just like you."

"Yes," said Jasen, rising. He sat on the edge of the bed, turned to her. "We're here. Just like I was still there after my house burned down. I lost everything—*we* lost everything," he added quickly, as Alixa's mouth opened, "but I had to keep going. Now we have to do the same. We have to … to start anew, even after everything we knew is lost. We can't just be paralyzed."

"I am *not* paralyzed," Alixa said, her frustration giving over to hotness now. Tears threatened, warbling the edges of her words. She clamped down on them, holding them back as she took a steadying breath. Sitting taller, she said, "I am *in mourning.*"

Jasen opened his mouth to answer—but he had none. Maybe that he was too?

Before he could find any words, though—

A thunderous wave crashed against the ship. The sound was barely dulled by the hull; for the noise, the waters might as well have been crashing over Jasen's head. The ship gave a terrific lurch.

Jasen barely had a moment to think. One moment, he was staring at

Alixa. The next, it was like the world exploded, for the second time in as many days; the room tipped and he was on his back. Alixa yelped, landing heavily next to him in the V-shaped channel that now was the floor. The bunk groaned after her, covers thrown off—

BANG!

That impact was worse, somehow. The wooden bed frame sprung free from its moorings—damned thing was only screwed in on one post—and, anchored only by that lone corner, it swung around and crashed into him. He cried out, thrusting uselessly with his hands as if somehow he might stop gravity from taking its natural course.

A distant *PING!*—and the screws holding it were torn free as gravity overloaded them.

The frame rolled, hitting hard into the heels of his palms. An angry stab of pain radiated up both arms—

The bed was falling right way up again, the room evening out, floor returning to its rightful place.

Jasen's eyes bulged. Barely a few seconds, the whole thing had taken—oh, and now he was racked with pain, all over.

Something moved alongside him.

Alixa, he thought.

He twisted to ask if she was all right—she would have taken the impact from the bed frame too, or perhaps the trunk as it skidded along the angled floor—but she was already up, a blur of motion.

"Wait—" he began.

She thrust open the lock. And then she bolted out, the door swinging madly behind her. Voices filtered through it, all the same: panicked.

Jasen stumbled to his feet, using the jamb for support.

He was aware of something wet underfoot, welling up through a puncture he hadn't been aware of in his boot.

The porthole.

A terrible, dark maw, Jasen only saw churning beyond. Skies and sea had merged into one incomprehensible whorl.

The hatch had not quite maintained its seal. Seawater had flowed in through an imperfect edge, staining the wood dark—and coating the cabin floor with a half-inch of liquid.

Scourgey can't swim, Jasen thought.

He knew where Alixa had gone.

Another wave slammed the side of the ship. They were focused on this side—starboard, Jasen thought, though he had no idea if that was right or not—and the concussive blow threw Jasen backward. He crashed half against the door jamb, sending a tremor up his spine.

Then the door was flying toward him, swung around on his hinges.

He took the blow against his palms—another stab of pain up his arms, into his shoulders.

Another spurt of seawater flowed in around the porthole.

The hold was underwater. If that first impact had compromised anything, it would be filling even now.

And Alixa was racing toward it to save Scourgey.

Jasen set his face. Turning on his heel, he pushed into the cramped corridors of the *Lady Vizola*, alive with shouting voices, and chased after his cousin.

5

Men were hurtling through the corridors. How many cabins there were down here, Jasen did not know. But they were many, and doors were thrown open as Jasen passed—most by the force of the waves, but more than a couple by sailors who beat furious feet down the halls to—wherever it was they were going.

A man with wide palms and frenzied eyes gripped Jasen as he ran past.

"*Dagot-bah? Ootohp cahnayh!*"

Jasen stared wildly back. "My cousin—"

The man with frenzied eyes said something, but another wave slammed the *Lady Vizola*, and they were sent sideways. The wall of a cabin broke their fall—painfully.

One last bark from the man, when the ship's movement had steadied. Then he released Jasen, turned, and hurtled down the tight confines toward stairs that would take him up.

Jasen moved in the opposite direction, running hard. More portholes had been inadequately sealed, or perhaps just knocked out by the first fearsome wave, for water spilled past doors and out into the main corridor.

A crash rocked the ship again and sent Jasen sprawling. He thrust his hands out, grunting as he collided hard with the corner of two walls.

He groaned—

The ship was groaning too.

It's going to come apart, he thought, a low pulse of terror moving through him.

What happened when a ship broke apart at sea?

He racked his brains desperately for an answer that might assuage him here. But in none of the stories he had heard, none of his

41

imaginings, had the possibility ever occurred to him. His mother had read him tales of pirates and sailors who were wrecked onto deserted islands. Battles happened at sea in some stories, and boats were invariably sunk. But how their people escaped, what their options were if the worst happened … no story had ever detailed it. The bad guys were simply felled and drowned.

Now, Jasen realized, they would want to live—

How, though?

The ship groaned again, plummeting sideways. Jasen clawed for a nearby door jamb, holding firm.

The wet was rising to his ankles now.

How the hold fared, he dreaded to think.

The damned scourge—and these damned people, with their superstitions and cages. If the beast had just been allowed to stay with him and Alixa, Alixa would never have gone charging off … and he wouldn't be charging off after her.

He forced himself back into motion again. For now, the water was not deep enough to drag on his legs, but he'd need to make haste, the way it kept rising.

Around the next corner, and the stairs leading down were in sight. No Alixa, though.

"Alixa!" he shouted—

The ship rocked again, groaning under the surging sea hitting against it—

From out of one of the side corridors lurched—something. Jasen barely had time to brace—

Hands grabbed him from behind, pulling him clear.

A crate crashed to ground. Half the size of Jasen, it landed on an edge. The noise was like the crack of a whip. The impact threw up its own wave, soaking Jasen with a frigid spray. The crate did not buckle or split, falling heavily onto a side and stilling.

"What're yeh doin'?"

Kuura had him. Jasen turned to see the man, who gripped him fiercely. His madman's leer was gone. His eyes bulged, mouth twisted down haggardly.

"Alixa," Jasen began—

"That crate could've crushed yeh!"

"My cousin is down there!"

Kuura stared. "What?"

"Alixa went down to get Scourgey."

"Yer—Jasen, that's madness. The hold—the cages aren't all secured, and any water fillin' this deck, it'll run down to the bottom—"

"I need to get to her," Jasen said, and broke free.

"Jasen, wait!" Kuura called.

But Jasen was already over the crate that had nearly knocked him through death's doorway. He leapt over, landing with a splash, then sprinted for the stairway.

Kuura was after him. "It's not safe!" The ship shuddered again. A door swung open, impacting hard against the wall as the hinges let it travel a full hundred and eighty degrees around. Jasen braced on the opposite wall—

The cabin was a mess. The bed had splintered. A trunk lay on its side, contents spilled into the water.

Dark liquid sluiced from under the porthole.

All the more reason to hurry to Alixa.

Jasen regained his footing and hurtled for the stairs. He mounted them—water was flooding down them like a miniature waterfall in a stream—and sprinted down—

"Jasen!" Kuura called from just a couple of paces behind—close, but not close enough to grab Jasen's shoulder.

He turned at the landing halfway up, looked down—

Jasen's fear that the *Lady Vizola* would come apart was replaced by another as he stepped foot into the hold. Seawater had flooded in from some burst seam in the hull. Already it came up to Jasen's knees—and still it rose.

The ship would not break. No, it would fill, and then sink to the bottom of the ocean—taking him and Alixa and everyone else with it.

"Can't you do something?" he asked Kuura as he joined him on the stair.

"Men are patching holes as we speak!" he answered. "Now come to safety before—"

Another furious crash rocked the ship. The world turned sideways. Jasen, still on the stairs, was shunted off. His head rebounded from the ceiling. Stars erupted—then were doused as he landed headfirst in the icy water filling the hold.

Kuura fared better, somehow. When Jasen spluttered into the air once more, Burund's first mate was pressed low to the steps, gripping them with one hand. He had a pained look on his face.

Jasen had no time to see if he was okay. Alixa was somewhere down here—and the cages were not as secure as Jasen had thought. The aisles carved through them were a mess where they'd shifted. Where the ship was thrust to the side over and over, the water coming to Jasen's knees was whipped into a frenzy. It rose and fell in mad waves that came from all directions, meeting and cancelling each other out, or joining and building in the small space, washing over entire cages.

Animals squealed madly, cries only adding to the relentless churn and the ship's near-ceaseless groaning. Those that could clawed at their cages, using human-like hands or strong clawed paws to hold themselves as high to the top as they could manage.

The animals in the smaller cages would have been long drowned by now.

They were not Jasen's concern. "Alixa!" he shouted.

Her voice came back, panicked and shrill: "Help!"

He bolted after her before even knowing where the cry had come from. Shoving cages aside, he forced his way forward. The water pushed at him in all directions, yet still seeming to drag him backward with every step. It was so terribly cold, his flesh broke out in goosebumps. No winter had felt like this in Terreas.

The impact of another wave shoved two cages hard into Jasen's body. He stumbled, almost landing on one knee.

The long-armed thing obsessed with the sow occupied one. It screeched, reaching out and clutching to Jasen.

"Let—go!" he wheezed, prying its hands loose.

It screeched at him in reply, holding tighter. It had claws, and as Jasen pried a finger loose, it readjusted, dragging them along his skin painfully.

"Get off!"

"*Jasen!*" Alixa cried, from somewhere out of sight.

"I'm—coming! *Would you just get—off!*"

Kuura appeared. He wrapped the creature's arm in one fist, then pulled—hard. It screeched again, baring fangs—but its hands were loose, and Jasen was free to move again, to find Alixa—

Kuura shoved the animal back and pushed its cage away, letting the water take it back toward its original resting place. He cast Jasen a manic look. "Yeh're mad," he said. "Both of you."

"My cousin—"

"Come on," Kuura grunted. "But then we're gettin' yeh out of here."

He forced the way ahead, shoving cages aside. When another wave rolled the boat sideways, he snatched out for Jasen's arm. His fingers were calloused and dug hard into the skin beneath his armpit. But it stopped Jasen from going sideways and getting soaked again.

The aisle had been vanquished entirely toward the rear of the hold. Kuura muscled through. Fortunately these cages were smaller, or empty. The cage with the cow, two down from Scourgey, was weighed down enough not to have moved—yet.

Alixa was fighting with the door to Scourgey's cage. Soaked through, her hair plastered to her body, she had a wild, deranged look about her. Her fingers clawed at the bolt.

It would not move.

"Please!" she cried to Jasen, Kuura. "Let her out!"

Scourgey was pressed as close to the front of the cage as she could manage. Her nose stuck out of a hole. Mouth wide open, she made a ceaseless, keening whine, rising in pitch every time a wave rushed in.

The water rose to her haunches. Heavier waves churned by the *Lady Vizola's* shifting were enough to reach her chest.

"The men won't like your beast out," Kuura said. "They already think it brought this upon them!"

"Scourgey is *safe!*" cried Alixa. "She wouldn't hurt anyone! And *we* haven't died!"

"The storm—"Another wave rocked the boat sideways. Jasen stumbled; Kuura held firm. Alixa kept herself upright with clawed hands around Scourgey's cage.

Scourgey seemed to scream.

"*Please!*" Alixa cried. "*She'll drown!*"

"So will we!" Kuura roared back.

"*Then let her out of here!*"

Kuura sighed, a gruff, unfriendly noise that didn't seem anything like him. He pushed Jasen aside with one big paw, Alixa too—and then he worked Scourgey's lock with hard fingers.

For a few seconds, it was stuck—

Then it burst open.

The door flew apart—and Scourgey lurched out, shrieking madly.

Alixa wrapped her arms around the scourge's neck. "I've got you!"

Kuura clamped a hand on her other arm, by the shoulder. "And I've got you. Now get out of here, both of you!"

"The other animals—"

"You got the one yeh wanted! I'm not freeing anymore! Now follow!"

And he forced his way back across the hold, dragging Jasen and Alixa, who in turn dragged Scourgey. She fought, seeming not to understand that safety lay ahead. But with Kuura pulling her, Alixa had no choice but to tug on Scourgey harder than she would've otherwise, and the scourge had to move across the deck.

Kuura didn't stop on the stairs to the next deck, instead dragging them round to mount the next flight.

"Where are we going?" Jasen asked.

"Top deck," Kuura grunted.

"But—why—the storm—"

"Just follow, would yeh?"

They rose and rose. The deck directly below the *Lady Vizola's* topside, the largely empty one with those strange metal contraptions, was driest. Men were shoving the metal things back on runners, and checking the seals on the holes aligned with them.

Into the short top deck—through the door—

Jasen stopped dead.

The noise was calamitous.

Sheeting rain fell. It came almost horizontally, and hit Jasen so hard he recoiled. It was like being stung by wasps, over and over and over.

Men worked furiously on the deck. Shipmaster Burund was yelling to them, but a shrill wind blew through, obscuring his words. He was shouting commands, surely; and between him and the dozen or so men on the deck, they fought with the sails on each of the three masts—perhaps for control, perhaps to steer them out of this nightmare somewhere.

And it was a nightmare. The sky and sea were almost equally wild and dark.

But most terrible of all was—

CRACK!

That noise broke through it all: a lightning strike, so close to the ship that Jasen could almost have touched it. Instead of forking through the sky, it connected directly from stormcloud to rioting seawaters, in a long line.

A long, *bright green* line.

Jasen stared in horror.

Another bolt rent the air in two, red, like the flowers of a budding rose. It left a dazzling after-image on Jasen's retinas.

"What's happening?" he cried.

"Hell if I know," Kuura answered. "Come on!" He dragged Jasen and Alixa along the deck, Scourgey following in their wake. If she was whimpering now—and surely she was—the noise was inseparable from the wail of the wind.

Burund gave them nary a look as they passed.

The men, however, cast eyes their way, their faces hardening at the sight of Scourgey.

A bolt of vibrant blue lightning arced from the heavens. It exploded on the water no more than five hundred feet distant.

Jasen ducked.

Burund's shouting intensified, vying for volume with, and briefly overpowering, the wind.

The men tugged their attention from Scourgey and pulled the sails, which billowed and tilted sideways on their vertical axis.

"What are they doing?" Jasen asked.

"Shipmaster is bringing her around!" Kuura shouted back. His words were barely audible in the whipping gale. The elaborate folds of fabric that set him apart from his crewmates caught it and filled, like the sails, making him look misshapen and much larger than usual. If a gust blew strongly enough, surely it would carry him with it, dumping him somewhere in the whorls.

Jasen had no time to think of anyone's safety but his own and Alixa's. If Kuura was snatched, so be it.

Kuura led them to one of the stubby top decks. A ladder was built alongside it. "Up!"

Jasen hesitated. "Why—"

"*Get up there!*" To Alixa: "Follow your cousin! I'll bring your bloody dog!"

Jasen clambered. The steps were slick.

Alixa followed. Then came Kuura, Scourgey slung over a shoulder.

"Stand against it," Kuura ordered, pointing at the mast, "both of you."

Jasen stared. Rain came slanting down, stinging his eyes.

"But what—" Jasen began.

"Just do it! Quick, now! Yeh want a wave to wash yeh away?"

Jasen looked to Kuura, panicked.

"Yeh'll be safe," Kuura promised. "I'll secure you. Just do it, would yeh?"

There was desperation in his words—and another rolling wave crashed against the ship, canting it over. Jasen stumbled; Kuura caught him before he spilled over the edge.

Foam had spilled over the main deck. It sloshed about the feet of the men down below.

A bigger one might come at any moment—and, like Kuura said, could wrench them from the deck and cast them into the waters.

He'd drown.

"I promise," Kuura said, "yeh'll be safe."

Alixa moved for him. Clutching Jasen's wrist, she said, "Come on." Her eyes blazed, wide with fear—but with the choice removed from him, an external force pulling him forward, Jasen allowed his paralysis to leave him so that Kuura and Alixa could move him over, press his back against the mast.

"Yours too," he said to Alixa when Jasen was still.

"Scourgey—"

"I'll secure her too," Kuura said gruffly.

The words came to Jasen from a great distance—as did, some seconds later, the feel of Kuura wrapping a cord of rope around and around his midriff, pulling it tighter, tighter … He was barely aware of any of it. All he saw was the rain, pelting him, stinging his skin like thousands of angry wasps; and the lightning, ripping the sky open in unnatural pulses of fantastic, terrifying color. Bright green—blue—yellow—it strobed madly, breathing life into fresh waves that assaulted the Lady Vizola.

"Stay," said Kuura. He'd finished, apparently—the rope was out of his hands, his circling complete, a knot tied—somewhere. And then, after another word which Jasen did not catch, he gave them a final look, and descended to the main deck.

Purple lightning boomed. A faint smell like spent gunpowder wafted past on the wind, little more than a ghost as it was carried away.

Alixa gripped Jasen's wrist.

She said something, but he wasn't sure what. Not because her words had been overpowered; he surely should have heard them. His senses were just … shutting down. Overloaded past the point they could continue working, they had all just given up, leaving him a shaking, shivering mess—and afraid. Terribly afraid. Like a wave he'd kept at bay over the past days, as he ran from scourge, then saw Terreas buried in fire, then ran again; then this ship, and chasing Alixa, and seeing the storm, and climbing—

It was all too much.

He sat and stared.

Alixa rubbed his wrist. Talking, talking.

Jasen heard no words.

But he saw the strikes as the heavens opened, again, and again, and again. Saw their colors: blue, green, yellow, pink, red, purple—

Felt the rain. Felt the wind.

Felt the sway of the *Lady Vizola* as waves displaced it, and the foremast canted, Jasen and Alixa and Scourgey lashed firmly to it but tilting all the same, toward an ocean that was black as the throat of a beast, and just as ready to swallow them.

For hours, it went on, and on, and on.

And Jasen shook.

6

Dawn came.

Jasen and Alixa lay at the bottom of the foremast, still lashed to it by Kuura's rope round their middles. Only in the early hours had the storm receded, the sea quieting. Yet still thundercracks cleaved the air for hours, striking the surface of the water. Each bright bolt seemed to set off a new barrage of waves, radiating out from the impact point like ripples from a stone. They buffeted the *Lady Vizola* for ten, twenty minutes, until slowly giving over to calmness.

Eventually, Jasen and Alixa fell into a muddled sleep.

They were woken by Kuura's voice.

"Yeh survived, then."

Jasen cracked his eyelids.

Kuura filled his vision.

Behind him, the sky was cloudless and blue..

Jasen squinted, frowning.

Kuura laughed heartily. "Wond'ring how the sun could ever shine again after that? Trust me, boy: see it enough times and yeh won't question it, yeh'll just thank your gods that yeh made it through. Right then—both of yeh in one piece?" He gave them a cursory look over. "Well, are yeh? I'm not Medleigh—I need confirmation."

"I think so," said Alixa weakly.

Jasen wasn't so sure. His insides felt as though they'd been rattled to pieces. Kuura was looking at him for an answer though, so he ceded with a nod.

"Good. Let's get you out then."

He untied them. The knot was a tangled mess, and Jasen was not convinced he would be able to pry it open at first. When he suggested a knife, after a solid minute and no discernible progress he could make out as Kuura's fingers worked, he was answered with a laugh.

"Yeh think we c'n afford to cut our ropes when we can't be bothered untying them? Where's this limitless supply space yeh've found on this ship then, Jasen? Shipmaster'll be pleased to hear about it."

The rope loosened, fell away.

It was like a weight had been pressing down on him. He hadn't realized just how constricted his lungs felt. Now, he sucked in a full breath. The saltwater air felt revitalizing.

It also hurt. Confined for so many hours, his body flailing against his bonds, his entire midriff must now bear a belt of bruises.

"Right," said Kuura when Scourgey was finally released. "Burund would like to speak to yeh."

Alixa cast Jasen a nervous look. "About what?" she asked.

"Speak to him an' see."

The shipmaster was on deck, as were a number of other men, most of whom were taming the sails or—from what Jasen could glimpse—assessing damage. As for the rest of the hands, Jasen could only assume they were inside the *Lady Vizola*. The alternative was that they had gone overboard during the night—not a very pleasant possible outcome, even for Hamisi and company.

The first steps were difficult. Jasen's body seemed to have forgotten how it worked overnight. Alixa stumbled too.

Scourgey wouldn't move. She just quivered at the foremast's base. Her eyes were unreadable for their perfect blackness. If they were, Jasen was sure he'd see her staring off into infinity.

"Come on, Scourgey," Alixa gently coaxed.

She wouldn't move—nor at Alixa's soft tugging against her shoulder.

"Storm's spooked her," said Kuura. "Does with some beasts."

"What do we do?"

"I've got 'er." And before Alixa could protest, offer up a more careful approach, he stooped down, scoped Scourgey up around the middle, and clambered down to the main deck with her.

She screeched like her life was ending.

"Be careful with her!" Alixa cried, leaping down after him, ladder be damned.

Scourgey bucked against Kuura's shoulder. He tightened his hold— "Whoa, now!"—and then a claw tore through the fabric of his tunic, across the shoulder. He hissed, dropped Scourgey—she landed with an ungraceful *plop*—and clasped it.

The scourge pelted for Alixa, wrapped herself around the girl's legs.

Alixa bowed to wrap her arms around Scourgey's neck. "Oh, Scourgey …"

Kuura grunted. "That bloody—" Lifting the flap of fabric Scourgey had torn, he revealed three red lines, carved from his shoulder toward his neck.

"You scared her!" Alixa cried at Kuura's dark look.

Kuura bit off something in his native tongue. Then he stalked away, waving to Burund.

Burund was corralling men with the mainsail. Between them they tackled a set of ropes, pulling it into position. The fabric fluttered softly in the light breeze. That and the sky suggested there had been no storm at all—though Jasen's soaked-through clothes attested otherwise.

Mainsail back in place, Burund tied off his rope to a metal hoop built into the deck, brass-colored but worn with a mottled layer of rust. He gave some instructions to the remaining two men, and then approached Jasen and Alixa. Close by, he nodded.

Scourgey made a sad sound in the back of her throat, and pressed lower.

Alixa patted her gently. "It's okay."

"You are in one piece," said Burund.

Jasen nodded. "I think so."

That drew a very small smile from Burund, one corner of his mouth lifting just fractionally.

"My crew is no longer suspicious of your pet," he said to Alixa.

She stuck her bottom lip out. "No?"

"No death has befallen us. The storm was intense, but we are all accounted for and in good health."

"And they know she's not responsible for last night then, do they?" Alixa challenged.

Burund nodded. "Yes," he said simply.

She huffed, like that wasn't good enough. Still, her shoulders seemed to relax, to loosen.

"What was that?" Jasen asked. "Last night."

"I do not know."

Jasen hesitated, waiting for more. None came, so he said, "Is it normal?"

The shipmaster shook his head. "In all my years on the sea," he said, "I have never seen anything like it. Many storms, yes, for the sea is alive with them. Monstrous ones have come too, threatening to capsize us as last night's did. But those colors … never have I witnessed something like that."

Burund stared away, lost. His held-together expression lifted, just for a moment. He appeared in equal parts awestruck and spooked, his gaze lost into the distance, mind surely going over those vibrant flashes as the night was split and the waters churned.

"It was a terrific display," Burund muttered, coming back to himself. "But not one like any I have seen before, no."

"Yesterday," said Jasen, "it looked like the clouds spread out, to—to seek us out."

"It looked like that," Burund agreed. "But that is not what happened. They simply spread."

"But the storm built on the horizon, alongside us … and you seemed to know we would be riding into it."

"I read the weather. Perhaps, if you sail as long as I have, you will learn to do the same."

Jasen nodded, a little disappointed at Burund's answer. He wished to believe the storm was something more, and that Burund had the answers to it, answers Jasen could unlock if he tried. But the shipmaster's responses seemed genuine; he was an experienced sailor who could read the sea and skies, but who had been dumbstruck by the crazed, frenzied show of brilliant lights throughout the night.

"In any case," said Burund, "we are past it now. We have endured the storm."

Jasen's stomach sunk a half-inch farther. That was it? Such a frightening, mystifying experience—and except for a brief reflection on it, Burund was to move past it because the storm had passed him by? Where were his questions? Where was the man's sense of wonder, or fear?

Jasen would have opened his mouth to voice these questions himself—but Burund had already gone on.

"Our damage has been patched up. You may find some wetness remains inside, but do not worry: we are not leaking any more."

"What about the hold?" Alixa asked, a little sniffily. "It was almost to my thighs before the storm had barely started." She added pointedly, "Scourgey would have died if I hadn't gone down there."

Would've died anyway, if Kuura hadn't been there to help, Jasen thought. He didn't think this was the time to insert that little detail, though.

"The hold is being emptied at present," said Burund.

"Of?" Alixa asked. "Water? Or corpses?"

"Water," Burund answered simply.

"And the dead animals?"

"They have been disposed of."

"Excellent," Alixa huffed angrily.

Jasen figured this was the point to step in, before Alixa's newfound propensity to forget holding her tongue led to a blowout between the only Luukessians aboard a vessel of seafaring men who would cast them out at a moment's notice.

"Where are we going now?" Jasen asked. "To Aiger Cliffs?"

"Yes," Burund confirmed with a nod. "Our course was little changed last night. We have lost some time, but will still arrive within a few days."

Jasen scanned the horizon. No sign of anything—just the sea, smooth as glass, as if no storm had come at all.

"Which way is it?"

Burund pointed. "You will not see it for some time yet, though."

Jasen racked his brains for information about Aiger Cliffs. Kuura had told him some, he knew, but in the overload that was the past few days, he was having trouble getting it nailed down straight. He remembered the names Arkaria and Firoba ...

"Where," he began slowly, "are we?" He wasn't certain how to ask the question, and Burund did not appear to understand, for he did not answer immediately. So Jasen tried: "These aren't Luukessian waters any more, are they?"

"No. We are crossing the sea between Luukessia and Chaarland."

Chaarland. That was it.

He repeated it to himself silently. It was strangely enjoyable, the feel of his tongue forming the name of a new place, one wholly disconnected from Terreas, from Luukessia.

"Have you heard of Chaarland?" Burund asked.

Jasen shook his head.

Burund considered this for a long few seconds.

"Your lands were overrun by the beasts you call 'friend,'" he said carefully.

"Scourgey *is* our friend," said Alixa hotly. "She saved us." She gripped the scourge's neck hard, as if afraid Burund might swoop in and drag her away.

"She fought other scourge," Jasen told Burund. "She's ... not like the others. For some reason." He peered at her, frowning.

"Peculiar," said Burund quietly.

He tapped his chin, thoughtfully watching Scourgey. She simply stood behind Alixa, mouth open and tongue lolling. Her black eyes could have been pointing anywhere.

"You're all wrong about her," said Alixa.

"Indeed," said Burund. "But still ... we heard stories of these creatures."

"What kind of stories?" Jasen asked.

"They filled your lands like a plague," Burund answered, "We heard tales that they would set upon anyone who dared to approach the land. They'd be ripped apart."

Jasen nodded. "It's true, at least as far as my father said."

Alixa blustered—

"It is," he said, looking at her quickly and apologetically. "Scourgey is different, but the rest of them … they were everywhere. If we crossed the boundary at the edge of our village—they'd come." Shaking his head at the grim memories—of being chased, of the things crawling across their path as they rode to Wayforth, of them gnawing at trees and devastating anything living they could find—he added, "They laid Luukessia to waste. Our village was the last …the last…"

Jasen stopped, the thought leaving him cold: *And now it was gone.*

"Yours is an interesting specimen," said Burund to Alixa.

"She's not a 'specimen.'"

Burund smiled faintly. "I hope you can understand why my men were fearful of her when you arrived."

Alixa just replied with a *humph*, averting her gaze to watch Scourgey.

Jasen looked back to Burund. He mouthed "sorry," lifting his shoulders in a low shrug.

A small, crooked smile back.

Then—

Shouts from the rear of the ship.

If Jasen had been shipmaster, he would have gone running. Even now, he was tempted, for the voices to the front of the ship sounded excited about something. But Burund only strode to them with his usual measured, calm paces.

He asked something that Jasen took to mean, "What is it?" as he went.

The sailors, leaning over the railing, answered, craning back to address their shipmaster before leaning out again.

Jasen exchanged a look with Alixa, then followed. Begrudgingly, she came too, coaxing Scourgey along.

There, laid out between the *Lady Vizola* and the infinity that was the horizon, was the wreckage of a boat. Rendered into little more than matchsticks, its fragments were spread across the sea, still some distance away.

Burund exchanged words with his men. Then they rushed off, back to the sails, where they began to tug at ropes.

"What's happening?" Jasen asked.

"We are altering course to investigate," said Burund.

"Do you think it was destroyed in the storm?"

"That is possible, yes."

The sails were pulled around. Wind pushing them at a sharper angle now, the *Lady Vizola* gently twisted in her path, so that she was moving toward the wreckage head on. Without the storm's gales pushing, they relied on the normal flow of wind to push them. Standing by Burund's side, Jasen watched as the wreckage slowly came closer.

Nearer, it was clear just how extensive the devastation was. Though the rough shape of half a ship had been clear to Jasen when it was farther out, as the *Lady Vizola* drew into its vicinity, Jasen saw that barely more than a vague frame was left. It bobbed, lopsided, much of the ship gone, leaving a wide open view of its interior—or at least what was left of it. The decks and some outlines of cabins were recognizable thanks to wooden beams that hadn't completely splintered off, but the rest of the ship was in pieces. Flotsam littered the water, spread out like algae on a pond. Barrels and crates bobbed in the water, but most of the debris was just splintered scraps of wood. Burund ignored the broken wood, pointing instead of barrels and apparently giving the order for them to be brought aboard. Sailors obliged, hurling nets down to ensnare those floating nearby.

"You're *looting*?" Alixa asked. She turned her nose up.

"Yes."

"What about looking for survivors? What about rescue?"

"There are no survivors."

"How do you know? You've hardly looked. That boat could've held any number of men on it, and—"

Jasen tuned out the beginnings of an argument. Instead, he stared. Something had struck him, something that was not like the rest of the wreckage floating around the *Lady Vizola*, something deep blue and lumpy in a way that everything else floating was not.

"There's a man," he said suddenly, realizing."What?" Burund's voice was sharp.

"A man," said Jasen. He pointed—and as Burund and Alixa stepped forward to look, his heart raced. Because it *was*, he was certain of it. A man was out there, dressed in full armor, floating face down on a hunk of wood that lay half submerged, ready to give out on him.

Someone from this boat remained … alive?

No telling, from here.

The possibility of a survivor was enough for Burund. He shouted an uncharacteristically urgent command to his men—whoever was out there might have their face in the water, or close to it.

Every second was valuable.

The *Lady Vizola* began a new path. It carved through the debris, barrels, and detritus that knocked against the hull, ready for picking through later.

The ship's pace slowed as the armored man drew closer.

Jasen squinted down at him.

"Is he alive?" Alixa murmured.

"I don't know."

Burund shouted new commands. Sailors rushed to the edge of the deck, with ropes—

A ladder, like the one Jasen and Alixa had climbed.

They slung it down. Its wooden rungs bounced against the side of the ship, like an over-long, flexible, tuneless xylophone.

"*Ach-tan sa!*" Burund called to the man below.

He did not answer. Did not move, in fact.

The same call. The same response.

Alixa pressed a hand to her lips. "Oh no."

Another instruction. Two men descended the rope ladder.

They're bringing him up, Jasen realized.

They jumped out onto the panel of wood the armored man floated on. It sunk momentarily under their weight, wobbling them on their feet, then rose, settling into an easy up-and-down bob.

They bowed, taking the armored man by the underside of each arm. Lifted—

But he was far too heavy, and they couldn't pull him far at all.

"*Tre-sangkt,*" one called to Burund. "*Ec pul-ve sa.*"

Burund ordered two more down the ladder.

Jasen watched tensely as they descended it, then landed on the wood, keeping the armored man afloat. It could take all their weight easily enough still, but it was becoming very crowded now, especially with the man in armor sprawled out and occupying so much of it.

Between them, they managed to move him over, onto his back—

Jasen's eyes widened. This was a *white* man, with a swarthy skin and a lantern jaw. A small mane of hair flowed out and around his helm, which was pointed and sharp. He wore a white surcoat that bore a black lion, soaked and matted to his blued armor. His eyes were closed. A lance, taller than he was, was strapped across his back.

One of Burund's sailors leaned over, face sideways to the armored man's.

"What's he doing?" Jasen asked.

"Checking that he breathes," Burund answered.

Apparently he did, because the cry from the sailor was excited.

Burund must have instructed them to bring him aboard, for as one the four sailors pulled the armored man up. Even with so many, they struggled with his weight. The fact they weren't on the most stable of ground was not helpful either. But they managed it, somehow, returning to the rope. Then, between themselves they managed to array themselves upon the rope, propping the armored man up two from above and two below. The lance rattled against the armor as they lifted.

"*Hay!*"

Men on the deck pulled the rope ladder.

It rose.

Jasen waited, heart thrumming.

The men spilled over the edge, pulling the armored man with them and hauling him onto the deck. He work with a jerk, as if he'd been rudely awoken from a deep slumber.

Jasen's heart thrummed.

The man looked up. His eyes were unfocused. Like a drunk's, they shifted wildly, taking in everything and nothing at once.

Then he collapsed—

But before he did, he wheezed one word in a lilting accent, different from the accent of the men on this ship. It was a word that sent Jasen's heart into a frenzy, made his breath catch in his throat.

"*Baraghosa.*"

7

The armored man was, according to Medleigh (and translated by Kuura) suffering from low-grade hypothermia. His face was pale, his fingers cold. His teeth chattered violently during his brief moments of wakefulness, and his mind seemed confused. He said no more for the first twenty-four hours, at least as far as Jasen was aware.

And he was aware of everything the armored man did. Evidently there was only one spare cabin in the whole of the *Lady Vizola*, so Jasen and Alixa, plus now Scourgey, were joined by a fourth in the little space. The man took up the whole bed. Might've broken the frame, if Medleigh and Kuura hadn't stripped his armor to soak him in a bath of warm water.

It did not cure him, but did seem to ease a little of his sporadic tossing and turning. When he did open his eyes and look groggily about or mumble incoherently, his teeth no longer chattered.

Good enough for now, apparently; after an hour of soaking, he was removed, dried, placed into a poorly fitting set of spare clothes scavenged from somewhere, and dumped on Jasen and Alixa's bed.

"Where do we sleep now?" Alixa had asked.

"Floor," grunted Kuura. Ever since Scourgey had scratched him, he had been decidedly short with them.

Alixa huffed when she and Jasen were alone again with Scourgey and the armored man. "*He* should sleep on the floor. Not like he'd know about it."

Jasen had watched him for long hours. That one word rung out and echoed like a bell in his mind: *Baraghosa*. He had so many questions, all fighting to top the heap. First, how did this man know Baraghosa? Had he wrought the same destruction upon him and his people? And from where did they hail? Was Luukessia possessed of more survivors than just Terreas? Had there been other boundaries out there, other places spared?

The moment the man drew into semi-consciousness, it was all Jasen could do not to burst out with his muddled, desperate queries.

But the man could not answer them, falling once more into unconsciousness.

Scourgey was peculiar with the armored man. She, too, watched, her head bowed.

Once, she pawed at his hand, like a dog might its sleeping master.

"She knows you're worried about him," Alixa murmured.

The night's sleep was poor. But there were no storms, no violent waves crashing against the *Lady Vizola*, so Jasen's slumber was only interrupted by the hardness of the floor, and his constant checking on the armored man's status.

Sometime in the early morning, the man's teeth started chattering again.

Jasen told Kuura so when he arrived in the morning to see to them. He bit off something that might've been a curse in his native language and disappeared without a word. When he came back a few minutes later, it was with Medleigh.

They lumbered him back out of the room, to the washroom where he'd been bathed yesterday. A metal tub sat in a groove in the floor, the water in it cool and dirty. Medleigh hollered for someone, who came to clear it, and then they dumped the armored man inside.

Jasen hovered by the door. He and Alixa had followed, Scourgey in tow.

"Make yourselves useful if you're going to loiter," said Kuura gruffly.

Alixa asked, "By doing what?"

Another of those plosive sounds that Jasen took to be a curse, or at the very least something not particularly polite. "Bring pails of water." And off he went, pushing past them without an instruction to follow.

Hadn't thawed today then either.

The water was heated via a metal furnace, by which pails of water stood. The furnace was almost utterly black. It belched smoke out toward the ceiling, where a very small vent had been cut. The heat seemed to be dissipated enough by the vent so as to prevent the *Lady Vizola* from catching fire, but if an appreciable amount of smoke was permitted clear, Jasen couldn't see it: much of the ceiling above the furnace was stained with soot.

The round trip, going back and forth, reminded Jasen of the last time he'd run a loop with buckets of water—trying to save his home from going up in smoke.

He tried not to think of it—though it was hard to ignore one thought:

Even if he had been able to save it, all of the effort would've been for naught anyway.

But then, would that have been better for Adem, dying in a place where his loved ones had lived with him? Surely it would have, if his father could have chosen. Not the Weltan home, if he were still there … or some unoccupied, unused new building on the outskirts of Terreas, which did not feel or smell like home.

Stop it, he told himself. *You said you were going to stop thinking of it, not keep on.*

When the bath was full to the armored man's midriff—he'd been stripped by then, and Alixa refused to step any closer than just inside the doorway for fear she might "see anything improper"—Kuura and Medleigh deemed it to be enough. The armored man was lolled back by then. His skin, though it appeared naturally swarthy, was pale, still covered in a layer of gooseflesh.

"Will this help him?" Jasen asked.

"Might," said Kuura.

"It didn't last time."

Kuura shrugged. "Medleigh knows what he's doing."

Jasen wasn't entirely convinced, but stifled his questions. Loony Kuura was hard to deal with at times, but he would take that over gruff Kuura any day.

Medleigh kept an eye on the armored man for all of two minutes. Then he shuffled off to busy himself elsewhere. Kuura waited maybe thirty seconds longer, watching with his arms folded and a stern look on his face. Then he announced, "I'm off. Find me if there's a change."

He paused at the door before exiting, scowling at Scourgey. She had perched herself alongside the tub. Resting her muzzle upon her forearms, she looked at the armored man longingly.

"Stupid thing," he muttered, then went.

Alixa harrumphed.

"Don't follow," Jasen warned. "Please, no arguments."

"I wasn't going to." She stuck out her bottom lip.

Jasen and Alixa watched—or, rather, Jasen watched. She grew restless as the minutes ticked by.

But then, gradually, so did the armored man. At first it was a few twitches here and there. At some point, though, Jasen was aware that he was definitely moving more, a lot more than he had been—and color was gradually coming back to his face.

His heart began to race.

"He's waking up," he said breathlessly.

Alixa frowned. "I don't think … okay, Jasen."

He waited, five minutes becoming ten, becoming fifteen. The armored man was moving maybe once or twice a minute now. He'd slumped sideways after one particularly violent jerk, and now his face was twitching too, the way a cat's did when something disturbed its whiskers or it caught a particularly interesting scent.

"He's definitely waking up," said Jasen.

Alixa couldn't deny it this time. "Should I go get Kuura?"

Jasen was about to answer—though if he meant to say yes or no, he did not know—when the armored man's eyelids shot open.

He stared, face a mask of confusion. Blinked, blearily—

Then his pupils moved, drifting as if they had not been working until this moment. They found Jasen, Alixa.

Jasen's heart threatened to pound a hole right through his chest.

The armored man's mouth fell open. It worked, up and down, like he was finding words, or perhaps simply testing that the muscles controlling it still worked.

"You're awake," Jasen whispered.

"Who …" the man began. His vocal cords weren't entirely up to the task though, and so his voice had a stretched sound to it, like worn leather. "Who are you?"

"I'm Jasen," he answered. "And this is Alixa."

She raised a hand very slightly.

The armored man frowned, shook his head. "Where—are you from?"

"Luukessia."

His frown deepened. He stared off into the distance, past the walls of the ship. His forehead was lined, his expression twisted, as if he were trying to recall something from the darkest recesses of his mind.

He opened his mouth for a new question—

And then he saw Scourgey, propped by the side of the metal tub.

"*MONSTER!*" he roared, standing up in a rush.

Water flew—

Scourgey whined at the spray that landed over her, but otherwise did not move. Alixa gasped and threw up her hands in front of her eyes, her modesty offended.

"*GET IT OUT OF HERE!*"

His vocal cords were working perfectly now.

Jasen stepped forward, arm out. "What's—"

"*BEAST—BY MY SIDE—!*"

The armored man stepped backward. He had forgotten he was in a tub, though—or perhaps was unaware of it completely—for he tripped over the rim. Staggering backward, he fell heavily onto his feet, barely keeping his footing. His arms wheeled around to help retain balance.

"*WHERE IS MY LANCE?*" he demanded. His head turned frantically in all directions, searching the small washroom. Yet he was also determined to keep Scourgey in line of sight; he snapped back and forth, staring at her with wild eyes.

"She's not—" Jasen began.

"*VIOLENT BEASTS! IN THIS—THIS PLACE I AM IN, AND—*" He hit the rear wall. Panicked look at it, then more desperate searching. "*I WANT MY LANCE! WHAT'VE YOU DONE WITH IT?*"

"Me?" Jasen asked. "I haven't done anything!" He took a step forward. "If you just calm—"

"*STAY AWAY FROM THAT MONSTER!*" the armored man roared, jabbing a finger at Scourgey—who *still* sat with her front legs resting upon the edge of the tub, regarding the shouting man with blank indifference.

From behind her improvised shield, Alixa shouted back, "Scourgey is *not* a monster!"

At the same moment, Kuura and Medleigh burst in.

"Just what is this—" Kuura began—

His gaze met the armored man's.

"*CAPTORS! WHAT'VE YOU DONE WITH MY LANCE?*"

"Why didn't you find me to tell me he's awake?" Kuura shouted.

"He just woke up a moment ago!" Jasen answered.

Medleigh approached the armored man—

He thrust hands out, fingers clawed into curls. "*STAY BACK! FRIENDS WITH A SCOURGE—WELL, IF I'VE NO LANCE, I'LL FIGHT YOU MYSELF!*"

Medleigh understood none of this. Only the gesture meant anything to him. Rather than pay it full heed, though, he held up his own hands, as if surrendering, and came nearer—

"*BACK!*"

Closer—

The crazed look on the armored man's face became only more wild. "*SO BE IT!*" he roared—and stepped forward, and punched Medleigh hard in the mouth.

Kuura surged in, barking off something in his native tongue.

The armored man wheeled about to hit him, too—

Kuura ducked the swipe, then latched onto his shoulders.

He shouted an instruction to Medleigh, who came in from the other side.

"*UNHAND ME!*" His voice was teetering on the edge of a scream now. He clawed, desperately—and still shot looks at Scourgey as if she might launch at him and tear his throat out, though she hadn't moved a muscle since he'd woken. "*I SAID UNHAND—NO, KEEP ME AWAY FROM THAT MONSTER! GET—OFF! WHERE—IS—MY—LANCE?*"

Jasen watched the struggle from the door in horrified fascination.

The man was eventually subdued. Kuura and Medleigh tried to force him back into the tub. But with Scourgey there, he would not go.

"Order your pet away," Kuura told Alixa.

Jasen expected a sardonic, "Please," in reply. But Alixa came to Scourgey, still shielding her eyes—

"*Careful!*"

—and placed a hand just above her shoulder. "Come on. Let him be."

Scourgey lowered herself from the tub and let herself be led back to the wall by the door. There, she sat behind Alixa's legs. Her mouth hung open. Her tongue lapped at the air.

"There we are," said Kuura. "Now get back in this bath, would you? Medleigh says you've hypothermia. The warmth will do you good."

"Hypothermia," the armored man repeated. He allowed himself to be walked into the tub again, and then sat.

When the soft *splosh* announced he had sat down again, Alixa dropped her hand. "Finally." The man and Scourgey were at an impasse. She stared at him, and he stared back at her. Scourgey, at least, seemed relaxed about it. He was all coiled tension, ready to bounce into action like a spring.

It was impressive, Jasen thought, considering he'd been unconscious barely five minutes ago.

"Why'd you let that—that *thing* upon your ship?" he asked in a hoarse whisper.

"She's safe," said Alixa before Kuura could answer.

"They're violent—"

"She's not."

"—all of them."

"*She's* not," said Alixa.

The armored man shook his head. "A scourge, here. They bring death."

"Stink of it too," Kuura muttered.

"*She* saved us," said Alixa, "more than once." She patted Scourgey's head. The scourge didn't move; just panted, watching the armored man. "The rest of them might be violent, but this one is different."

"All scourge are the same! Murdering, corpse-defiling—"

"Excellent," Alixa grumbled. "A male Shilara."

Jasen winced. The image of her falling to the army of scourge on Luukessia's beach filled his mind for a moment starkly, her arm thrust up to the sky before they crushed her down—

"They kill at any and every opportunity," the man was saying.

"*She* doesn't," Alixa said harshly.

Medleigh said something.

"Maybe you should—" Kuura began.

But Alixa just cut across him. "She has been in with you the whole time you've been in here—and all of yesterday, and last night too."

That caused a hesitation. But the armored man recovered: "Left unsupervised—"

"You're bunking with us," Alixa said, "as is she. She was unsupervised *plenty* while you slept on our bed and we were relegated to the floor."

Another hesitation, longer. For the first time, the armored man glanced away from Scourgey, to Alixa, Jasen, and then Kuura and Medleigh. "Is—is it so?"

"It's true," said Alixa. To Kuura: "Tell him."

Kuura's scowl came back, though not as intense as before. "It is true," he conceded. "You have been in a room with that thing for a day now."

"See?"

"Though if it was left unsupervised," he added quickly, shooting Jasen and Alixa a pointed look, "I could not say. The children might have slept in shifts."

No thaw in the forecast then, by the look of it.

"We were both asleep," Alixa said. "Scourgey was unsupervised. So if you think they kill at every opportunity—think again. Because you are still here."

A thoughtful expression crossed the armored man's face. He frowned again. His was a particularly hard frown. Every muscle in his face seemed to throw themselves fully into it.

After a few long seconds, he said, "Perhaps this one … knows better."

"She's different," said Alixa. "She's our friend."

Tense quiet.

Kuura broke it, nudging the armored man's shoulder. "It'll be yours too, the way it's staring at you. Think the thing's in love or something." And he cracked a smile, the first Jasen had seen in nearly two days. Too wide, too many teeth—but he was smiling. Medleigh laughed along with him, a low guffaw between the two crewmen that seemed to set the pale man slightly more at ease.

"What's your name?" Jasen asked.

The armored man looked at him, frowning again. "Excuse me?"

"Your name. We told you ours. What is yours?"

"My name," he said, slow, like he was trying to comprehend the words as he repeated them, to parse them. Then: "Yes," he said. He took a deep breath, steadying himself.

"My name," he said, with all the dignity he could muster in his half-chilled, naked, sorry state—

"… is Samwen Longwell."

8

Shipmaster Burund likely had a hundred questions for Samwen Longwell, when he was capable of answering them.

Jasen had only one: How did this man know of Baraghosa?

But between his waning hypothermia, the effort of fighting off Scourgey's non-existent advances, and the energy it took for him to rise up and set his shoulders back as he introduced himself, he looked immediately worn out. So, when Jasen opened his mouth to ask—

Kuura would not permit him. "Out," he said, "the both of you. He needs time to recuperate."

"But—" Jasen protested.

Kuura shooed him away with a mighty wave. "Go on, get out of here. Let Medleigh tend to his patient."

"I just wanted to know—"

"Come on," Alixa said, pre-empting Kuura. She tugged gently on Jasen's sleeve and patted Scourgey, gesturing her forward with the other hand. "You can ask him more later."

Jasen begrudgingly followed. Though not before frowning at Kuura and Medleigh. He had questions, damn it, burning ones—that he would've had answered by now if Longwell hadn't had such a violent reaction to Scourgey's presence. And seeing as how the past twenty-four hours had been so agonizing, the thought of even a moment more was almost unbearable.

Still, he had to wait—and so he would.

The best place to wait was beside the washroom. Maybe by Medleigh's improvised doctor's station, a converted cabin Jasen hadn't yet been into but which he had stalked past yesterday as Medleigh and Kuura spoke. It was a squashed little room, with barely the space for two people to sit. A locked crate in one corner was dented, presumably by the waves' assault on the *Lady Vizola* the other night. Jasen didn't know what it contained—remedies of some sort, he supposed.

The problem was Kuura's mood. If he saw Jasen waiting—*loitering*, as he called it—then Jasen thought him likely to turn grouchy with them all over again, biting off—whatever unpleasant things he'd been muttering in his native language since Scourgey's scratch.

Best to leave them to it until Longwell was deemed satisfactorily well, then.

With nothing to do, Alixa suggested they spend some time on the upper deck. So they did, sitting upon it with Scourgey down below the foremast, where they were suitably out of the way of sailors milling about, performing whatever shiply duties Burund had entrusted to them.

A cluster of islands was in view today. But they could not be the Aiger Cliffs—they were much too small.

The past days—in Luukessia, and here on the *Lady Vizola*, butting against storms as it had been—Jasen had forgotten that summer approached. He remembered now though: as the sun drew higher, and the shadows shorter, he broke out in a sweat. The too-large clothes he wore didn't greatly ease things.

The heat wasn't doing great things for Scourgey, either. She stank to high heaven—a new reason for the sailors to skirt her a wide berth now their suspicion had faded.

Burund strode onto the deck sometime after noon. Jasen and Alixa had eaten by then—biltong and hardtack respectively—and returned, now sitting in the small strip of shade afforded by the forecastle's slight overhang.

He smiled at them, nodded.

"Shipmaster," Jasen greeted.

"You are looking hot," Burund said.

"It's sweltering out here," said Alixa. She'd cast an arm over her head to improvise shade, as well as to keep sweat from dripping past her eyebrows and into her eyes.

"It is cooler inside."

Was it? It hadn't seemed much better indoors.

Or maybe it was that being indoors reminded him of what he was waiting for, and his impatience grew while they lingered below deck.

"You are waiting to speak with Samwen," said Burund knowingly.

Jasen nodded. "Is he any better?"

"Medleigh says he is improving. You will be permitted to speak with him later."

Jasen wanted to ask, "How much later?" His heart quickened at the promise.

"Come inside," said Burund. "I will show you some things."

Jasen and Alixa followed, Scourgey in tow. If Burund minded her, or was offended by her deathly, rotten scent, he neither said nor showed it. The deck on the aft of the ship—this one called the poop deck, Jasen had been told to a snicker from Kuura which he did not understand—housed an office for Burund. Jasen had seen in through the windows—it was from these that the candlelight had bled that first night, when he and Alixa had been fished up—but that had been only a glimpse of the wonders within.

Inside was a veritable treasure trove. The room was equivalent to maybe two cabins adjoined on the long end, forming an approximate square. Burund had a desk, which was not useable: its surface was carved with maps. Though it had taken a battering over its use, it was still beautiful. Jasen puzzled at it momentarily, wondering how it looked as though the islands' outlines seemed to have been carved by flame; the hollows appeared burned, not just inked.

Alixa's attention was immediately drawn by a copper kettle resting on a shelf. It was concave toward the middle, with a wide, oblate bottom and top. The spout was very long, a good seven or eight inches. A line of gold material wended its way around the upper third of the kettle. It was uneven and bright, enough to make the rest of the kettle look dull by comparison.

"You like it?" Burund asked.

She nodded self-consciously. "I like the gold." She pointed, tracing its path without touching. "Why is it like that?"

"It comes from a seaport on Bithrindel," said Burund. "In their culture, breakages are mended like so."

Alixa nodded. But she frowned, apparently wondering more. Whatever question she had, she did not ask it.

Scourgey nosed her way in, sniffing at the object of Alixa's fascination.

"Uhm," she said, shooting an awkward glance toward Burund. "Do you mind—?"

A faint, crooked smile appeared at one corner of the mouth. "No."

Jasen busied himself with eyes roving deeper into the room. Most of Burund's items were fabrics or wooden carvings, colorful and elaborate. Pinned by its corners on one wall was what appeared to be a flag cut from animal hide: it was mottled with camouflaging spots.

"Did you get these on your travels?" Jasen asked.

"I did," Burund confirmed simply.

He took up a seat on the other side of the desk, and remained there.

Jasen hesitated.

"Feel free to look," Burund said. "I am sure something may catch your interest."

Something had: a locked cabinet in a corner. Coming up to Jasen's lower rib, it had three distinct compartments if the locks on the front were an indicator. The dark wood was stained—and, like the desk, had its fair share of markings from the beatings it had received in storms past. Curling patterns had been worked in the edges of each of the compartment's panels, very small and subtle.

"What's that?" he asked.

"Ah." Burund smiled again—and this time, it was with both sides of his mouth. He rose, and came round the desk. "That, Jasen, is a bookcase."

Alixa frowned at it. "It's not like any bookcase I've ever seen. Where are the shelves?"

"Books would fall off if they were on shelves," Jasen told her.

"Oh. Yes." Face reddening, she turned away, feigning disinterest yet listening nevertheless.

Burund reached to his belt. Hidden by an overhanging fold of his tunic was a ring of keys. He unhooked it, and began slowly but methodically moving through them.

When he found one that was maybe an inch long—barely a third the size of any others—he slotted it into the keyhole of the first compartment. It unlocked with a click.

The panel opened downward.

Inside were two shelves of books, both filled.

Burund looked at Jasen expectantly.

He looked back, confused.

"Go on," said the shipmaster.

"Err ..."

"You may take a book."

"Oh! Uhm. But these are ... are you sure?"

Burund nodded. "One for each of you." He added wryly to Alixa, "And one for your pet ... if she could read."

The pink flush in her cheeks rose a little at this joke. Interest piqued, though, she stepped forward to look at the pickings. "Are there any written in Luukessian?"

"Perhaps one or two," said Burund.

Alixa tilted her head to read the spines, what words were legible on them anyway. After a few seconds she withdrew a book with a very faded cover with an equally faded title: *The Petticoat Owned by the Sand-*

Colored Rabbit." A children's story, Jasen figured, though a lengthy one: it was at least a hundred pages.

He scanned for text he recognized. Not finding any, and not willing to ask Burund to open another compartment to scour, he pulled out a book with moss-green binding. Flipping through yielded no language Jasen understood. But it did reward him with pictures of plants, very detailed and marked with many arrows and scrawls.

He thought of Aunt Margaut.

Alixa appeared to do the same. He caught her looking at it, a wistful, melancholy look on her face. When their gazes met, she smiled wanly and turned away, sifting through pages.

"You may sit a while and read," said Burund, "if you would like to."

Jasen nodded. Better this than sit outside and being bored.

He pulled up a seat, as did Alixa. She began to read. He flipped through idly.

Burund tapped his fingers together behind his desk.

It was quiet, but not in an uncomfortable way. Yes, it was somewhat strange, sitting in the shipmaster's office … but it was a companionable sort of quiet.

Without understandable text to read, though, Jasen grew bored … and Burund noticed. So he began making conversation, asking about Jasen's village, the people, the scourge … Alixa's ears pricked and she listened, book forgotten and no pages turned for a long time.

Jasen tried not to answer too sadly.

It was difficult.

Eventually, when that line of questioning had ended, and the silence had fallen again, Jasen asked,

"Why'd you bring us in here?"

Burund's mouth crooked up at one corner. "You have time to kill." They whiled away the afternoon like that, sometimes in conversation—about the world around them, Burund's travels, the things in his office. As the sun dipped low, though, Kuura came to summon him, and Jasen and Alixa had to leave.

"Keep the books," Burund told them. "As they have enlightened me, so too may they enlighten you."

And the waiting resumed.

The evening's meal passed. Kuura did not return. Medleigh showed his face once, passing through the mess hall and taking a handful of biltong and hardtack. He shoved it all into his mouth, swept the room with a look, then passed through. Not that he'd have been able to provide any information to Jasen if he did stay.

He and Alixa sat in their cabin for a time. She lost herself in the pages of her book, eyes devouring the words. Jasen tried with his own, but it was harder: written in another tongue, he could only study the pencil drawings of herbs and plant life scattered within. Another day, they'd have fascinated him. Today, none would hold his interest for long before he cast a look back through the porthole.

The sun dipped.

"Maybe he's out now," said Jasen.

Alixa blinked. Her eyes tracked to the end of a paragraph. Then she looked up, gaze flickering as if coming out of a dream. "Longwell?"

"Yeah," said Jasen. "He must be."

"Where?"

"I don't know."

"Want to look?"

"Please."

Alixa studied the double page she was open to. Without a mark of any kind, and unwilling to fold down a corner, she recorded her place visually before shutting it, and led Jasen and Scourgey out into the deck of the *Lady Vizola*.

The ship was still busy at this time, and would be for hours to come yet. A few sailors met their eyes; to these, Jasen gave low smiles. A handful were returned. Most sneered—Hamisi included, who was coming down the tight stairs just as Jasen, Alixa and Scourgey were climbing up. He looked like he might bite off something nasty in his native tongue, but then caught sight of Scourgey rounding onto the landing, and bustled past with a frown.

Jasen wouldn't try smiling at him again.

Onto the top deck they went—

There, standing at the *Lady Vizola's* portside, a few feet from the edge, was Samwen Longwell. Dressed once more in his armor, he clutched the three-pronged lance that had been slung across his back when they'd dragged him from the sea. Color had returned to his complexion.

Against the banded orange of the setting sun, he looked magnificent—nothing like the guards in Terreas, who protected from scourge but had no duty other than watching what stalked beyond the boundary.

No, this man was a warrior, born and true.

"Hello," Jasen said on approach.

Longwell did not turn around. "Hello," he said back.

Without Kuura or Medleigh to stop him, Jasen dove in:

"Baraghosa," he said. "You said his name yesterday."

Jasen saw one eye twitch. "What of him?"

"How do you know him?"

Longwell adjusted his hold on the lance. He was not just gripping it, but leaning on it, just slightly. He shifted uncomfortably, then leaned on it again.

"He destroyed my ship." Longwell's words were tight. "The storm," he said, glancing backward at Jasen and Alixa, "it was his doing."

The storm—that abominable force that had threatened to tear the *Lady Vizola* apart with its howling winds and fearsome waves. Its brutality might have been natural, but those vibrant, glowing bolts of lightning that had struck the sea's roiling surface, whipping up new waves—those were not.

Of course, Jasen thought. A man with the power to cleave a mountain in two—he could easily whip the ocean and sky into a frenzy.

It brought a new string of questions, ones this Longwell could not possibly answer. Had Baraghosa followed Jasen? A curse was laid on Terreas—but two of Terreas's people had escaped.

Perhaps the storm had been meant to snuff out the last of them.

"How do you know Baraghosa?" Jasen asked.

Longwell turned to him with a shake of the head. "It is my turn. Where in Luukessia do you hail from?"

"Terreas," Alixa answered. "It's not there anymore."

Longwell frowned, that intense look coming across his face again. "How can that be so? Luukessia was overrun by scourge decades ago. How is it your village ..." He trailed off.

"We don't know either," said Alixa.

"There was a boundary around Terreas the scourge wouldn't cross," Jasen explained.

"A boundary?"

"A wall."

"But the scourge wouldn't cross it before the wall was there," said Alixa. "The wall was built after—to mark it for the village."

Longwell shook his head again. He eyed Scourgey a long moment, lapsing into silent thought.

"We didn't know why it kept the scourge away," said Jasen. "Nor did we question it."

"No," Longwell ceded, "I don't suppose you did. Probably just grateful the bastards didn't come roaring through and devour you all...as they did the rest of the land."

"It's gone now, in any case," said Alixa sadly. At Longwell's raised eyebrow, she said, "The mountain tore open and buried the village in lava. We're all that's left." She took a shuddery breath, pushed her shoulders back—fighting to remain stoic. Jasen recognized it now; she'd done it plenty these past days, more than anyone should have to.

"We," she said sadly, "are the last of our kind."

"Hardly," Longwell said. "The Emerald Fields, in Arkaria, are filled with Luukessians." There was a pause, as though all the air were sucked out of the room. "It is the place where countless of those folk fled when the scourge came, over the endless bridge to Arkaria. They live there now, some hundred thousand and more – a last, growing refuge of the people of that fallen land."

Jasen's breath caught.

"What?"

Alixa's reaction was less muted. "*Excuse me?*" she exploded. Before Longwell could answer, she turned to Jasen, and grabbed him fiercely by the shoulders. "We *have* to go there. Wherever it is—a whole world away, even two—*we have to go to the Emerald Fields, Jasen. We have to be with our brethren.*"

"But—"

"You could take us," she said to Longwell, "couldn't you?"

Barely before he had inclined his chin, she was on Jasen again. "We can go! The Emerald Fields—we have to go there! We can rebuild! We can carry on the line our ancestors started for us!"

"But …"

"The Luukessians are not dead!" Alixa cried. She released him then, throwing her hands to the sky. Then she danced in a circle, hooting to the heavens, more animated than Jasen had seen her—ever. Round and round she went, crying out: "The Syloreans still live! We are not the last of them! *We are not the last of them!*"

Longwell watched with a faint trace of amusement.

Jasen felt like his gut had been torn out of him.

He swallowed hard.

"Alixa."

She heard, answering with but a look as she spun around madly, like a top.

Jasen said, "We can't go."

Now she stopped with a jolt. "What?"

"Alixa, I …"

"What?" she prompted again, when he did not continue.

How to say it? How to break apart all that he had been feeling? How to show Alixa this—this *guilt* upon him?

"I have to find Baraghosa," he said.

73

"No—" she started.

"I do," he cut across. "I have to. He did this to us—the mountain, and the storm. He has to pay for that."

Alixa shook her head, kept shaking it. "Jasen, no. You can't."

"Terreas is dead because of him. We can't let him get away with that." His jaw settled into a tight line. "*I* can't let him."

"No—"

"He killed our families, Alixa," Jasen said. He needed to make her see this, make her see just how momentously important this was.

But she just looked hurt—and suddenly very far away.

She shook her head once more. "I will not be part of it."

Impasse.

Tense quiet.

Alixa recovered herself. To Longwell, she said, "Will you take me to the Emerald Fields?"

He nodded slowly, glancing warily between the cousins. "I will. Both of you, if you wish it."

"Thank you."

"But it will not be until this is over."

"Until what is over?"

"I too have business with Baraghosa," said Longwell.

Jasen felt his heart swell—saw Alixa's expression fall.

"Baraghosa destroyed my ship," Longwell said.

His face hardened with determination.

Looking out to sea again, rippled with orange-red light from the setting sun, he said, "And this account must be settled—now."

"Where can we find him?" Jasen asked.

"He may be anywhere," said Longwell. "He is a flighty warlock. Rumors have come to me of him in many places, going about his business, always followed by strange lights that danced in the sky above him."

"Business?" Jasen wanted to ask—but Longwell had carried on without pause.

"One rumor, though," he said, and here he slowed, twisting back slightly to regard Jasen, "places him where the shipmaster sails us to as we speak."

Jasen's eyes widened. "Aiger Cliffs?"

Longwell nodded. "The very same."

9

The port of Aiger Cliffs jutted out from the main city, which was nestled in a great shadow from the surrounding rock crests. The sun was peeking around them now as it moved across the sky, bathing the port and some of the beaches in yellow light. The farther reaches, though, would likely never receive a drop of sunlight.

The cliffs themselves ... those were what took Jasen's breath away. They were grand, enormous things, dwarfing the buildings laid out at their feet. Jutting skyward hundreds, maybe thousands, of feet, they rose in jags, twisting and turning upon themselves. Bare rock shimmered where the sun caught it. A scaffolding had been thrown up against part of the cliff, mere pencil lines against the vast rock face. Jasen squinted to make out the levels, and thought he could count at least eight, with more hidden by the buildings rising ahead of it. Any movement upon it was impossible to discern from this far.

Above the city, where the cliffs leveled out, towers of rock rose in jagged spires and arches, a mountain range in miniature that, except for the passages Jasen could see where erosion had carved holes open, walled the Aiger Cliffs off from the rest of the continent. Twisting paths were etched up them.

Jasen watched out of the porthole in their cabin, crouched beside Alixa. Both had on their old clothes. Dirty still but dry, Jasen appreciated them immensely: finally something that *fit*.

Alixa had one hand on Scourgey. For the past half-hour of their approach, she'd fallen into silence.

Jasen broke it. "When do you think we can go out on deck?"

Alixa just shook her head. For now, nods and shakes were what passed for answers.

Jasen and Alixa had been shooed away early this morning as the *Lady Vizola* made her final approach to the Aiger Cliffs. Many hands were on deck, following swift orders from Burund. What they spoke of, Jasen did not know. Only some of them worked the sails to direct their course toward the port, and the waning shadow overlaying the nestled city; the rest were back and forth like ants, doing who knew what.

Either way, Jasen and Alixa (and faithful Scourgey) had only clogged the deck and gotten in people's way. A kinder Kuura than two days past suggested they retire to their cabins until the ship was moored. "Unless yeh want to be trampled." Another massive belly laugh.

So they'd reluctantly gone down to their cabin, and there they remained.

At least Longwell was no longer sharing with them. It would've been tight, with the three of them watching out the porthole. Especially given his armor, which he insisted upon wearing at all hours … and the lance too, which had not left his side since the evening of his recovery.

The port alone was almost the size of Terreas. Jasen could only marvel at the bustle of ships that made their way in and out of the harbor. The vessels were all quite similar in their approximate silhouette, plus or minus a mast or two. Yet some were huge. He'd thought the *Lady Vizola* was a fairly large ship when he first arrived— even more when Kuura told him that it housed some eighty men. But compared to some of the ships anchored at port, it was a tadpole. Just the next ship over had to be three or four times the *Lady Vizola's* size, easily. It housed at least four interior levels above the water's edge that Jasen could count, two of which had holes like the *Lady Vizola's* next deck up, metal protrusions jutting out of them. The main deck had a forecastle, but then to the rear had *three* smaller decks all stacked one atop the other. Four masts towered, its sails billowing. With their mammoth size, they must've needed a dozen men to manipulate just one edge.

No one was upon it that Jasen could see, much as he craned his neck. Shame—he longed to see just who came from this behemoth ship, what lands they might hail from. Perhaps their skin was another color entirely—pale brown, or yellow, or … green?

The *Lady Vizola* gradually moved alongside the dock, which teemed with people. Dark-skinned, fair-skinned, everything in between, there were all manner of them, bustling in every direction. None of them paid any mind to the *Lady Vizola* pulling in.

But then, why would they? Ships crossing the seas, arriving to their lands—or maybe doing the very same themselves—was nothing new or exciting to them.

"Do you think we can leave yet?" Jasen asked.

Alixa shook her head.

Jasen bounced on his knees, impatience growing. "When?"

"I don't know."

He breathed. First words Alixa had spoken in all this time—and they were not remotely helpful.

More maneuvering.

A faint clunking resonated through the hull.

The ladder?

Jasen could stand it no longer. Whether it was or wasn't, he was getting to the top deck *right now*. There were things that needed doing, damn it!

He pushed onto his feet and ran from the room.

Alixa called his name—but he didn't answer. And in any case, she was coming after him a moment later, Scourgey hot on her heels.

Up the stairs—

The main deck exploded into view with a *BANG!* as Jasen thrust the door open.

Blue skies—

And the Aiger Cliffs.

It floored him, stopped him sharply in his tracks. Upon its doorstep, he felt smaller than he had ever felt in his life. Even sailing open seas, the whole world out of sight, replaced by only water, had not caused him to feel as infinitesimally minimal as he was now, on the *Lady Vizola's* deck.

The city was *huge*. Ten times Terreas's size, it rose in layers toward the mountains. To Jasen it looked as if it had been built upon a hill. That hill had been terraced, then built upon, with winding stairways put in to allow access from one level to another.

Huge walls separated the city layers, with crenelations overlooking the streets below. Massive arches hung over those stairways, all grey stone on white, with spiraling patterns like the waves themselves rendered in masonry.

In the shadows, metallic extrusions were visible, shimmering.

And those rods at the very tops of the rocky towers overlooking the city … they seemed almost tall enough to pierce into the sun itself, and Jasen could imagine the yellow running out like a broken yolk. Smaller details were more visible now, like short horizontal rods crisscrossing them toward their feet, and again at the tops. But those were outshone by the sun, and even squinting Jasen could not pick out anymore about them.

Jasen absorbed it—devoured it.

There is a world beyond Terreas, he thought.

And he was here, in it.

A stray thought went to his father, and Terreas. It hollowed his stomach, dulling his wonder.

He ground his teeth. Before, he'd wanted to see the world just because. Now, he had a reason to be here.

Baraghosa.

Longwell had said Baraghosa was known here. If the sorcerer was anywhere, it would surely be here.

And Jasen would find him.

The deck was emptying. Burund oversaw. A ladder had indeed been thrown down the side—two, in fact—and men formed a queue to descend.

"Come on," Jasen said to Alixa. He sprinted over.

Burund turned as he was joining one of the queues.

"Jasen," he greeted, nodding slightly. The same to Alixa.

"Shipmaster," she said.

"Where are you going?"

"Emerald Fields," said Alixa—

At the same moment, Jasen said, "To find Baraghosa."

They silenced. Turned to each other. Glared. Alixa folded her arms across her chest and huffed.

Burund did not comment. But he did hesitate, for a rare moment.

"Before you go," he said slowly, "I must say two things. First: pursuing the man you seek is dangerous."

"Baraghosa?" Jasen asked.

Burund nodded. "He is known to all who sail these waters."

"What can you tell me of him?" Jasen said. Why hadn't Burund *said* all this time? Why hadn't Kuura? For *days* he could've been pumping them for information that might allow him to find Baraghosa, more than Longwell's scant exposé. Burund had *heard* Longwell mention Baraghosa, for crying out loud! And if Baraghosa had made the storm, as Longwell said, surely Burund knew that. Jasen had discussed it with him! He had sat in his office, waiting for Longwell to wake, looking over his trinkets from a world travelled—and all the while, Burund had kept his knowledge of Baraghosa silent.

Burund shook his head at Jasen's question. "I have no more to say but my warning."

This new wad of frustration joined the tangled ball of it in his stomach.

"Fine," he said, "then I'll ask Kuura."

"Neither will Kuura tell you anything more than I have done."

Jasen pursed his lips. His internal temperature was rising.

Unlike Alixa, he'd not let off the steam with sarcastic remarks. Better to just let it simmer and then die of its own accord, unvented.

"Second," said Burund, "I rescued you from the waters. In the eyes of my people, that makes you my responsibility. I cannot let you wander into the Aiger Cliffs."

"But—"

Burund spoke over Jasen's protestation. "Were you to die, it would be a stain upon me, an abdication of my responsibilities as a man and a shipmaster."

"So …" said Alixa, "we can't go."

"You may. I understand you both must go … wherever it is you are going. If you are to join with another vessel, though, I must speak to its captain. This is my responsibility."

"So we can go."

Burund nodded. "You may."

"Right," said Alixa. "Where is Longwell?"

"Samwen has already left."

Jasen's stomach hollowed, again. "What?"

"He will be back."

"But … he knew we were waiting."

"He indicated he might encounter trouble," said Burund. "He did not wish to drag the two of you into it." He leaned forward. "Trouble is plentiful in Aiger Cliffs."

Jasen looked to the cliffside city once more. Its majesty was suddenly less grand. Underlined by that remark from Burund, the place took on an almost sinister look, and Jasen realized that, for all his excitement at stepping out into the world, he did not *know* that world, or the dangers it presented.

Terreas was boring, but it was home, and safe, and trouble generally only came in the form of squabbles with his peers—and Baraghosa.

Here, every step was unknown.

"Be wary," Burund warned. "And watch your purse."

"We don't have any money," said Alixa.

"It will not stop a thief from trying."

Well. That just about muted every last shred of excitement that Jasen felt.

But he had come here for a reason, and Longwell believed the cliffs were connected to Baraghosa in some way. Burund had all but confirmed it by warning Jasen of the danger he posed now they were here.

Jasen steeled himself. Whatever dangers might lie in Aiger Cliffs, he would face up to them. The threat of a thief or two was not enough to deter him from the desire he harbored, and shared with Samwen Longwell:

Revenge.

Revenge, he repeated to himself.

And down the ladder he went.

10

The port overwhelmed Jasen almost immediately.

Hundreds of voices carried from all directions. Conversations went on in dozens of languages. Here and there Jasen would get a snippet of words he understood; most, though, were incomprehensible, not only because Jasen had never even heard another language outside of the walls of his village, but because the general bustle and hubbub drowned them out.

If the rest of the world had only fair-skinned people like Terreas, then tagging along with the *Lady Vizola's* crew would've been easy. Look for dark skin, and follow. But here the crowd was made up of people with skin of every shade of brown and peach, white and black. Some in headdresses, others in flat, dull armor, some with barely any clothes on at all—wherever they came from, it was *not* the *Lady Vizola*—and so Jasen and Alixa, the moment they dismounted the ladder, were alone in this new world.

"Where do you think Longwell is?" Jasen asked Alixa. He had to lean forward to be heard.

"How should I know?" she shot back. "Have *I* ever been here before?"

Jasen didn't answer. Alixa's mood was already sour. Like an agitated nest of wasps, it would not do to go kicking it.

Looking up and down the port, he was at a loss. There was so much going on, and the people striding by seemed not to be going in any one specific direction.

On the right, however, maybe a few hundred feet up the way past stalls with tented tops, was a grandiose brick arch. Primarily white, it was huge enough—three quarters the height of the *Lady Vizola's* main mast, at least—that grey stone had been inset to form writings in many languages, one line above another.

Jasen found their own. Written in Luukessian were the words, "*AIGER CLIFFS—THE CITY OF LIGHTNING*".

"There," Jasen said, pointing.

"Fine," said Alixa. "Come on, Scourgey."

They wove through the people filtering about—although "wove" was perhaps putting it kindly. Almost everyone here was an adult. Jasen was slight, Alixa slighter; and without the force to simply push through the throngs and cut their own path, Jasen and Alixa were shunted about. They slotted into gaps when they opened and moved ahead. But then a group would make way in the opposite direction, or someone would step across heading for a docked boat, and their progress would be stalled until they could find a new eddy to follow. It would have been impossible—if not for Scourgey.

She, at least, helped. When people noticed her, reactions were varied. Two men with their hair tied in short, stiff braids practically leapt aside when Scourgey crossed their path, biting off words Jasen didn't understand. Farther up, Scourgey nosed the palm of someone who had, just before, been winding linked sausages. She distractedly went to pat the animal she assumed was a dog, then froze, staring bug-eyed upon actually taking Scourgey in. Her companion asked her what was wrong. Jasen didn't hear the reply; they were already past.

The tang of salty air was rich here on the dock, but every few feet, it was overpowered. Stalls served food, mostly hot, from giant, round pans over burning coals, wildly different every few steps. Jasen couldn't help but salivate, as well as stare in fascination; one was serving what must be chunks of rabbit, mixed with peppers and onions and something green and sprouting that Jasen didn't recognize; the next was like biltong, all hot spices that warmed the back of the throat without true heat. Then there was a baker, dispensing hot loaves and buns to a rabble of customers; and then cheese, thick rounds of it, the smell almost overpowering but so wonderfully good. Jasen eyed them all hungrily, even the foods he did not know, wishing that he had money—enough to try a morsel from each and every vendor on the port. If not that, at least enough to fill his belly with more than cured meat and dry crackers.

The archway stood tall over stairs as wide as a full house, back in Terreas. There were two dozen steps up, easy.

"City of Lightning," Alixa murmured, looking up at the inset text.

Jasen peered at her, knowing what she was thinking. "Longwell said the storm—"

But she leveled a weary—and guilty—look. "Stop it." Then she fell into tight-lipped silence, not letting any of her thoughts slip.

Everything here was large. The city itself, its buildings—even its roads were much wider than any Terreas had known. It was like they'd been sized to allow a boat—one of the smaller schooners, mind—to be tugged right through the city. Jasen pegged the streets at near fifteen feet across. In spite of the increased space, it was still a chaotic tangle of people moving in all directions.

"Where now?" he asked Alixa.

"Again: how should I know?"

Someone collided with Jasen's back. He looked up apologetically. The fat, balding man who'd hit him barely cast Jasen an eye though, moving past without looking.

Jasen tucked himself closer to the side of the top of the steps. Looking about, peering over the heads and up the levels of the city itself, he said, "Well … Burund said Longwell expected trouble. So if we just …"

"I am not looking for trouble with you," said Alixa flatly. "You may seek it out on your own, but I am not getting involved in any more misadventures with you, Jasen Rabinn."

"What do you mean, misadventures?"

"There have been *plenty*."

Jasen pursed his lips. "Fine." Alixa's foul mood was quickly dragging his own into a downward spiral. "Well, I'm going this way." And off he marched, forking left just because.

In spite of her complaining, Alixa trailed along behind. Scourgey lumbered along too.

After stopping to ogle a busy fishmonger's stall—it stunk to high heaven of fish like Jasen had never known, and he was baffled at why so many patrons did business there now; didn't they know the sea was teeming with them just two hundred feet away?—he said grouchily, "Why are you following?"

"I'm looking for Longwell too." It was a sniffy reply, clipped.

"Why? You heard what he said. He's seeking Baraghosa."

"Well, he's an adult. Maybe he's more open to reason."

Jasen's nostrils flared.

Instead of replying, he forked down the next side street. This was a little tighter. The buildings immediately to either side of the junction had strung twine between them in zigzags. Triangular sheets, all different colors, flapped in the sea breeze.

Music drifted from somewhere, and Jasen followed the sound.

Someone behind him shrieked.

He turned to see a woman in an elaborate, wide-bottomed dress jabbing a finger at Scourgey.

The scourge just regarded her blankly.

"She's safe," said Alixa.

The small, impromptu crowd, gathered as people paused and turned in the direction of the cry, did not look so sure. A man with a teenaged son put a hand on his back and forced him on a wider path around Scourgey. As they were already on the other side of the street, Jasen couldn't see how the extra two feet of space would make much of a difference.

The music came from a man playing a stringed instrument. It was a stubby little thing, resting upon his shoulder. The fingers of one hand worked the strings against its neck, while the other plucked them.

To his side was a dancer. Dressed with many-folded clothes that would make Kuura's tame in comparison, he spun on his toes, then leaped, and spun again.

A few people watched. Some chucked coins onto a piece of green cloth apparently for that purpose. It was fairly well covered, though what the actual value of the coinage upon it was, Jasen could not be sure. These men might be terribly rich. Or not. Probably not, he decided.

He walked on.

And Alixa still followed.

"Longwell sees sense perfectly well," Jasen said after a while.

Alixa just huffed.

"He does."

When she still didn't answer, Jasen turned back.

She shook her head, giving him a withering look. "You heard Shipmaster Burund. Baraghosa is dangerous. So why you think chasing after him—you, of all people—"

"What's wrong with me?" Jasen blustered.

"—would do any good—"

"I can fight him!"

Alixa huffed again. "No, Jasen, you can't."

The heat burning in Jasen's midriff mounted—again. He was teetering on the edge of an explosion, he could feel it—

Instead, he made another sudden turn, this time down a narrow side street. This was much more reminiscent of Terreas now, and less busy. It was darker too—they'd well and truly entered the shadow of the cliffs now.

Alixa scoffed. "Baraghosa's down here, is he? In this alley?"

Jasen whirled on her. She'd exhausted the last of his patience—or maybe he found himself exhausted from holding back the frustration tugging at him from seemingly every direction.

"Just what is your problem?" he burst out. "You think going to the Emerald Fields is—is going to bring our families back?"

Alixa's face seemed to flare, like a sudden spark in a fireplace. "Those are our people—"

"They are not our people!" he shot back, shouting her into silence. "The only people we knew have joined our ancestors—because Baraghosa—" he jabbed out with a finger here, as if pointing to the man, wherever he might be "—killed them."

"Our ancestors—" Alixa began.

"*Our ancestors* would want vengeance."

Alixa shook her head. "You've gone mad."

"I have not." But it felt as if he had. All the building frustration—all his guilt, churning and churning inside like the stormclouds that had tried to rip the *Lady Vizola* apart just nights ago—it had pushed him to some invisible brink. And now, as this all poured out of him, he was suddenly aware of it, aware of being there, at its edge, and staring down into the abyss.

"I have to stop Baraghosa," he said. "I have to kill him."

"Jasen," Alixa began—

"*Coinpurses,*" said a voice—and they turned to see a pair of men blocking the alley's lone exit. A heavyset one stood back, apparently keeping guard, head twitching back and forth.

The other, a skinny little man with spindly wrists, approached. He leered at Jasen and Alixa … and then shifted, just enough to show an eight-inch-long blade. He held it close to his trousers—hiding it from passers-by.

He licked his lip, took another step nearer.

"Give me your coinpurses," he said again, voice tremulous and quiet, yet threatening all the same. "Now."

11

Jasen's heart pumped into immediate overdrive.

"W-we don't have anything," he stammered.

The man wielding the blade advanced another step. A leery look in his eye, he sneered at Jasen's words. "Hand them over, boy. I ain't asking again."

Alixa had maneuvered behind him. She clutched his wrist, tight, fingernails driving crescents into his skin. He could practically feel the *thud-thud-thud* of her heart against him as she pressed close—

But what protection was he? He had no weapons—neither of them did—except for fists. Thin as the man was, Jasen might be able to match him toe to toe … but there was a height difference that probably meant a gap in reach, too, that would disadvantage him by a few inches.

None of it mattered anyway. Not when the thief had a knife. Nor when his blubbery friend kept watch at the head of the alley, alternating looks between the road for passers-by, and the unfolding mugging.

If Shilara were here, she could deal with this. Both men, easy. An arcing swing of her spear's handle, across the skinny one's nose, then around to whip the other in the neck—

Shilara was dead though, and no use to them here. Her last stand had secured their escape from Luukessia. It did not extend to Chaarland.

The skinny man licked his lips. "Last time I'll tell you." He was maybe six feet from them now, and closing, even as Jasen and Alixa stumbled backward.

Scourgey bared her teeth. A rattling noise warbled from her throat—her approximation of a growl, possibly. Crouching low, she poised herself to spring.

The man at the head of the alley's expression had turned nervous. He snapped something to his comrade in another language.

The knife-wielding man cast Scourgey a momentary glance. He replied. Then, to Jasen: "Call your dog off."

"She's not a dog," said Alixa.

Jasen's chest swelled as a flood of hope surged through him. Scourgey would protect them.

"Don't come any closer," he warned. "She'll hurt you."

The man with the knife's eyes flashed. *Threatened?* Jasen could almost hear him thinking. *By this boy?*

He stepped again—

Scourgey's rattling sound grew louder.

Somehow, the stink emanating off her body grew more intense. Not just the wretched scent of death; something animal and dangerous bled into it now too.

Knuckles tightened on the blade's hilt, turning the white of bone. He gritted his teeth.

From the alley's head, a shout—

The heavyset man's attention was not on Scourgey, though, but something outside. Whatever he said to his partner was panicked and quick. Then he was bracing, and—

He ducked as someone barreled into view, swinging a fist.

The dodge wasn't quick enough. A dark-skinned hand slammed into one ear with a crash. He stumbled back—but another was sailing in already and caught him under the chin.

The man with the knife spun—

Kuura clocked the heavyset man once more. Then he whirled, a blur of fabric.

Eyes flashing at the man with the knife, he grimaced and shoved up his sleeves. The heavyset man staggered behind him, casting one last frightened and bloodied look down the alley before running out of sight. Kuura cracked the knuckles on both hands.

He bit off something in his people's language—it sounded threatening and angry.

Failed-mugger responded. He brought up his knife, ready to strike—

But Kuura just kept coming. And so, when the distance between them had just a couple of seconds till it closed, the thief cried out something Jasen could only assume was a cowardly last threat, dropped his knife, and bolted past Kuura as close to the alley's edge as he could.

Kuura stuck out a leg.

The man tripped, went over hard. He landed on his palms, a sound that was almost comic.

Then he was up and running at a hobble out of the alley and in the direction of his friend. No looks back, and no last words.

Kuura scowled at his back.

Then he turned, looking over Jasen, Alixa, and Scourgey.After a long moment, the disgust on his face dissolved. Letting his sleeves fall loose again, he approached. "Are you okay?"

"Yes," said Alixa. Jasen agreed with a nod. "He didn't get close enough to do anything. And Scourgey would've stopped them if he had."

Kuura eyed the scourge. "Hm."

She was still on alert, body pressed low to the ground. Her rattling growl had ceased, but if those eyes could be read despite their utter blackness, Jasen believed they were pointed at the mouth of the alley, pupils as wide as they could go to absorb anything and everything that might become a surprise threat.

Alixa consoled her with a pat to the shoulder.

Scourgey didn't soften her stance.

"Thank you for saving us," said Jasen.

Kuura stooped to pick up the fallen knife. He looked it over without much interest. Then he handed it, handle first, to Jasen.

"Err …"

"To protect yourself."

Jasen looked at it uneasily. Long ago, he had thought that he might be a soldier, and wield a sword or spear through the lands of Luukessia, cutting the scourge down and reclaiming its lands. It was a child's dream, one that had died, replaced with the tamer desire to simply explore a world beyond his village. He knew nothing about how to wield a dagger—

But then, what more was there than a stabbing motion?

Shilara would have reacted scornfully to that, Jasen thought.

He felt another pang of sorrow—for her, and his father, who'd done the best he could with Jasen.

They're with the ancestors now, he thought, and it brought some peace.

And they would want Jasen to be protected.

Carefully, he reached out. Taking the blade by the hilt, he wrapped his fingers around it.

It felt …

Unnatural. To some men—*and women,* he amended, again thinking of Shilara and what she would say were she still here with them—a weapon was a natural extension of themselves. It was perfect, it was right, to clasp one, to brandish it. Good men—and bad, like the muggers—for some it simply seemed…right.

Jasen was not one of these people. Holding the blade up in front of him, his arm rigid and almost straight—as if he were afraid it would turn upon him and stab him of its own volition—he was certain he never would be.

Burund's warning echoed: the city was dangerous.

So Jasen carefully tucked the blade into his belt. He did it at the very side of his hip, so there was no chance of it cutting into flesh as he walked.

"We'll find you a scabbard for that," said Kuura, nodding to it.

"I don't have any money," said Jasen.

Kuura waved him off. "Ways around it."

"How did you know we were here?" Alixa asked.

"Shipmaster Burund had me follow you," Kuura answered.

Jasen deflated a little at that. Now the moment had passed—and now he was armed, too late to deal with it—a sense of shame had come over him like the fine mist that settled at the base of the mountains overlooking Terreas. That Kuura had saved them just by luck was a fine enough coincidence he would accept …

That Kuura had saved them by tailing them at some distance, on Burund's orders … that made Jasen feel like even more of a child than ever.

And when he was searching for Baraghosa, to exact revenge for what he had done to Jasen's home …

A sour taste lingered in his mouth, coppery, like blood.

"Thank you," said Alixa, genuinely grateful. "We really appreciate it."

"Right," said Jasen. "Thanks."

"We'll be sure to thank Shipmaster Burund too."

Kuura cackled, spreading his lips wide and showing off as many of his teeth as he possibly could manage. "I did not simply follow you because my shipmaster requested it of me," he said. Growing very serious all at once, he said levelly, "Though I would always honor the instruction of my shipmaster. But the truth is …" And here his lips parted, flashing many white teeth again. "I have grown to feel a certain affection for you orphans."

Alixa shot Jasen a glance. "Oh?"

"You are like strays," said Kuura pleasantly.

Alixa's lips thinned. "Oh," she said flatly. "He's comparing us to dogs."

Kuura bellowed laughter, throwing his head back. Bear-like hands spread out over his stomach, clutching it. Hard to think that, perhaps a minute ago, those hands had been devastating, fearsome fists.

"Well, you know what it is like," he said. "You take them in, and they are wary and scared for a while. Then they get better—and then they bite at your hands again as you feed them, and you think, *Why, oh why, did I take this stray in when it bites me so?* But you remember that they do not always bite, and if they do, it is because they have felt something that has scared them, or made them angry—and it passes, and you remember why you took them in in the first place. Do you see?"

Jasen looked blankly at Kuura's grinning face.

Alixa hesitated. "Uhm."

Kuura erupted into laughter again.

When he had quieted some, he said, "You are but children in the woods here in the Aiger Cliffs."

Another stab went through Jasen, this time at being called children. It was true, of course, but … still.

"And the Aiger Cliffs," Kuura went on, oblivious—or perhaps simply ignoring the hurt look that crossed Jasen's features—"is no place for unsupervised children. Even," he added, "ones as brave as the both of you."

Oh. Well, that dispelled some of Jasen's feeling of uselessness.

He eyed Kuura's face. Was that a pointed, purposeful placation? Jasen could not tell. Nor, he thought, would Kuura be forthcoming if asked.

Whatever the case, it eased some of the unpleasant feeling in Jasen's chest enough that he raised a small smile.

"Now come," Kuura said. "We have talked in this alley for too long. Let us step out into the sun again and evaluate the next steps."

'Stepping into the sun again' was only figurative. The sun had not moved across the sky far enough that its light could fall upon these streets yet, and probably would not for another hour hence. Yet the alley's tight quarters seemed to have dampened the light yet further, so it did feel as if they stepped out of the dark when Kuura led Jasen, Alixa and Scourgey back onto the street proper.

Scourgey's hackles were still up. She looked in all directions, teeth bared. No rattling growl—not that she wasn't threatening enough without it. Upon their arrival from the alley, a cluster of children loosed panicked yells, turned on their heels, and sprinted away.

Alixa looked crossly at their receding backs. "Just ignore them," she told Scourgey, patting her above the shoulder softly.

Scourgey did not appear to care.

Jasen's walk was careful. The knife stuck into his belt was awkward—and felt, the moment he moved, perilously sharp. He was afraid to stride at his normal length for fear the blade might shave a layer of skin off.

He needed a sheath for it, as Kuura had said, and soon.

"So," said Kuura, "what is your plan now?"

Jasen cut in before Alixa could speak. "Finding Baraghosa."

Alixa groaned. "Nooo, Jasen."

He rounded on her. "Baraghosa—"

"Yes, yes," she said, "I've heard it all before. He destroyed our lands, destroyed our people."

"Which is exactly why—"

"We should go to the Emerald Fields," Alixa said, with a finality that suggested that the conversation had concluded, and nothing Jasen said or did could ever bring her around—so it was worthless to try.

But try he would. "I'm not just dropping this."

Alixa folded her arms. She huffed a breath, turned away from him. Conversation *definitely* closed.

Jasen wheeled around her, trying to catch her eye.

"Baraghosa has to pay for what he did," he said.

"And you are the very person to stop him," Alixa retorted, voice flat. Casting him a sideways look, she said, "You didn't even have a knife until two minutes ago." Looking away again: "Though if you expect a knife to get you far against a sorcerer with the power to rip open mountains and whip up the sea …"

Jasen gritted his teeth. Was everyone intent on making him feel pathetic today? So he hadn't had a great deal of thought over the logistics of his battle with Baraghosa. Did it matter how he would do it? Surely what was important was that Baraghosa be smitten, be utterly destroyed, for what he had done to Terreas?

And Jasen could do it. He could—he *would*, if he could lay his hands on him.

All he had to do was find him.

"I'm searching for Baraghosa," he said quietly, calming the rage that had started to fester and boil in his stomach again, "whether or not you like it."

Alixa humphed.

Let it drop, Jasen told himself.

… and still he couldn't. He needed Alixa to see him eye to eye on this, to see reason.

He dredged deep, looking for something, anything, that might bring her around, make her see that Baraghosa had to be brought to justice—and that he, Jasen Rabinn, was the person to do it.

He thought back to the night Baraghosa had come to Terreas; thought back to how Jasen had been singled out; thought back to how Adem had refused him—the first child in—how many?

Pityr had gone easily. That, Jasen remembered. He was smiling—troubled, yes, but he went, even as his parents refused.

But then, his parents hadn't been councillors. They could not reject Baraghosa's deal the way Adem had.

Pityr had to go.

Maybe …

Jasen licked his lips. He said, carefully: "What if Pityr is still out there?"

Alixa didn't turn. But the question, asked in low words, had to have struck her in the chest like a lead cannonball. Jasen was attuned enough to her to detect the mental flinch—it came out in the slight, hard breath she exhaled from her nose, the way her fingers tensed around her arms.

Jasen had hit his mark.

He waited, breath held.

Finally she answered. "He's not."

Jasen's chest hollowed. He had been so sure that that would bring Alixa around.

It hadn't.

At least … not yet. He still had hope. She had not come around to see things reasonably, but maybe talk of Pityr would start the process.

Either way, Jasen had not been totally defeated. Longwell, too, was searching for Baraghosa, to exact his own revenge for wrecking his ship. As Longwell was Alixa's key to getting to the Emerald Fields; unless she chose to go it alone—and she might, if pushed, for now she had no choice but to follow this "folly" along.

"If," Kuura said, taking the quiet as an opportunity to re-insert himself into the conversation, "Baraghosa is here, I know of a way we might find out."

Jasen's head whipped around. "Oh?" He ignored the little huffed sigh from behind him—and the murmured curse that was begun and unfinished.

"There is a man named Stanislaus, down at the docks. He knows everything that goes on here."

Jasen's heart skipped. No Longwell to guide them for now—but this Stanislaus, he would surely know better than Longwell would anyway, if he saw the comings and goings of the Aiger Cliffs' visitors.

"Can you take us there?" he asked.

Kuura nodded. "I can. But first—" He pointed at the knife, sticking out at Jasen's hip. Gravity and his movement had pulled it around, so now it hung at a stupid angle, blade pointing slightly forward as if ready to stab anyone who came too near.

"Oh. Right. But we'll go ask after Baraghosa next?"

Another nod from Kuura. "Come. Follow me."

Off he went, without checking that they would follow.

Jasen fell immediately into step—

Then he paused, looked round.

Alixa hadn't moved. Remaining stationary, she still had her arms folded across her chest. A disdainful pout twisted her mouth, brought her eyebrows down lower than normal, pressing a faint line between them.

She appeared not to wish to look at Jasen … but as he waited there, another few seconds, she glanced his way.

A long moment.

She sighed, dropping her arms. "Please, Jasen."

He brooked no argument. "I'm going." There was a sudden ferocity in his voice now, one he had not heard before.

Alixa's mouth worked, up and down on a silent hinge. She looked away, swallowed hard.

When she looked back, there was no more of her exasperation or fire. She just looked lost—

Like a girl whose only family now stood before her——and who threatened to abandon her, in not so many words, if she did not come.

She hesitated a long, long moment.

Then, with another sigh, she cast her eyes down. Shaking her head, she patted Scourgey gently. "Come, girl," she said—and then came in Jasen's direction.

He waited until she was close, then pivoted too.

If not for Kuura, their journey back toward the docks would have been silent.

12

Stanislaus worked a long way down the docks, where a promontory jutted a mile and a half into the water. A natural arch had been cut through it, leaving a shadow upon the beach and across pristine waters. It shielded the dock from some of the salty wind, so the smell was weaker under it. Still, boats congregated thickly on either sides of the arch. The vessels here were different: slimline boats with efficient sails, adorned with great lizard's heads at their prow and scaly, twisting serpentine bodies across their hull were side by side with heavier vessels, built thick and sturdy, with holes for a great many pairs of oars etched into their sides. The oars lay flat against the ships' sides now. As they widened into an angled paddle at the ends, and lay overlapping each other, they looked almost like birds' feathers.

Kuura told Jasen and Alixa where these boats and people hailed from, sometimes with descriptions that were downright unkind.

Jasen barely took this in. His mind boggled at the rocky arch—and, as they drew under it, the fear that the entire thing was an inch from collapsing upon them.

Kuura spotted Jasen's pale-faced look after realizing he had not been replying for some minutes now.

"What is it?" he asked.

Jasen nodded upward shakily. "What if it falls?"

Kuura exploded with laughter. The boom drew the attention of some passers-by, but not many. Scourgey was responsible for far more looks shot their way, none of them particularly pleasant. By comparison, Kuura was fairly banal.

"What's so funny?" Jasen asked.

"Fall on us?" Kuura asked, wiping a tear from his eye. "Why would it? What are *you* going to do to knock it down? Just 'cause yeh've a knife now, it don't mean yeh c'n fell the gods' creations!" And he descended into howled laughter once again.

The fact that it was a laughing matter assuaged Jasen's worries, though he couldn't help but feel a little bit insulted—yet another embarrassment to add to the count for the day. At this rate, his self-esteem would be ground into dust by nightfall.

He glanced to Alixa, hoping she would share in his worry and make him feel better. But she kept her eyes ahead, downturned, and wouldn't meet his gaze.

Guess he was alone then.

Stalls were erected here too, much less regularly than those spread along the coast closer to the *Lady Vizola*, yet close enough that air was still suffused with the scents of cooked meat and sweet pastries and rich cheeses.

Where the arch grew most narrow, no boats were moored. Instead, an expanded pier reached out from the dock. Workers bustled about it, most of them light-skinned and blonde, moving crates and barrels.

As Kuura approached, he said to Jasen, "There he is." He cupped his hands around his mouth. "*Stanislaus!*"

More than one of the men moved. But for most, it was only a glance to see who had shouted, before turning away and continuing to move their shipments. A man with a tattooed face, though, straightened to look at Kuura with a sharp eye—then he dropped a crate heavily at his feet, and sidestepped it.

"Kuura, you old loon," he called. "What's an old scrote like you doing on my dock?"

"T'ain't *your* dock," someone grumbled.

Stanislaus answered by sticking his middle finger up.

He came round to the edge of the pier. A rag was tucked into his belt. Once white, it was now creased and dirty. Nevertheless, he fished it out and gave his hands a cursory wipe with it. Stuffing it back into place, he appraised Jasen and Alixa without much interest. Scourgey was not of interest either, apparently, because she garnered little more than a glance before Stanislaus's attention returned to Kuura.

"Surprised to see you back at the cliffs," he said. "What's brought you? Your wife shacked up with your brother yet?"

Kuura guffawed, like the thought of his wife's infidelity was the funniest thing he had ever heard of. "Yeh're a wretch, Stan." He planted a wide hand on Jasen's back and shoved him forward. "Meet Jasen. Jasen, this is Stanislaus."

Jasen looked up at him nervously. Even discounting the black patterns tattooed down one cheek and around his eye, Stanislaus was an intimidating figure. At least six and a half feet tall, he was blonde-haired, blue-eyed, and rippled with muscle all over. His face was hard, even when he grinned. With practically zero fat clinging to him, his jawline was all angles, his chin very square. The clothes he wore—a thin white shirt, and dark shorts clutched tight to his midriff by a fibrous belt—were just loose enough not to appear glued to his frame.

His hand was even bigger than Kuura's. Calloused too, Jasen felt when he shook, the skin so hard and dry you could cut glass with it.

"And Alixa," said Kuura.

She shook too, then backed off.

"Stan Yalow."

That was the full extent to which Stanislaus appeared concerned with the children, for his introduction was said very shortly. Almost immediately his attention was redirected to Kuura, whom he looked at unflinchingly, nary a glance for Jasen and Alixa now that their handshakes had concluded.

"You know the city's that way, don't you?" He pointed over Kuura's shoulder, back the way they'd come. "Or that captain o' yours chucked you off the ship and now you're bartering for dock work?"

Kuura grinned. "You think you know everything, don't you?"

Stanislaus looked him up and down. "Got to say, I don't think you've got dock work in you."

"No?"

"Nah. Too fat round the middle."

They both laughed at that, Kuura in his usual, head-thrown-back, hello-world-here-are-all-my-teeth way, Stanislaus with clipped barks that did not sound very amused at all. Jasen and Alixa stood nervously to the side. Unsure what to do, exactly, Jasen forced a smile, although it felt more like grimacing.

"You have me all wrong," said Kuura. "I am still employed—and my wife and brother remain only good friends." He smiled, wide. "What about you, Stan? How has life treated you since last I was here?"

"Well. I'm still haulin' boxes around for the likes of you day in, day out." Turning, Stanislaus spat over the edge of the dock. The glob sailed in an arc and landed in the sea with a heavy *plop*, as if he'd dropped a stone in the water. "That about sum it up?"

"Driven as ever," said Kuura.

Stan chortled in that hard way again. "You arrive today?"

"Aye," Kuura confirmed. "Just a couple of hours ago."

"Cargo?"

"None today."

"Thank the gods for that." Stan spat again. It landed farther out this time. Jasen watched the minute ripples that radiated away with a disgusted fascination. "You run into storms out there?"

"Several these past few days," Kuura said.

"Yeah? Normal ones?"

Jasen's breath caught. He glanced back to Stanislaus, waiting.

"The first was," said Kuura. "The second ..."

"Not so much, I'm guessin'. Bolts of crazy lightning? Waves like you wouldn't believe?"

"You had the same here?"

Stanislaus shrugged, then shook his head. "Well, sort of," he amended. "We got the edge of it. Darkened the skies right good and proper though; didn't let up until next morning. Not much lightning here—but we saw it, out on the horizon, at least when the waves weren't damn near reaching for the heavens. Colors like I never saw." Turning his head back slightly, he said, "Romily here thought the world was endin', didn't you?"

Romily, the man who'd told Stanislaus that this was not his dock, said, "That the storm you're wittering about?"

"Might be."

"Meant to be working."

"I'm on my break."

Romily shook his head. He hefted up another barrel, holding it round the middle. He had to almost waddle to carry it away, as he was shorter than Stanislaus by a good ten inches.

As he was passing, though, he said, "Yep. Thought the world was ending." Then he passed and made his way to the other end of the pier.

"Scares easy," said Stanislaus, pointing a finger behind him. "Not your standard fare though, is it? Glowing lightning like that ... never seen it before. Impressive as it was, I hope not to again."

"No," said Kuura. "I agree with you there. The storm nearly upended the *Lady Vizola* many times."

"Proper caught in it then. What about you, little man? What'd you make of it?"

Jasen was taken aback. Stanislaus had an intense look about him, probing, and not in the quiet, gentle yet commanding way that Burund had. Taking a question from Stanislaus felt more like being a rabbit cornered by a fox.

"It was frightening," Jasen said weakly.

"Think the world was endin', did you?"

Jasen shook his head. Although, under the steely gaze of Stanislaus, he was not sure exactly what he had believed—just that he had better find an answer and give it *now*, thinking be damned.

"Braver man than Romily, then." Back to Kuura. "Unfortunately, stick around the city and you might find more than a few strange happenings still unfoldin'."

Kuura raised an eyebrow. "Oh?"

"Been going on now for a few days," said Stan, "ever since that little boat pulled in down here the morning after the storm."

Little boat? Jasen made to ask, wondering at the same time, *Baraghosa?*

Stanislaus had not paused, though, and kept on without query.

"Pair of lights, there were," said Stan, "floating probably fifty feet above it. White, glowing orbs, they were—like someone'd taken the sun right out of the sky, shrunk it down small, and perched it on the back of a firefly. They kind of drifted about, sort of lazy, you know?" He motioned with his hand, waving it gently up and down. He might've been describing the soft ebb of waves—

But Jasen knew better. Alixa too. They had seen those lights many, many times.

"Where's the boat now?" Jasen asked.

Stanislaus answered him without looking. "Hell if I know. Didn't come down to my part of the docks—gods be praised. Flynt saw it though—dinky little thing, and didn't have a sail, but it floated along all by itself, no one working oars or anything. And the man who climbed out of it—well. We see plenty of types working the docks, but ..." Stan shook his head. He worked at his chin with a calloused paw, rubbing the hard edges of his jaw. "Skinny thing, but tall. *Long*, like he'd gone through a press and it'd stretched him out—know what I mean?" He asked this of Jasen.

This time, Jasen knew exactly what he meant. "Yeah," he said, nodding. "I know."

"Do you know where this man went?" Kuura asked.

"Do I know?" asked Stanislaus. "Damn near everyone in the Aiger Cliffs must've known about it. It was those lights—they followed him. Even when he'd disappeared into the crowd—and that wasn't easy, for everyone who he passed gave him a bloody wide berth—you could track where he went by those floatin' lights." Another shake of the head. "Unnerving, it was. Least we'll get a good bit of notice when he decides to make his way back to that boat of his to leave the rest of us normal folk alone. Him and his tricks."

"What tricks?" Kuura asked.

Jasen clamped his mouth closed. He'd been about to repeat the question: *Where did he go?*

"Air feels weird. Sort of *charged*. Comes and goes—rarely in the mornings—but in the evenings or at night, when twilight's comin' down … that's when it feels wrong. Like electricity's going to spark at any moment and burn it all down."

"But this is the City of Lightning," said Alixa.

"That's not why they call it that," Stan replied. "The name comes because power runs off those conduction rods up on the clifftops." He nodded toward them, and Jasen turned. He could barely see them pointing skyward in the distance, atop the towering rock spires and arches, with their metallic, yet somehow crystalline extrusions.

"What we're feelin' now, though," Stanislaus went on, "it's something else. And him, with the lights … he's the cause of it."

"Where did he go?" Jasen asked. His heart was hammering hard in his chest. This answer, he needed now, damn it, *now*, like no other.

"Flynt said he went that way." Stanislaus pointed along the dock the way they'd come. "Just carried on walking up the docks a long time, he said."

"But where's he going?"

"Don't know." Stan paused to spit again. "But from what Flynt said he heard—I'd guess he went there." And nodded again, up—at the conduction rods overlooking the city.

13

"I like Stanislaus," said Kuura, smiling in that too-wide way of his.

Alixa frowned. "Why?" she asked in her pointed, blunt way, as if the idea that anyone could like Stanislaus was utter madness.

Kuura had led Jasen and Alixa back along the docks, past all the food stalls and the *Lady Vizola*. The docks spread almost the entire length of the extended beach, giving way only now and then for access to the sands. Unlike the Luukessian shoreline, these sands were much disturbed. There were dozens of people in each sandy nook, stretching their legs. Mostly these were children, running from their parents and impressing small footprints in the sand. Not long ago, Jasen would have longed to kick off his boots and step through it like them, feeling it on his toes.

But his headlong crash as the cart collapsed a few days ago, then Shilara's last stand as scourge overwhelmed her, was burned into his mind. Sandy shores no longer held any great appeal to him.

Kuura had led them off the docks at the same arch Jasen had used to enter the city. But instead of going left, he directed them to the right, up a wide road that curved gradually out of sight in the direction of the looming cliffside. The sun had broken past it now, shining with brilliant light. The metals jutting from the cliffs' sheer walls glared with refracted light. Jasen had to shield his eyes.

"He talks," Kuura said in answer to Alixa's question. "A great deal—more even than me, yes?" He hooted a laugh, three quick owl-like noises, then continued: "It takes little effort to extract information from Stanislaus, and he sees and hears much, working on the docks. Useful features in a contact, no?"

Alixa pursed her lips. "I thought he was scary."

Kuura rumbled with laughter.

Always laughing. Always.

Jasen ignored it. The road leading to the cliffs began a steady rise. Having started by caressing the coastline, it now moved inland, up the remnants of the natural hill that had been split into levels for the city. Farther ahead, he could see the road's terminus. It climbed the cliffside itself, winding up and up. Then, when the cliffs gave over to cones of jagged rock, flattening at their dizzying apex and littered with conduction rods, it clambered up and around those too. How high that was, Jasen didn't want to think about. He thought instead of the pathways under the rocks, where another path must lead through an arch and farther inland. Kuura said these routes up the cliffsides were the only ways past the Aiger Cliffs and to the rest of the mainland. That meant a little foot traffic, most of it directed the way that Kuura, Jasen and Alixa were going. It also meant horses and carts, which announced their arrival in advance enough to move to one side of the road so they could pass.

The exertion was taking its toll already. A subtle cramp had started in his midriff, just above his hipbone on the left-hand side. If he pushed on it, it might ease—but then he would look terribly unfit, and after a day of being insulted, effectively being called useless, he didn't wish to invite any more comments.

Lucky for him, although Jasen was the reason for this excursion to the clifftops, he was not the focus—not with Kuura dominating.

"So what do you think of the Aiger Cliffs?" he asked. "Is it everything you had hoped for?"

"It's amazing," said Alixa, turning to look across the city. Not so high up yet, they hadn't yet scaled even a quarter of the lowest cliff wall, and so much of the city was still level with or above them, toward the rear. But this vantage point gave a bird's-eye view of the docks receding behind, and the first layer of streets. The hubbub was even more impressive from above. So chaotic, it was incredible that anyone managed to get anywhere. "Are all cities like this?"

"Are all people like you?" Kuura countered.

"Excuse me?"

"Are all people teenaged girls, like you? Are they all your height? Do they all have your braids, or your freckles, or your nose? Do they unpick knots the same way as you, or sniff at new foods and take tiny little bites?"

"Well, obviously not."

"Exactly." Kuura grinned. "So, no, not all cities are like this. The Aiger Cliffs is but one. There are many—and you will see them, if you should choose."

A horse and cart approached from the rear. As he moved over to let it pass, Jasen used the pause in conversation to think about other cities. He could picture them vaguely, based on the same drawings and hand-me-down tales that had fueled his imagination before leaving Terreas. But he'd never have been able to picture the Aiger Cliffs, not in a thousand eons—and he found now that he could not arrange his mental image into any meaningful permutation that *might* represent a city.

The old Jasen would have thought that this meant he had no choice but to visit more, to discover them first-hand.

This Jasen, stifling his wheezes as he climbed higher, hoping that Kuura and Alixa did not turn their attention to him, did not much care. One quest and one only was Jasen's now—and if Stanislaus was correct, it ended here.

He gripped the handle of his knife, tucked semi-tight into a scabbard not made for it, scavenged from a storeroom on the *Lady Vizola* as they had passed en route back from their visit to Stanislaus.

This one was leather.

The blade's next sheath would be Baraghosa's throat.

"The Aiger Cliffs," said Kuura when their climb had resumed, "is nothing like the cities where I am from."

Alixa said, "Shipmaster Burund said it's a place called Coral ..."

"Coricuanthi," Kuura corrected. "Yes. But that is the continent, like your Luukessia. The place I am from is called Nunahk. But this is not a city," he said, shaking his head. "Nunahk is only a village. Yet, isn't that how all cities begin?" He smiled broadly at Alixa and Jasen in turn. Spreading his hands wide to encompass the Aiger Cliffs, he said, "This city was once just as small as a baby is to a full-grown man. And look at it now: it bustles with life, people visiting it from the world over." Dropping his arms, he said, "And so, maybe one day Nunahk will be a city too, with houses spread over the hills for miles and miles to see."

"Would you like that?" Alixa asked.

"No," said Kuura, very earnestly. "Coricuanthi has enough cities. If its people wish to build another, then they may build another—but I wish that it will not be Nunahk."

Jasen's eyebrows pressed close together, low. Even without his wild swings from seriousness to laughing like a lunatic, Kuura was a struggle to follow.

Apparently Alixa felt the same, after his singing about the growth of a village, for she asked, "Why don't you want Nunahk to grow?"

"It can grow!" Kuura said, and Jasen felt his confusion increase another increment. "But in a little way, yes? Slow, and gradual, so it retains what it is today, and what it has been in the past. When places become cities, though, they become watered-down. All their character becomes muddled."

"I don't follow."

"Stop," Kuura said, halting.

Jasen obeyed, more than happy for the pause. Halfway up now, and still so far to go—a rocky spire coiled above the next plateau, the path winding around it three times before reaching its apex. A sweat had broken upon his forehead and the small of his back already, his tunic clinging to him uncomfortably. He'd be drenched by the time he reached the top …

Assuming, that was, his legs didn't give out on him first.

Kuura gestured back over the Aiger Cliffs, all its hustle and bustle filling the streets. "You have seen the city first-hand now," he said. "Maybe not for long, but you have seen it. You have seen the faces of people from many far-off lands—lands like your Luukessia, or my Coricuanthi, or a dozen others. They are all here in this place, doing their business, mixing their cultures."

Alixa was frowning. "What's wrong with that?"

"Nothing is wrong with it. In fact, it is a beautiful thing."

Her frown only deepened. "So …"

Kuura laughed. Resuming their journey upward, he said, "Nunahk has a special place in my heart. It has a culture all of its own, a history. And so, selfishly, I do not wish for Nunahk to grow beyond that. Its culture would endure, I know, and it would be shared with the people who came to make it home … but it would also be forever changed. It would not be the Nunahk I know anymore. Does this make sense?"

Alixa mulled it over. "I think so."

"It is a beautiful place, Nunahk. Not the same as this—the buildings are smaller, the paths are dirt … but it straddles the Locau River as it bends—it is a glistening blue river, the Locau, alive with fish of every color you can imagine—and my people have crafted tributaries of their own so that our fields are wet, and our crops plentiful. They have planted fruit trees, with the most wondrous bark that shines like the wings of a moth in the moonlight—and there are thick grasses, perfuming the air, which we would run through as children."

His eyes twinkled. "And then, when we have our own children, we chase them through it too, laughing and playing—so they know it is okay, yes? So they know not to be afraid of the world outside of our village. It is this philosophy that led me here, now. You see?"

Alixa nodded.

"I am very fond of Nunahk," said Kuura, somewhat wistfully.

"Stanislaus mentioned you have a wife?" Alixa asked.

"I do," said Kuura—and he grinned again, showing almost all of his teeth. "Asha. And two daughters: Imami and Ada. They are all so beautiful."

"Do they live back in Nunahk?"

"Oh, yes. I would not endanger their lives at sea! That would make me a bad husband and father indeed, a very bad man. Maybe if I did not love them." He barked laughter. "But they are fortunate that I do love them, very much—so they stay in Nunahk, and they wait for me when I come back to visit."

"How often do you go?"

"A few times a year, if we can manage it. Never for very long—a week, maybe two."

"It must be hard," said Alixa.

"Aye," Kuura confirmed. "For me more than them, I think. They make my life so much richer. But me—I am just the crazed old loon who comes around every few months with far-fetched stories of the places he has been to." And again he laughed, like it was the funniest thing in the world to him.

Jasen's mouth twitched down at the corners.

"If I could stay longer, I would," Kuura went on. "They are my family, and I love them dearly. But our trade does not pay great riches, so I must return to work that I may support them the best I can."

When he was not breaking into laughter, he spoke very seriously but also very plainly. Almost businesslike, it was as if he was not speaking of the melancholy. If his heart ached—and surely it did—he made no show of it.

Alixa said, "You're a good man, Kuura."

He did not acknowledge this. Instead, he said, "I have told you of my village. Perhaps you can regale me with a story of yours as we climb?"

Alixa glanced to Jasen. He didn't say anything—was too busy sucking in breaths as his legs fought the increasing slope. Three quarters of the way up this lowest cliff now—maybe a third of the total distance. He saw why people took horses and carts up here—although it was hard to ignore the fact that men and women and children on foot made up probably eighty percent of the traffic moving in either direction. None of them were even a fraction as out of breath as Jasen was.

It had been a long day, he reasoned.

Scratch that. It had been a long *week*. When was the last time he'd eaten properly? Biltong and hardtack did not a meal make. He'd probably lost fifty ounces of body fat already—and it was not fat he could spare.

Sooner or later he had to stop pushing himself, or he would push himself too far.

Baraghosa went up here, he thought. *I'll stop when I've killed him.*

So he carried on and listened as, after a long pause, Alixa spoke.

"We lived in Terreas." Her voice was soft. Idly, she ran a hand across Scourgey's haunch—comfort, for herself, not the scourge. Her eyes, downcast, did not appear to take in the cobbled pattern of the road, but stared an infinite distance away—to a past, perhaps, where the world had not been turned on its head, and Terreas still stood.

"It was a village at the base of mountains—seven of them, arranged in a curve. In the mornings, you could—you could see the mist come in as the air condensed through the gaps between them, around their bases. I'd watch, sometimes. Monsters roamed in them ... but that wasn't what I was watching for. Not always."

Jasen remembered that first morning when they had sat on the rock together, back at the start of this—not when Baraghosa arrived, but in the days before, when he had traded dares with Alixa and vaulted the boundary, saving Tery Malori and then clambering over again to retrieve his mother's necklace.

He touched it now, feeling the stone pressed against his chest.

Strange; for the past days, he hadn't thought of her, or the amulet, this last thing he had left, much at all.

A great wave of guilt washed over him.

Alixa gave Scourgey an idle pat, lost in her memories.

"We were small," she said. "And comfortable, even in the corner of our land where we eked out a life. But it *was* a life," she said fiercely—and Jasen looked up to see that tears glistened in her eyes. She'd squeezed her hands into tight fists, pressing hard crescents into her palms, knuckles yellow-white as she tightened. "We might have been boxed in, and there might have seemed to be nothing left for us in the world beyond the little boundary the scourge were afraid to cross ... we might've been slowly running out of space as the mountains ate up our crop fields, and mothers and fathers fought back against the world by having more babies than we could ever hope to feed ..."

Without Baraghosa, she didn't say—but Jasen tacked it on all the same, in his mind.

"But we had a life," she said. "We loved, and we lived, and we fought for every day we had together."

She looked down. No tears had slipped out. Those saltwater droplets clung to her eyelashes though, held there.

Alixa thumbed them away.

Softly, she finished, "They're with our ancestors now, may their souls find peace."

Quiet, for a time. Even talkative Kuura, inappropriate as his mood tended to be at times, did not break it.

Jasen thought again of Terreas—the corner of a blighted world which they had fought for, as Alixa put it, in which they dared to live when monstrous beasts had overrun the rest of their land, wishing only death upon them.

He'd longed to leave it, never appreciating till now how much he loved it.

All of it was gone. Not diluted, the way Kuura feared Nunahk would grow over time; simply extinguished in fire and rock and ash …

Were he not breathing hard through his mouth, Jasen would've ground his teeth.

Again, that name reverberated in his skull. Again, his rage built at every echoed syllable.

Baraghosa.

He heaved hard.

Baraghosa.

The top of the cliff cupping the city loomed, the path splitting in two directions: rightward, a smaller route that took a circuit of the higher rocks; and ahead, where horses and carts receded to a village outpost a few miles distant, toward roads that led out into a world Jasen had once dreamed of exploring.

He saw none of it, heard none of the slow conversation that resumed between Kuura and Alixa.

All he saw was that man, his thin, gaunt face; the long, spindly fingers; the lights dancing above him like a beacon, signalling him for miles to see …

Baraghosa …!

And he heard his voice, like grass whickering in the wind, just a little too high-pitched for a man. So very unnatural, yet so sinister and frightful.

Jasen would kill him. *Had* to kill him. He had to—

Nearing the fork in the path, his legs gave out. One moment the world was upright; the next it had tilted, as if the ground were pulled out from under him. He pushed his hands out to catch himself—but it was too late; he'd already slammed into the cobbles, fallen into a sweating heap.

"Jasen!" Alixa cried.

"I tripped," he lied.

Her hands were on him, pulling. A moment later, Kuura's joined. He eased Jasen up so he was sitting.

The world had taken on a slight spin, just at the edges.

Jasen sucked in steadying breaths, trying to ease it.

"You're sweating," said Alixa.

"I'm tired," he said.

"And not very fit," Kuura chuckled.

"It's been a long …" Jasen started to say. He'd run out of breath though, and cut himself off drawing for more air.

"Your cousin struggle like this very often?" Kuura asked Alixa over the top of Jasen's head.

"We've not really stopped for almost a week now," she answered, looking at him with concern. Scourgey, at her heels, apparently felt it too, for she edged up to Jasen and pressed her nose against his temple, sniffing.

She whined.

"Just … give me a minute," Jasen said.

His breath caught, he allowed Kuura to pull him back onto his feet. Slightly wobbly, maybe … but he could stand. And after the first step, it was like he hadn't just scaled a whole cliff at all. (A quarter of it, maybe—no use pretending he wasn't still kind of exhausted—but the pause was appreciated.)

"Next time just ask to have a breather," said Kuura as he led them along the rightward path, to the highest plateaus, and the field of conduction rods. "Not all of us c'n walk as hard or far as I can." He laughed.

Jasen laughed politely too.

Around they went, and around. This winding path, etched right along the twisting rock face, was thinner, more perilous. Jasen stood on the inside edge, and Alixa followed behind. They'd still got four, five feet of space between themselves and the edge. Yet there was no fence. And though Jasen would not let on, he did not trust his legs to remain stable.

His knees began to wobble as they corkscrewed by the city spread beneath them for the second time. By the third and final pass he was panting hard again. Sweat stuck his tunic to his entire back. What he wouldn't give to take up Kuura's offer of a breather …

But Baraghosa had come up here. That was what Stanislaus had said.

The sorcerer would be here—and Jasen would kill him.

This thought was what kept him putting one foot in front of the other. Left foot—right. Left foot—right.

His breathing was haggard, hard.

Left foot … right.

Around and around …

The conduction rods swelled. From down at the dock, this portion of the cliffs had seemed minute. Here, climbing to its peak, though, Jasen saw the truth: it was enormous, easily the size of Terreas from boundary to mountain foot. And there were more, where the spires and arches rose elsewhere too, all lined with great steel rods with bulbous tips and metal crossbeams tilted up to the heavens, channelling lightning strikes.

Cabling ran down the cliffside. A vertical trench had been gouged out, the thick cables inset and tethered. Here there were mesh fences, so tight only a finger could be stuck through, and then nowhere near close enough to touch. What the effect of that might be, Jasen could only imagine. Each time they passed a coil, the air felt like it filled with static. Gooseflesh rose of its own accord. A hum filled the air with it, low, barely discernible yet unsettling. Jasen less heard it than simply felt when he'd passed through the electric field. His heart, beating hard, let up a little.

Step after step:

Baraghosa. Baraghosa.

The peak loomed. The last thirty feet now. Jasen pulled on every last drop of energy he had. One hand reached for the hilt of his blade and rested there. Palm slick with sweat, he tightened his hold, ready to unsheathe it, to brandish it skyward, to run at Baraghosa, to thrust—

They climbed—and Jasen pushed ahead as the top dropped before him, coming to eye level, down—

He took four steps, eyes wide, surveying—

The field of conduction rods stretched out before him, grand behemoths that were as thick as his waist and taller than the *Lady Vizola's* main mast.

… and that was all.

No one was up here—no one except him, Kuura, and Alixa.

14

"*No.* No, no, no …"

"Jasen …"

Alixa's hands were on him.

He shrugged them off. Carried on legs that hardly could hold him any longer, he lurched forward into the field of conduction rods. All of them hummed, infusing the air with electricity—perhaps like the sort Baraghosa had brought upon Aiger Cliffs since his arrival. A spark could jump at any moment, from rod to rod—or maybe rod to Jasen, using him to reach the earth and neutralize itself, one last cacophonous explosion of energy that would do away with him in a blinding flash of light.

He searched desperately, eyes jerking back and forth like he was looking through a forest, trying to catch a glimpse of his quarry through trees and undergrowth.

Yet, in all directions: no one.

Baraghosa was not here.

"Nooo …"

Alixa caught him again, by the shoulders. "Jasen, please—"

He thrust away from her. Whirled.

Kuura stood at the end of the path. Somehow, Jasen had traveled past a half-dozen of these huge rods, with their wide bases, like a miniature set of steps. Thinner cables than the one snaking down the rock spire spilled off them, held to the ground by metal staples. Each rod they passed, another filament was added, until they gathered into one vast coil that wended down toward the city.

Kuura watched with a half-opened mouth—

Pity. He pitied him.

Jasen staggered toward him.

"Where is Longwell?" he said.

Kuura said, "Jasen, perhaps you ought to …"

"*Where is he?*"

Jasen was on him now, and he clutched at the elaborate, oversized flaps of Kuura's tunic. His grip was weak, but desperation turned his hands into claws that tangled and held fast.

"I need to know where Longwell went," Jasen panted. "He said he was after Baraghosa too. He said he'd be here. Stan said he'd be here."

Alixa tried a third time: "Jasen—"

"*Where is he?*"

This, a shout. It was stark, in the near-quiet of the clifftops.

It seemed to take long seconds for the background hum to return.

Kuura answered, "I do not know."

Jasen whirled. Again, he scoured desperately, as though perhaps Baraghosa had concealed himself behind a conduction rod. His form would fit, it would, unnaturally thin and long as it was …

He stumbled through, looking—

Finding no one, he craned skyward.

No lights.

There had been no lights.

Never had been. Just blinding sun.

Climbing here—it was a fool's errand, said the voice of Hanrey, the crabby old village elder of Terreas, loud in his mind—and always right, always. *And you are a fool for doing it.*

"No," Jasen wheezed.

His breath was catching.

Damn it. How had this happened? Baraghosa was seen—he had come here, brought a strange veil down upon the Aiger Cliffs. Longwell knew—yet Longwell had just up and left, abandoning Jasen, after promising that he, too, sought vengeance for Baraghosa's cruelty.

Jasen needed it, he craved it.

Yet everywhere he looked—no Baraghosa, no Baraghosa, *no Baraghosa*.

"Please, Jasen," Alixa said. "Please, just drop this, and come to the Emerald Fields with me."

"No," he whispered.

"Please."

"I said *no!*"

She flinched as though he'd raised a fist to strike her. He'd not … but he had stopped his ceaseless pirouetting, turned to face her, eyes bulging in his ashen face, accusing and hard and mad all at once.

"I have to find him," he breathed. "I have to find Baraghosa. Why don't you understand that? *Why?*"

"Longwell wants to find him," Alixa said. "Perhaps he has gone alone, to—"

"He can't have! *I* have to do it! Understand? *Me!*"

"But why?"

"Because we lost Terreas," Jasen said bitterly. "*I* lost Terreas."

"I lost it too."

Jasen laughed, the crazed laugh of a man teetering on the edge of an abyss he was moments from tumbling into. "Don't you see? *I* lost Terreas. *I* destroyed it."

Alixa's face contorted, a frown pulling her eyebrows down. "But how did—Jasen, Baraghosa tore open the mountain."

"And why? Why did he do that?"

He'd crossed to her without realizing. She flinched again as he drew near, reached out, clasping her shoulders in those clawed hands. Maybe he was hurting her—surely he was, the way his fingers were angled and spread—but he couldn't let go. His cousin, his last remaining relative, the last surviving link he had to the home he'd lost, was the last thing keeping him upon his feet as his mind ruptured, the way the mountain over Terreas had, and all the fiery magma of his guilt overspilled.

"Because of *me*," he said.

"Jasen—"

"I should've gone with him."

"No, Jasen—"

He loosed his hold, somehow staying upright. Backpedalling— almost tripping over the square base of a conduction rod—he boomed in a voice not at all like his own, "*I SHOULD HAVE GONE WITH BARAGHOSA! I SHOULD HAVE BEEN LIKE PITYR! NONE OF THIS WOULD HAVE HAPPENED!*"

He fell to his knees.

He was crying. Didn't know when he'd started.

Claws dug through the hard earth. Sunbaked, it allowed only narrow troughs to be drawn through it.

"Ancestors …" he choked out.

Alixa was on her knees too. She clutched his face. Looked at him with a wild fear.

"You're not thinking straight," she said.

But he didn't take her in. He'd gone blind to all but his plight.

"Please," he begged, his mother, his grandparents, their parents— the whole long, storied line of his people, whose bodies were gone and whose souls rode the winds.

Alixa was speaking still.

"What do I do?" he whispered to them, to their faces, floating just out of sight as they always did.

They had to have answers—had to.

"*Where do I go?*"

Kuura was over him too. He clutched Jasen's shoulder.

Scourgey was there.

"*Ancestors,*" he begged. His throat was raw. Tears turned his words into shuddering breaths.

He cried like he never had cried before, enormous, racking sobs that felt like they would rip his body in two—

Just as Baraghosa had torn open the mountain, buried his village, his people, in slag.

"*Please,*" he called to them, shaking. "*Please, answer me …*"

The ancestors crowded round, out of sight, pressing in … he could feel them, feel their ethereal hands, reaching for him … felt the hands of his mother and father, reaching out to the son who had outlived them sooner than he was meant to …

He begged and cried, cried and begged …

Yet none had an answer for him.

*

After a long time, Jasen's fit tapered off. He stopped shaking. The lightheaded feeling that had misted his mind eased away, like a fog gently dispelled by the breeze.

He sat in morose quiet at the base of the conduction rods, arms folded around his knees.

Alixa perched beside him. She rubbed a hand up and down his back. On the other side sat Scourgey. She leaned against Jasen's shoulder. For the last fifteen minutes, she had pressed her nose gently against his forehead without moving it. Her breath, rancid as it was, was almost comforting against his cheek.

Kuura sat opposite. He'd pulled the legs of his trousers up, so they bunched around his knees, ending only a few inches down the calf.

"No one could endure things like you have," he said. "To go through such turmoil … it is a terrible thing. Heartache breaks all of us—and you have seen so much of it, both of you. It is only natural that you would feel as broken as you do."

"I don't feel broken," said Jasen bitterly. "I feel guilty. I *am* guilty."

"You're not," Alixa said.

He ignored her. No sense arguing. Alixa wouldn't see things reasonably, he knew now. And all her protests would not cause Jasen to reconsider what he knew was truth.

"So what now?" Kuura asked.

Jasen lifted his shoulders in a small shrug. "I don't know."

"We can't take him on," Alixa said. "Not us. Probably not Longwell." She turned to Kuura. "You know that, don't you? You must see?"

Kuura sighed, a long exhale. "This Baraghosa …" he began. After a pause, he restarted another way. "I'd never have believed what you said about the volcano, days ago. But after the storm …" He shook his head. "There are magics, and I would never had denied that. But … the sheer *force* and *power* of what I have seen … these are not magics I have even heard of. The scale, it's … it's unprecedented."

"He has to be stopped," Jasen said.

"We aren't the ones to do it," Alixa said, hard. "A man who can rip open a mountain will not be felled by a fifteen-year-old with a dagger he picked up off the street."

Jasen gave her a hard look.

"I'm sorry," she said, "but it's true. What you want, and what you can reasonably achieve … they're very different things, Jasen. And you need to listen to that—before it's too late for you."

He pursed his lips and looked away.

She was wrong. So wrong.

Kuura repeated, "So—what now?"

Jasen glanced around the forest of conduction rods, humming quietly as they waited for a storm to unload upon them.

"Back to the city, I guess," he conceded after a long time. Sour-faced, he added, "Not like there's anything up here for us."

"Then come," said Kuura, rising. He stuck out a hand, and helped Jasen to his feet. "You can walk?"

He moved—but Scourgey slipped in under his legs. She swept him off his feet, so he sat—very awkwardly—upon her dangerously curved back.

She looked up at him with black, coal-lump eyes. Her tongue lolled in her mouth.

Kuura shook his head. "Your pet confuses me more by the day."

"I told you she's different," Alixa said.

"Aye, you did. Right. Ready?"

"Ready," said Alixa.

"Jasen?"

He shrugged, then nodded. "Mm."

Kuura led them back to the path.

Jasen held onto Scourgey. She walked unnaturally, each step sending a jarring little jolt up his spine. These, he ignored, though, same as he ignored Alixa's presence alongside him, and her furtive looks.

Just before the conduction rods slipped out of sight, he looked back one last time.

No Baraghosa.

Their trek had been for naught … and Jasen was out of ideas, again.

But it was a long way down, at least … and maybe he could come up with something by the time they were at the bottom.

Maybe.

15

Back in the city, Jasen, still riding Scourgey's back, moaned.

"Where could he have gone?"

He'd been squinting his eyes the entire way down the path, searching the constantly moving throng for any sign of Baraghosa. He searched, too, for those dancing lights that would give him away. Finding neither, he still could not stop himself from taking in face after face as he sought the sorcerer. Woman; man, but his nose was the wrong shape; another man, dark-skinned; that man was too old ... Each appraising glimpse was a second long only—but though Jasen had seen Baraghosa for perhaps the sum of only two hours across his entire lifetime, one second was all it would take to identify him—and to pursue.

"Perhaps he traveled farther inland," said Kuura. "Stanislaus said he spoke of the heights. He may've been talking of them as the road we climbed is the only way out of the city."

"He can't have," Jasen dismissed immediately.

"But you don't know that," said Alixa. "He arrived days ago."

"It is plenty of time to have moved elsewhere," Kuura agreed.

"No!" Jasen breathed heavily. He shook his head slightly, but without stopping. "He had to have gone to the conduction rods. They harness lightning—Aiger Cliffs is the city of lightning—and the storm—it all fits!"

"How?" asked Alixa.

"I—I don't know." He slumped. Exasperation built quickly, but after the explosion of emotion on the clifftops, it dispersed quickly again too, instead of mounting up. Possibly the exhaustion had helped there. Though Scourgey had allowed him to ride all the way down, he was only physically rested. The mental dams which usually kept everything pent up, for good or bad, had not yet recovered, and his mind felt blank and unfocused.

"He also split open a mountain," said Alixa. "Is that related to the conduction rods too?"

"He's a sorcerer," Jasen grunted back. "How should I know what he does?"

Scourgey looked up at him. She whined, twisting her neck farther than any normal animal's should go so she could nuzzle her cheek against Jasen's knee. He ruffled the spray of wiry hairs that stuck out at the base of her skull and looked away, conflicted at a show of emotional support from the scourge.

"I think," said Alixa, "we should just face the facts. Baraghosa came through here, muttering about the heights. But he was talking about them in reference to the roadways to the next town or city—nothing to do with the rods."

"That may be so," said Kuura, nodding.

"And what about what Stanislaus said?" Jasen challenged. "He said that a charge had come into the air since Baraghosa was here, that people saw the lights that trail him. He must still be here, or how would that still be going on?"

"He didn't say people were still seeing his lights," said Alixa.

"Yes, he did."

"No, he didn't. He said his friend Flynt watched where he went by the lights—but after that ..."

Jasen racked his brains, combing over the encounter with Stanislaus again. Certainly that was what Stan had said, wasn't it?

But now that Alixa claimed otherwise, Jasen was not so sure. Had he only heard what he wanted to hear? Made assumptions based on his wants?

Damn it, why couldn't he remember the full conversation?

"Alixa may be right," said Kuura.

"She can't be," Jasen said. "Remember—remember what Stan said about the air feeling charged? That's Baraghosa's doing."

"Baraghosa split the mountain apart without being there," said Alixa. "He could do this too."

Nostrils flaring, Jasen rounded on her—or at least twisted, on Scourgey's back. She wheeled around a second later so he could face her head on.

"How would you know he wasn't there?" he demanded.

"I—well, I wouldn't."

"He could be anywhere if he wanted. Remember the way he disappeared that night when he came for me? In minutes he just vanished completely—like he'd ... been carried away on the wind, or something, like the ancestors."

Now it was Alixa's turn for her expression to flare. "Do *not* liken him to them. He is an abominable, slimy—"

"I know," Jasen sighed. "Which is exactly why I want to find him. I just … I wish I could figure out where."

"It's not here," said Alixa. Before Jasen could open his mouth fully to protest, she said, "It's not. Whether he needed to be outside of Terreas or not when he … when he … destroyed it—" She paused, for a few seconds, to recompose herself after this quavering tremor.

When she resumed, she spoke more strongly, her voice more clear. "Whether that were the case or not, he cannot be in the Aiger Cliffs now. Think: the lights that follow him, they would betray him easily. We've been up to the clifftops and back, and seen no sign of them. He cannot be here any longer."

True, yes, and Jasen was horribly aware of it.

But he changed tack:

"His boat," he said. "Stanislaus said it's still in the dock—that they were glad of the lights, because it meant they'd know when he was on his way back. We could … go down to see it, maybe." To Kuura: "Couldn't we?"

Kuura looked uneasy. "What are you asking? To see it only? Or more?"

More, Jasen thought, though would not admit it.

Admitting it aloud was unnecessary. His face gave him away.

"Jasen, *no*," said Alixa fiercely. "You can't. If he comes back, and we're on his boat …"

"Then I'll kill him."

"Or he'll sink it and drown us without needing to lift a finger. Do you want that?" When he didn't answer, she repeated, even more harshly, "*Do you want that?*"

"No," he said, sullen and quiet.

"What?"

"I said *no*, okay? No, I do not want to be drowned." Folding his arms, he lamented, "I just … I need to know what he's doing, what it is he wants. Maybe that could help me find him."

"He wants children," Alixa reminded him. "That's all he's ever wanted."

"From us. But what of Longwell? Baraghosa sent a storm to wreck his ship. That's got nothing to do with children. So why?"

No answers, from Alixa or Kuura.

The only two people who could reasonably offer some conclusion to that mystery were Baraghosa—and Longwell. Baraghosa was missing, and when they clashed, Jasen did not believe he would give the sorcerer time to say his piece; the rage in his chest, now just a low simmer once again, would surely spill over, and he would be upon him, knife to his throat before Baraghosa could say even a word—

And Longwell had hightailed it off the *Lady Vizola* the moment they pulled into port.

Jasen cursed him.

"Jasen!" Alixa said.

Kuura tamped down a grin.

He wiped it from his face completely when Alixa jerked her head round to him, as if to say, *You're the adult here; reprimand him, won't you?*

Doing his level best to keep a straight face, and no mirth in his voice, Kuura said, "Why do you curse Samwen Longwell? I thought he was a friend to you. You have talked these few days together on the *Lady Vizola*, yes?"

"I thought he was a friend," Jasen lamented. "Or at least someone who was going to help us."

"Help *you*," Alixa muttered.

"He said he'd help you too."

"Second." She turned her nose up. "I am an afterthought to two boys dead set on petty revenge."

Rage bloomed, boiling ferociously in a moment. *"It is not petty revenge! He's a murderer!"*

The cry drew the attention of the people nearby, and more than a few faces turned to Jasen. In another life, a flush of embarrassment would have colored his cheeks red, redder than the sudden anger had made them. These, though, were people he would never see again, and he could not bring himself to care what they thought of him.

"Fine," Alixa said, "it's not petty. But you are two boys—"

"Longwell is a man, and I am *fif*—"

"—and Baraghosa is a sorcerer who can move the heavens and the earth. Between you, you have a dagger and a lance and one suit of armor."

Apparently the mental dams were still capable of holding onto his boiling emotions for longer than a few seconds. New anger was filling him, roiling as if someone had hollowed him out and turned that rage to boiling liquid and poured it into him.

It bubbled ominously. And all he wanted was to let it blow again.

He fought it back.

With a calmness he did not feel—a calmness he did not believe Alixa deserved from him—he said, "I have heard it all before. I don't want to hear it again."

"You should. You might listen to it one of these days."

Jasen ignored her. Turning to Kuura, he asked, "Do you know why Longwell left the ship?"

Kuura shrugged. "I was told only that he had things to attend to."

"Dangerous things," Alixa amended. "That's what Shipmaster Burund said."

"What sorts of things?" Jasen pressed. He leaned forward—and, following his movements as though she were a second (and third) pair of legs, Scourgey scooted ahead too, to bring Jasen and Kuura closer together. "Where did he go? What is he doing there? Does he know where Baraghosa has gone to?"

Kuura did not answer.

"He's gone to battle him, hasn't he?" said Jasen, knowing that it was true. "He's found him. He's gone to fight." The knowledge made his chest ache suddenly. He sagged back, mouth falling.

His eyes were hot. Wetness threatened.

Kuura placed a hand on Jasen's shoulder. "If he had, and I knew of it, do you think I would have led you on this wild goose chase along the docks and up and down the cliffside?" Shaking his head, he said, "I do not know where Samwen Longwell has gone. But if it is to battle … you are *children*."

Jasen pulled backward. Again, with that word …

Kuura went on, "Do you honestly believe he would take a child into battle with him?"

"I'm not—"

"If anything were to happen to you, his honor—it would be in tatters."

"But he said …"

Except—maybe he hadn't said at all. Maybe Jasen was putting words in other people's mouths. Maybe Longwell's battle was his alone, and Jasen was never to be a part of it. Maybe, like Jasen, Longwell's revenge must be exacted by himself, no one else—and to let Jasen along, hurt and angry and ready to commit his own murder, would prevent him from achieving vengeance the way Longwell envisioned it.

So he had left.

He had gone, departed the *Lady Vizola*, after his promises—promises that maybe he had never made, but Jasen believed in them nevertheless, had been fueled for days by them—

And Jasen was alone again, with no direction and with these two people who cared for him, yes, but who believed he was a child, engaged in a child's folly … that he was doomed to fail.

No.

He couldn't.

He had to find Baraghosa. Had to.

He must be here. He *must*.

So, wheeling Scourgey around, he leaned forward—pointing toward the center of the city, where it rose another level—

"Go," he told Scourgey.

"Jasen, what are you—" Alixa began.

The rest of her words were lost, though. Scourgey bounded forward, carrying Jasen deep into the crowds.

"*Baraghosa!*" he shouted, a piercing roar that cut through the chaos like a thunderclap. "*Baraghosa!*"

On and on, he shouted. Scourgey wove through them, deft on her feet. Impossibly twisted though her body was, the spine too curved, the opposite of streamlined, she moved with surprising finesse. The crowd made way for her with cries of shock or fear or disgust, or just plain irritation at this boy and his beast sprinting through the city. Where people did not shift in time, Scourgey bounded through gaps between, springing left and right to carve a path before Jasen even registered them.

Again and again, he shouted Baraghosa's name. His gaze roved, desperately, at the faces moving past. Woman. Man. Man. Man. Child. Woman. Woman. Man. Woman. Indeterminate, but not Baraghosa. Just a fraction of a second to take them in now—yet still he searched.

He was here. He must be.

"*BARAGHOSA!*"

Up the steps, to the next level.

Were Alixa and Kuura following?

He did not look back for them. He could only go forward, pressing closer to the city's heart, here in the shadows of the Aiger Cliffs.

Smells flowed over him, glimpsed and gone before he could fully process them. A flowerseller had a stall overloaded with bouquets. A tangy burst of sweetness clouded the air, and he and Scourgey surged through it, the scent mixing with the scourge's rotten aroma—the same deathly stench that had assailed him from over the boundary's edge, carried on a strangely hot wind when the air blew in from the mountains just right.

He was used to it now. Barely did he think of it.

Something meaty—gone before he could identify it. Nothing like Terreas's cookfires.

"*BARAGHOSA!!*"

Buildings passed, the smallest bigger than Terreas's largest. White stone; grey stone; neat thatch, pale yellow, like new … nothing like the aged roofs back home, long in need of replacement.

Back home.

He had no home now.

And—

"*BARAGHOSA!*"

—had taken it from him.

He screamed his throat raw, drawing eyes to him, eye after eye that he looked into, then moved on from, as though discarding that person.

Not Baraghosa. Not Baraghosa. Not Baraghosa.

He had to be here. Had to be, in this strange place that Jasen had longed to visit without having ever heard of, had dreamed of his whole life without knowing the first thing about it.

Baraghosa had brought him here—and Jasen hated him for it, just like he hated this place, hated it for no reason other than that it was not home, his house was nowhere on these streets or even upon this land, and Adem Rabinn, his father, was not waiting for him to come home, with a mother whose amulet bounced against his chest with every breath he took, every lungful he sucked into a scratched, pained throat, not to keep breathing but simply to *shout that name*, to find the man who had done this awful thing …

"*BARAGHOSA!*" he roared. "*BARAGHOSA!*" Through a throng collected outside a hall, the entrance wide open, upper level overhanging and supported by pillars. "*BARAGHOSAAAA!*"

"Wait!"

Scourgey thundered to a stop, as if she had understood it.

She wheeled around.

A man was pushing his way out of the small gathering in front of the hall. Light-skinned, his hair had been blonde once. Now it was turning a faint greyish-white color. Lines spilled out from the corners of his eyes and down an apprehensive face.

"Did you say 'Baraghosa'?" he asked.

Jasen dropped off of Scourgey. "Yes," he said. "I seek him. Do you know where he is?"

"Not right now."

Jasen's stomach dropped.

Yet this man, almost timid-looking, not just in his expression but the very way he held himself, slight and slightly slumped, barely any taller than Jasen … he had reached out for Jasen as he passed.

"You know something, though," Jasen said. "Don't you?"

The man cast a backward look. The people outside the hall

remained in their clusters. Some looked at him, most not.

Speaking lower, the man said, "I am a councillor here." He said it almost conspiratorially, as if being a public servant was some great secret that he was entrusting to Jasen.

"What do you know?" His heart was thudding hard in his chest. It banged against the base of his throat too, sending nauseating spikes through his stomach.

The man hesitated. Another backward look.

When he glanced back to Jasen, he opened his mouth and closed it without saying a word.

He looked away.

"Please," Jasen whispered. "Tell me. I need to find him."

The man gripped the back of his neck. He squeezed, looking pained.

He edged a half-step back. "I should …"

"No," Jasen breathed, closing the gap again. "*Please*. I must find him. What is it you know?"

The seconds were long. With each, this tantalising hope drifted farther away.

"Please," he whispered—begged.

The man bit his bottom lip.

He leaned forward. "None of us are very happy about it, you see."

Jasen nodded, kept silent, fighting desperately not to press—not to disrupt him now he was opening up, spilling this secret.

"He came through here two days ago, spoke to the council. He … made a request. Most of us voted against it," he said, and the sentence warbled with a nervous laugh. Those fingers working the back of his neck pressed harder, fighting a knot. "But we were overridden. He offered good compensation to the Aiger Cliffs—a donation—so …"

"What did he want?" Jasen asked.

"Use of the conduction fields."

So Stanislaus had been right.

But that was two days ago.

Jasen's stomach dropped a half-inch. "Has he used them already?"

The man shook his head. "No." He glanced away, around, looking for listeners.

Meeting Jasen's eyes again, he said, "But he will."

"When?"

The man answered, one word that sent Jasen's heart into overdrive:

"Tonight."

16

Alixa and Kuura had followed. They caught up as Jasen was chatting with Councillor Drue, who had to nervously reiterate what he'd told Jasen. By this time he was increasingly itchy to get away and kept shifting from foot to foot and looking about, more of his attention on the surrounding street than the people he was talking to. Kuura granted him leave after just a handful of questions, to which Drue's answers were vague—how much compensation Baraghosa had offered, what he might be doing in the conduction fields, and why tonight was the night of choice considering he had been in the Aiger Cliffs for days now.

Grateful for his escape, Drue scuttled away and disappeared.

Now Jasen sat with Kuura and Alixa at the front of a tavern. A round wooden table was erected outside, on the street. Though several around it had been occupied, they emptied when the three sat down—probably something to do with Scourgey's smell. Definitely, considering the fact that the barmaid had said quite firmly, "Do *not* sit in here with that wretched thing. You'll drive all my business away."

Sitting outside was going to do the same, Jasen thought: with Scourgey sat at the table's edge, anyone who eyed the tavern was put off of entering. If they sat long enough, it would empty out completely without refilling.

"Congratulations," said Alixa with all the sarcasm she could muster—which was a lot. "Now we know where Baraghosa is headed. I can't wait to go rushing up to the clifftops all over again, without a plan."

"I'll think of a plan," said Jasen.

"Think?" She laughed. "That's the last thing you're doing at the moment. Do I need to remind you that—"

"He's a sorcerer, and I'm just a kid with a dagger?" Jasen shot back laconically. "No, you don't need to remind me. I've heard it dozens of times today. It has sunk in, thank you very much."

"Hardly seems that way to me. If it had, you'd shrug off this ridiculous quest and see that the Emerald Fields are where we should be going. Not after a powerful wizard."

Jasen cast his eyes down. Lectures, lectures, from left and right today. How tired of it did he need to get before Alixa laid off?

He sipped from his glass. Three quarters full, it was topped by a head of pale green foam. The beverage, which Kuura had bought for him, was alcoholic, brewed from a plant called hops, and dyed the shade of young grass. The alcohol was weak, so it didn't burn. Didn't matter; Jasen couldn't enjoy it. The whole thing tasted just too green, somewhere between sweet and savory with every mouthful, never settling on one—never inviting Jasen back in for another sip, either.

Kuura had his own glass of it. Already half was gone. The foam clung to his lips. He smeared it off with a thumb, licking it clean.

Alixa, as was proper, had a glass of water. The barmaid wouldn't give her a bowl for Scourgey, so when they were outside she had ordered Scourgey to open her mouth, and then poured half of it in as Scourgey madly lapped at the air.

Jasen sniffed his drink. That last sip was almost earthy, and not in a good way.

Either it smelled of pondwater, or its true scent was mixing with Scourgey's aroma.

He set it back down and idly wondered how he could get away with not drinking anymore, even though Kuura had paid for it and would expect to see the glass emptied.

Maybe Alixa might be tempted to share ...?

Doubtful. Though, her thoughts on the other hand ...

"I'm serious, Jasen," she said.

"*I know.*"

"And I will keep saying it until you listen to me and change course. *You cannot beat Baraghosa.* And before you say it," she said quickly, cutting over him before he could interject, "that does not mean I don't want to see Baraghosa beaten. I am just saying, of all the people in the world, *you are not the person to stop him.* I mean, honestly—what are you going to do when you run into him? Yell at him for burying Terreas in magma and rubble? Write him a strongly worded letter? Maybe just ask him politely to draw and quarter himself for you?"

All through this, Kuura was nodding furiously.

Jasen ignored him.

"I don't know," he answered.

"Tell me."

"I don't know."

"No, come on. I want to hear it. You're so determined to find him that you've gone racing all over the Aiger Cliffs today, hoping to crash into him somewhere—outside a butcher's shop, you probably think, as if he's just going to be walking the streets like you and I. *Tell me what you'll do when you find him.*"

"*I don't know.*" This, a long, exasperated sigh. Because, after all Alixa's pushing … she was right. Baraghosa was a sorcerer. Jasen's only hope, really, was the element of surprise … and he had no way of banking on that. Even if he had it, who was to say the sorcerer would not outwit him?

Jasen *was* just a boy with a dagger.

Less, really: he was a boy with a dagger, and no experience to speak of.

He looked down at it, affixed to his hip, and wished Shilara were here. She would train him. Could have trained him for a good many years, if he had gone to visit her more often, instead of treating her, most of the time anyway, like the outcast Terreas had turned her into.

He closed his eyes on his regrets, willing them away.

"I thought as much," said Alixa.

"Whatever I'm doing," Jasen said, "it can't just be nothing. Baraghosa can't just be allowed to walk around, free to do his business, while we stand here idle and aimless. He was able to do that for too long—and now he's pushed it too far." He ran his finger around the rim of his glass, picking up a small blob of greenish foam. "He took Pityr from us, and dozens of other children over the years. Who's to say they're not out there? Our next of kin—"

"They're dead, Jasen."

She said this so abruptly, yet so gently, that Jasen was silenced. His breath stop-started, once, and he looked up, locking eyes with his cousin.

"He killed them," she said softly. "You know this."

He did. He knew it, knew it even though he had hoped for years that it was not true—hoped for the past year that Pityr still lived, his friend, so happy and jolly and then gone.

It stung him.

But then he steeled himself against it, hardening.

"That is exactly why he needs to be stopped," he said. "He is a monster."

Alixa seemed to strain under the weight of her incredulity. "And I ask again: *what do you expect to be able to do?*"

Another voice answered, from the street: "*I expect you to win.*"

They turned, and

Kuura gasped.

An ebony-skinned woman stood before them. Tall and imposing, she could measure and match Shipmaster Burund inch for inch. Straight-backed and standing proudly, she wore a thin, pale blue armor made of overlapping plates. It must have been custom-made for her, as it curved to her shape perfectly. A sword hung at her side, held in a ring by the hilt but not sheathed. It was curved, a brilliantly polished silver with a wicked edge.

Her hair was braided tight to her skull. A red tattoo adorned one cheek, a crescent moon, arcing around the edge of her left eye. Her lips were full, pressed into a short line beneath a rounded nose and almond-shaped eyes—brown, the same shade as her skin.

"Huanatha," breathed Kuura, and he dropped from his seat onto one knee. Then, without looking up, he whispered to Alixa and Jasen, "*Bow!*"

Alixa gave him a perplexed look. "Why should we—"

"*Because she is a queen!*"

17

"I am no queen," said Huanatha dismissively. "Rise."

Kuura obeyed, scrambling up to his feet as though, despite her refutation, she was still royalty, and worthy of being obeyed.

Jasen took her in. He had never seen a queen before, or a king. Syloreas had had one, once … but Shilara's stories of him were not flattering. Jasen's impression of the man was not a good one, thanks to her, and few others in Terreas spoke of him at all. In any event, by now he was a distant memory, and Jasen's concept of royalty was based mostly on stories and books.

Huanatha was not a queen as Jasen had ever imagined one. For starters—that armor. This was a warrior, surely, not a woman who sat on a throne.

Alixa evidently thought the same.

Worse: she turned her nose up at Huanatha.

And Jasen remembered those early days with Shilara … *Early days.* As if their time together had been more than a few weeks in all … when Alixa had been very clear: women were not made to be warriors.

Some of Alixa's propriety had relaxed, from being around Shilara and from the various disasters they had faced. But gradually she seemed to be reverting to her old self, going by the way she looked Huanatha up and down.

"What is a 'queen' doing walking the streets of Aiger Cliffs?" she asked.

Kuura's face fell. He did his best to recover. "I am so sorry, Queen Huanatha," he said quickly, bowing forward. "The girl, she does not know of what she—"

Huanatha cut over him, in their native language. A short sentence—maybe an order.

Kuura hesitated. Then he answered, slowly.

She said something else.

He replied, looking miserable.

Jasen followed, eyes moving back and forth as if following a ball batted from one person to another, yet with no sense of who was winning—or indeed what this conversation was.

One last word from Huanatha.

Kuura sat on his chair again. He folded his arms, letting them lay on his lap.

He looked like a child who'd been scolded.

Jasen glanced from him to Huanatha. "Uhm."

"I told your friend not to call me 'queen' any longer," she said. "It no longer befits my station."

"So … you're not a queen," said Alixa. It was half a question, though her tone suggested it was obvious.

"Huanatha *was* a queen," Kuura explained miserably. "The Queen of the Muratam—a widespread tribe in the Coricuanthi. They have been warring amongst themselves, though …" He trailed off.

"You were deposed?" Alixa asked Huanatha.

"Worse: exiled," said Kuura. He shook his head, frowning bitterly, his eyebrows a hard line. "I had heard that you had come to Chaarland," he told her, "but to see you myself, with my own two eyes …" He drifted off again, eyes misting, like he had lain them upon a goddess. "Already you have become legendary here, the tales say."

Huanatha said only, "I am not legend."

Jasen stepped forward. "Just now, you—cut in. Do you know who we're talking about?"

"The sorcerer Baraghosa," she said. "You speak of defeating him."

"You know him then?"

She sneered. "He came to our lands many years ago," she said, "spoke to our people. Struck deals. Whispered in ears, raised hackles … sowed discord."

Her accent was not quite the same as Kuura's, though it was tonally close enough that Jasen figured their birth places could not have been greatly separated back on Coricuanthi. Kuura's had been diluted though, in much the same way as he lamented the dilution of Nunahk if it grew out of its humble footprint. Travel, speaking other languages with the locals of many places, had softened his accent, as it had Shipmaster Burund's. Huanatha's remained harder, her vowel sounds clipped short. However long she had been exiled, it was not yet long enough to have blurred her way of speaking.

She went on, "I welcomed him when first he came. But soon enough ... he cost me my throne."

Kuura murmured, "So the stories were true. I had heard ..."

Jasen rounded on him. "You knew Baraghosa had done this too? Why didn't you say something?"

"I believed they were just tales," Kuura said.

"What else do you know?"

"Doubtless he knows many stories of that wizard's upheavals," said Huanatha. Her bottom lip curled. "Baraghosa is known among many people in many places. I can only imagine that others see him the same way I once did: wily, but an asset all the same, the benefits he brings outweighing the stormclouds he inflicts upon the lands he visits."

"He caught us in a storm too," said Jasen, "out to sea a few days ago." He made to add, *And our friend, Longwell,* but did not. Abandoned by him the moment *Lady Vizola* pulled into port, Jasen did not see him as much of a friend anymore.

In hindsight, he should never have assumed they were friends.

"The storms that rent my land were not physical," said Huanatha. "They were the human sort, dissent sowed among my people. I should have seen it coming. Yet I ignored the whispers of the dead—and now I must make my life in this frigid and rainy land, cut off from my people."

Frigid? Rainy? Jasen squinted into the sky. Blue, with little cloud. The ocean breeze blew in along the docks, and he supposed when the sea was cold, the wind carried that iciness upon its back ... but the day was warm, the sun shining and bright. Temperatures dropped in the shadows, yes. At the height of summer, though, they offered cool respite.

Kuura saw his confusion. "Coricuanthi is far south of here. Even its coldest days are equal to some of the warmest here."

Oh. Well, that made more sense. Though Jasen struggled to picture it—a place hotter than Luukessia. Sitting aboard the *Lady Vizola* two days ago, awaiting Longwell's awakening, they had endured a stifling heat. The same every day—that was madness.

"So there's another thing," Alixa said, and she rounded on Jasen. "He was able to overthrow a queen. It's mild, relative to the storm and Terreas—but does it give you a clue as to what we're up against now? One that you might take heed of?"

Jasen's teeth ground together. "I know what we're up against."

"So what do you expect us to be able to do about it?"

Before Jasen could answer, Huanatha drew her sword from its

resting place at her hip. She swung it around and forward, a precise arcing motion, bringing it to bear in an instant. The blade caught no sunlight, but still it gleamed as it sliced through the air.

A kerfuffle from the passing crowd. Gasps—shouts—the closest to the tavern on their way around backpedaled furiously, compressing the small pathways etched between these walkers. Someone had just been making their way from the tavern's confines. Stepping out to the sight of this armored woman lifting her sword to two unarmed children and their companion, he yelped and made a swift about-face, returning inside.

Huanatha ignored the commotion. She said, "You can fight."

Alixa opened her mouth to protest—

Jasen pushed past her, bringing himself out and ahead of her and Kuura. "I want to fight," he said, resolute. "And I know where he is now."

Huanatha appraised him, eyes tracking up and down his body. Beneath her gaze, he felt instantly very inadequate. His frame was too slight, his muscles not developed. Compared to her sword, the dagger hanging at his side looked like little more than a well-crafted children's toy. Somehow, he was certain she would even see through the sheath, knowing that it was not anywhere close to a perfect fit.

But he did not back down. Another person had presented herself who had a bone to pick with Baraghosa. And there would be more. Councillor Drue had been upset by him, as had a number of his peers. Stanislaus said Baraghosa had left an impression on the dock workers who saw him, and not a very good one. How many more were out there, longing to settle a score with a sorcerer who had scorned them?

Jasen might just be a child with a pilfered dagger … but he was set on vengeance for his people—for his father—and for himself, most of all, to atone for his guilt that had brought this grief upon him and Alixa, and his ancestors. And in a battle against the sorcerer capable of ripping open the earth, the more hands were willing to fight, the better.

So he stood as tall as he could, his shoulders pushed back, the way Huanatha's were. He steeled his face, set his expression, steadied his breathing.

"You want to fight," Huanatha said, her words slow. "Yes. I see it in you. I see it in your eyes—the fierceness of them, filled with determination—hatred." She stepped closer, looking deep, a penetrating gaze, like she could peer into his very essence and decipher it. "You wish to kill him."

Jasen nodded, not breaking eye contact. "I do."

She assessed for a moment longer, looking into his eyes, at—what?

Then she jerked her head to Alixa, and the spell was broken. Jasen felt himself relax.

"And you?" Huanatha asked. "You wish for your own revenge too?"

Kuura cut in. "Queen—Huanatha, no, you cannot. These are just children."

Her head whipped around, her burning gaze on him now. He almost recoiled from it—or perhaps it was the blade that made him take a step backward, poised and ready to strike any who opposed her. A quiver in his knee threatened another low bow. He overpowered it.

"Who are you?" Huanatha asked. "I do not recognize you from my own lands. Yet you bow to me, like I wield power over you."

"I am not from your lands," said Kuura. "Yet you are royalty; I must bow."

Huanatha bared her teeth in a cat-like sneer. "I am royalty no more."

"I am sorry, Queen—"

"*Enough.* Who are you?"

"I am Kuura of the Wantanwe," he answered, "from the city of Nunahk."

Huanatha nodded, knowing, possibly, where Nunahk lay in relation to her own tribe's lands. "And do you know how to wield a blade, Kuura of Nunahk?"

He hesitated, then nodded. "Yes."

"You do not carry one, when the boy does."

"That is—not true, Que—Huanatha," he corrected, speaking low. Glancing about, he licked his lips. "I have small weapons secreted upon me, should the need arise. It does not arise often, so they remain out of sight."

"Where you cannot reach for them at a moment's notice."

Now he bit his lip. "I do not wish to show you. Not here."

"Fine." But her look at Kuura was disbelieving. "And you two? You can fight?"

"I can use a sword," Jasen lied quickly.

"No, you can't," said Alixa hotly. "He cannot."

Huanatha raised no eyebrow. But she did look at him, hard, another penetrating gaze that did not sift through his basest feelings, but rather demanded he share the truth with her.

"I have practiced several times in my life," he said.

"With a dagger," Alixa added. "And only rarely. You can no more wield a sword than I can."

Shame threatened him.

Just a child with a pilfered dagger.

Still, he fought it back. Setting his shoulders again—they had slumped, his back too, taking an inch off his meager height—he said resolutely, "But I will draw on all the experience I have so I may defeat Baraghosa."

Apparently that was good enough for Huanatha. She turned her attention to Alixa. "And you?"

"Unlike my cousin, I would not claim to be capable of fighting a *warlock*," she answered sniffily. The daggered glare she fired at Jasen was well practiced though, even if her hands were not.

"You have weapons of your own?" Huanatha asked.

"No. And I don't want—"

But Huanatha just spoke over her. "Then we must get you some. Follow." And she stowed her sword at her hip once more, tucking it through the loop that held it at the handle with fluid grace. Pivoting on her heel, she made her way back through the crowd, which parted around her.

"No way," said Alixa. "I am not being roped into this."

"Come on," said Jasen. "We have to do this."

"*I* have to get to the Emerald Fields. And so do—*Jasen!*"

He had strode away as she was mid-sentence.

Scourgey followed. Jasen heard Alixa's shrill voice calling her name. Scourgey hurried alongside him.

He looked down at her. She returned the gaze, lifting her head to meet his eyes with those black voids. Her mouth open, tongue lolling, she made an almost strangled sort of noise that Jasen could only take as support.

"Good Scourgey," he said. "Thank you."

She padded alongside, and so he too had a path cut for him through the crowd, following the back of Huanatha's receding head, with its tamed braids strung through colored wooden beads that hung against the backplate of her layered armor.

A glance behind showed that Alixa was following, a harried look on her face.

So too came Kuura, muttering to himself. Just before the crowd closed between them and again blocked his sight, Jasen was sure he heard him say:

"*What have I done to offend the gods that I find myself at the mercy of two children?*"

18

Huanatha occupied an apartment two thirds of the way up the leveled hill where the city was built. Here, foot traffic was lighter and there were fewer market stalls. Storefronts sold expensive fineries. Restaurants were open here and there, nowhere near as common as the stalls on the docks, or even those arrayed in the first couple of levels of the city. The folk dining in them wore silk dresses and tailored suits.

Though such a separation had not occurred in Terreas, given its small size, he recognized this immediately as a district for the richer travelers to the Aiger Cliffs.

So who lived in those grandest of buildings on the uppermost level, Jasen could not imagine. Neither could he imagine that he would be welcome there if he were to wander up and take a look. Certainly he, Alixa, Kuura, and Scourgey had drawn looks of a mildly offended sort as they made their way to Huanatha's apartment. Were Huanatha not with them, her position as a woman of wealth obvious in her attire if not simply the way she carried herself, they might've been ordered to turn heel and return to the lower portions of the city.

The scaffold erected about the cliffside was much more obvious here. Actually, it was something of an eyesore, compared to the white stone buildings erected so perfectly on these streets. Miners climbed up and down it, harvesting the metals shining in the cliff wall. A patch on the right, spanning some two hundred yards or so, had been picked mostly clear. Such a minuscule span of the cliffs, it was only noticeable here this close to it—Huanatha's apartment lay on the edge of this level, not long a walk from the scaffold at all. From so near, the barer stretch of cliffside was unmissable.

"We are here," said Huanatha, beckoning them to a door.

"Great," Alixa muttered. Arms folded, face dark, this was the first she had said since catching up and being forced into an introduction.

Huanatha led them up. Her apartment was in a building housing many more—something Jasen could not fathom, as he looked up a set of steps that had been turned into a smooth spiral, up to higher levels.

The doors were locked, with a key and mechanism like that of Burund's book chest. Huanatha's door, though, had two keyholes. She produced both keys from separate locations somewhere on her body—though her doing so was so smooth, likewise in vanishing them after the door was unlocked, that Jasen might have sworn she were a sorcerer herself.

The place was sparsely decorated. It was bare, in fact, as far as Jasen could see. Her small rooms had essentials only.

"You don't entertain guests often, do you?" he asked as they passed a living area with only one chair. Opposite, where Jasen would expect a fireplace in a traditional home, stood a rack for a suit of armor. It was empty; she had only the one set, apparently.

Kuura marveled at it, sadness in his expression. "Did your people not allow you to bring any keepsakes from your lands?"

"I did not wish for them," said Huanatha, and no more.

At the back of the apartment was another closed, locked door, this time with three keyholes, spaced above each other at a separation of maybe six inches. Again, she produced keys from somewhere as though conjuring them. The locks, she did not open from top to bottom; instead, she opened the middle first, then the bottom, then lastly the top.

Only when the key twisted in this one did Jasen hear a *click*.

Huanatha's keys vanished.

The door opened ...

Jasen's eyes bulged. He breathed a curse word that made Alixa gasp in response. He clapped a hand to his mouth, as though doing so would stop it from having fallen out.

Kuura cracked a grin, but Huanatha did not smile. "Come in, and you may choose."

Inside the room were racks, set up at every wall. And on them hung dozens of weapons, the likes of which Jasen could have never imagined. Oh, there were swords, but only some were like the thin blades he would have recognized. A whole rack of them were curved; some just fractionally, others curving greatly. Some had hooked ends, and these came in their own varieties too: one had a straight hook, jutting off at a forty-five-degree angle from the main body of the blade. Its neighbor's hook was curved, like a crescent moon had been affixed to the sword's end.

There were fat yet stubby swords, and terribly long ones that were so thin that Jasen could have sworn their maker had affixed no more than a thread to a hilt, hardened it, and sharpened its edge. A person run through with a blade like that would never even feel it.

Kuura's gaze had lingered on a rack of axe-like weapons. Yet only one of these was even close to an axe as Jasen would imagine it. Many others were pronged, so a strike would impale at two points, or three. One particularly vicious axe had an additional prong pointing in the opposite direction, so it could be sunk into an attacker at the front, then impale another from behind as it was withdrawn.

"I see now why yeh did not fill your boat with keepsakes when yeh fled the Muratam," Kuura said.

Huanatha said nothing to this. Instead: "Take your pick."

Jasen's eyes had hardly gone back to their normal size. Now they bulged again, wide and full of whites. "Sorry?"

"Choose a weapon."

His gaze swept through the room. So many. And he could just take …

"Any?"

Huanatha nodded. Then she stepped forward, to a rack of spears, and retrieved one with a three-quarter-length handle and a bronze barb upon its head. "For a beginner, perhaps this one." She lifted it from its resting place, and swung it. Kuura, who'd edged toward the rack of axes, had to flinch back as the spear's tip lanced through the air just inches from his face—although, the swing was so controlled, Huanatha's poise so precise, that Jasen believed it could have come a half-inch from slicing him from temple to collarbone and still he would have been safe.

"It is lightweight," she explained, "but the barbed tip will gore a man." Another swing, stabbing out at an invisible foe's guts. She twisted, then drew it back.

Jasen imagined a man's innards strung along the barbs, pulled out of him in meaty lumps.

"Would you like to try?" Huanatha asked. She held it out to Jasen.

"Uhm …"

The hesitation, however brief, convinced her that this was not the weapon for him. She reset it in its rack, then hurried to another, her stern demeanor giving way to excitement. "Or this," she said, and she withdrew a weapon resembling a pick, all fashioned from the same piece of dark metal. "It is small, but the points will smash through a skull with one strike." She swung it, two-handed. "Or you can grip it in one hand, and brace with a shield in the other." She mimicked this—though why she gave this piece of advice, Jasen did not know; shields were apparently of no interest to her, going by this room.

"Or—no. This one." She snatched up a billhook, with extra teeth along either side of its exaggerated blade. One in each hand, she whirled, a flurry of razor sharp edges.

Jasen stared. On the one hand, he understood why this woman had been a well-respected warrior in her own right.

On the other, his only experience of people with weapons were the boundary guards in Terreas as they drilled … and Shilara. She had had her own small arsenal and practiced each day, improvising targets and raining her patch of grass with the broken remains of weapons she had pushed beyond their limits. Yet even she was tempered, albeit in a different way to the boundary guards. Fighting was second nature to her, an intrinsic part of her being, but it came from a place of survival.

Watching Huanatha, Jasen did not believe she fought for the same reasons. She wielded blades because she had an insatiable passion for fighting, one that drove her from her very core. An addiction, perhaps, to be fed and fed and fed.

"You should really put those down, you know," said Alixa, as Huanatha again came within killing distance of Kuura, twisting her body so that the blades sailed past him on either side. He cowered, eyes wide, no smile on his face now. "You could hurt someone."

Huanatha stopped. Turning a beady eye onto Alixa, she said, "I only hurt those who I wish to hurt." She strode back to the racks, depositing the weapons again. Then, to Kuura: "You have eyes for the axe, yes?"

His gaze jumped to it guiltily, then back. "Aye."

"Then why do you not take it?"

"I … I am fearful, Que—Huanatha."

"Of what? Seeing the look in the eyes of a cruel man as you cause the life to drain from his grotesque, inhuman body?"

"I am … simply cautious. Alixa … her points are not invalid. We must tread carefully if we are to do battle with Baraghosa."

"Then tread carefully we will," said Huanatha. She reached for the axe, with its many prongs, and wrenched it out of the rack—then thrust it into Kuura's hands. "Now you are armed."

He swallowed, his Adam's apple bobbing. "Yes, Huanatha."

"As for the two of you …" She came closer—and again she looked into their eyes, in the way that Jasen had felt was her parsing through his most base components. She searched him first … then, her lips pursing just a fraction, she turned her attention to Alixa.

"You will take daggers," she said almost immediately.

"I will not," Alixa scoffed.

"When your life depends upon them, and you find yourself empty-handed, you will regret your decision."

"My life will not depend upon them."

"Will it not?" Huanatha bowed, so she stood only a head above Alixa. Looking very closely at her, she said, "What I see in you lies on the surface. You wish not to be swept up in this fight … yet swept up you are."

"That's because I keep being forced to follow."

"Who forces you?" When Alixa did not answer, Huanatha continued: "Baraghosa brought an act of greatest evil upon your people. I see this in you. I see it reflected back at me: the way magma poured upon your village as you watched, severing the people you most love from this earth."

"Is that supposed to be a … a medium's trick?" Alixa said. "Do not speak to me as if you can read what happened from my eyes. I *said*, by the tavern where you eavesdropped upon us, that Baraghosa could cleave the earth apart."

"You do well to question," said Huanatha.

"You do not have answers."

"No. Perhaps not. But I can tell you that it did not hurt them."

Here, Alixa drew a sharp intake of breath. Her eyelids flickered open wider, just for an instant. "Excuse me?" she whispered. Her voice trembled.

"As the mountain poured down upon them," said Huanatha, "they did know. It was so fast. The only knowledge they had of it was a distant rumbling, disrupting their sleep for an instant … then it disrupted them no more."

Jasen closed his eyes. Hot tears threatened to break past his lashes, trickle down his face.

He imagined his father, lying in bed—not awake, as he had believed, feared, but wrapped in a peaceful slumber, away from the pains of his waking life. Perhaps he was dreaming. And then that dream had just … stopped, Adem with it.

He did not feel. Did not hurt.

"Is …" he began—but his voice trembled too, terribly, and he had to clear his throat to make his words feel solid when he tried again. "Is my father at peace?"

Huanatha looked to him, into him.

"Yes," she said after a long time.

"Is … is he …"

"With your mother now. Yes. And the rest of your ancestors,

looking over you now."

His breath came out shakily. So close to crying, he forced himself to hold it together.

His father and mother—together again.

He was without them … but they had each other. He pictured them now, embracing, their spirits coming together after so long apart. Oh, how they'd missed each other …

He shut his eyes, tight. So wet.

His chest ached, an impossible pain. The gouges carved through his heart, his soul … they burned, like they were new all over again.

Huanatha touched his shoulder. "It is okay to cry," she said. "You may grieve. They understand. They grieve for you too, both of you … you who rose from the ashes of Luukessia. *And rise you must!*" she said, in a cry that made Jasen's eyes open. She was standing at her full height again, arms open wide, eyebrows high upon her forehead. "The both of you must continue on—for it is what they want—you, and the beast who has lashed herself to you."

"Scourgey?" asked Alixa. She'd been crying too, or come close to it; her eyes were tinged with pink. Frowning at the scourge who sat amicably at her ankle, she said, "What does she have to do with this?"

"Your Scourgey is as much destined to follow the road you both are on as you are," said Huanatha. "And she knows it, even if you yourselves do not presently see."

"She … knows …?"

"Oh, yes," said Huanatha. "She tells me so."

"She tells you." Alixa's voice had gone flat, disbelieving all over again.

"Do not harbor so many suspicions, child. I speak truth. Have you never met a shaman, speaker with the dead?"

"No …"

Huanatha smiled. "You have now."

Alixa frowned down at Scourgey again, her confusion only growing. "But Scourgey isn't dead."

Huanatha barked, a laugh that was distinctly unfeminine. Then she said, "Choose your weapons, child. You may pick any that feels right to you."

"You said I had to take daggers."

"These, I believe, will feel most right to you. But if you do not trust my judgment, test them all and see yourself."

Alixa pouted, for a moment. Then, glancing sidelong to Jasen, and down at Scourgey, she sighed. "I really have to do this, don't I? I don't have any other choice."

"You have plenty of choice," said Huanatha.

Alixa answered only with a, "Hmm." Then, body sagging, she joined Kuura at the rack of axes to begin testing them.

"What about me?" Jasen asked, meeting Huanatha's eye again. He trusted her, fully, for reasons he could not discern. Whichever weapon she said would fit best into his hands, he would take; she need only look deep into him, and say.

"You … you are more difficult," she said, slow.

"A sword? I think I could—"

"Jasen."

He stopped.

"Do you know what is behind you?" Huanatha asked.

He twisted around, seeing the empty hall—

Her hands on his cheeks brought him back around.

"I don't understand," he said.

"I see the souls of your ancestors," Huanatha answered, "those who came before you. They follow in a line, from the beginning to now. And they worry about you, Jasen. See truths about you that you do not yet know."

"What truths?"

She bypassed this. "They wish to see you succeed."

Jasen's heart swelled. "I do too. But … how?" he asked in a whisper.

"Pour your heart into this," Huanatha said. "Go after it with your full effort, like never have you before. Only then will you find your way. Your ancestors are certain of it."

He imagined them again, their spirits carried on a wind he felt but could not see, imagined them looking down on him. It made him lightheaded—every one of them, right back to the beginning—and there, at the forefront, clearest of all, his mother and father.

He would avenge them.

He would do them proud.

But now, for the first time, now he was waiting for a collision he knew was destined to happen this night, his assurance faded.

The smiled drooped.

Your ancestors are certain of it.

Jasen was thankful beyond measure …

He only wished he was certain too.

19

A storm was building.

Dark clouds had rolled in throughout the afternoon. Jasen had watched them, starting first as greyish puffs that marred the open blue of the skies, then growing darker and darker. A frigid wind blew in from the sea. It whistled and howled, carrying the spray of waves upon it, falling into the city like rain.

By late afternoon evening, true rain had started, falling from the heavens in fat spattering drops, almost weighty enough that they came down straight despite the wind blowing at them. The skies were almost fully black by then, as if nightfall had come five, six hours early. The darkest part of all was centered directly above the Aiger Cliffs themselves, as if the impending storm was targeting the city specifically.

Days without storms ... and here this one had come, on the very night that Baraghosa had agreed with the council he would access their conduction fields.

He'd known.

It sent a shiver up Jasen's spine.

For perhaps only the second time since witnessing the destruction of Terreas, he had another glimpse of Baraghosa's power, unobscured by his single-minded desperation for vengeance. Compared to the act of splitting open a mountain, it was a simple thing, that Baraghosa had foreseen this.

Yet if he could foresee a storm days out, what else could he see?

They watched well into evening, waiting.

"When are we going?" Alixa asked. She was restless.

No one was more restless than Jasen. His first plan—the frail beginnings of one, at any rate—had been to scale the towers of rock overlooking the city once again, and lie in wait for Baraghosa at the conduction fields. Huanatha agreed on this. But Kuura and Alixa talked him out of it, Kuura believing that it would be better to catch Baraghosa unawares, from behind.

"You say that as if we can guarantee an approach when his back is turned," Huanatha had scoffed. "Are your eyes on extendible stalks?"

"We may approach when his back is *metaphorically* turned," said Kuura. "He will be distracted with his business with the conduction rods. So we make our attack then, yes?"

"We might miss him," said Jasen.

"The lights you speak of will be easy to follow."

But Jasen did not believe that would be so, when the winds howled and the rain came down at a steep angle, stinging their faces and eyes and forcing them to cast their gaze toward the ground lest the frantic downpour blind them.

They agreed, eventually, that they would wait for when Baraghosa was atop the cliffs—or, if visibility was a problem, when he was likely to be on the cliffs. Then it would be Jasen to give the go-ahead.

They waited at another tavern at the bottom of the cliffside path. Unlike Terreas, the world kept turning in the Aiger Cliffs when the rained poured. Fewer feet pounded the streets—but these people had crossed seas, braved storms and enormous waves, leaks to their own hulls, perhaps naval battles in unfamiliar territories ... so the lashing of the rain upon their heads was nothing to them. At most they pulled over a hood made of loose fabric, or donned a cloak, then steeled their bodies and pressed their way through the city to the vendor or shop or tavern they were headed toward.

The vendors on the docks did pack up eventually, but only when the waves threatened their stalls. Still, they did not move far, retiring to streets up the steps and past the archway leading into the city proper.

The rain hammered. Sitting outside, on a table quickly soaked, Jasen stared up the cliffside. The twisting spires did not shine now with exposed metals.

There was no sign of Baraghosa's lights. At least, Jasen saw none. Shielded from the rain by a wooden awning erected around this tavern's side, he could at least look up without the rain pelting into his eyes, though still it blew into their shelter, angled so it wet them from the waist up.

Jasen kept one hand gripped upon the sword Huanatha had let him pick, one with a lightweight, blackened blade that she promised was sharpened to perfection. He held tight so no water would pass his knuckles and slicken his hold when it mattered most.

The sheeting rain made it harder to see. And the darkness of the sky made it harder still. Picking out the spires of contorted cliffside had been near impossible. But he'd found it, and his eyes blazed on the nigh-indiscernible edge that separated it from the roiling bruise overhead.

He watched for lights, waited.

Still none. But he would see them ... he hoped.

They all watched, Jasen knew. Between their eight eyes—ten, if Scourgey watched too, and he believed she did—they would surely catch Baraghosa as he climbed to those dizzying heights.

But Jasen watched most intently of all. His back was to the table they all clustered around. His legs were ready, at a moment's notice, to stand and propel him forward. He half-listened to the idle chatter behind him, enough to follow a conversation but not enough to be able to recount it thirty seconds later.

Kuura was storytelling—or maybe had been, trying to reduce the tension in the air. Yet Jasen was not listening very well, and Alixa's interest had been crushed out of her as the evening drew on. So now he spoke with Huanatha about Nunahk, and she talked of the Muratam in turn.

"... the *aihn*-blight affect your crops?" Kuura asked.

Huanatha frowned. "You ask of matters two and a half decades ago."

A nod. "Yes. But it was a bad blight, yes? Do you recall it? Our seeds were bitten by it. Many of our stores had to be burned, for the fungus spread too far before we were aware of it. If not for our river, I do not think many of us would have survived." He laughed, adding, "When we did have the grain again to bake bread, it was like a blessing from the gods themselves."

"The blight came to the edge of our lands only," said Huanatha. "Deudenwe had great foresight, and prevented it from damaging our resources."

"Deudenwe," Kuura mused. "He was a great leader, as we heard tell." Hastily, he added, "Of course, not as great as *you*, Queen—"

Huanatha cut him off with a throaty derisive noise. "I told you that I do not wish to hear—"

The door into and out of the tavern opened. Wind blustered in a particularly violent blast at that same moment, whipping it from the hand of one of the bar staff as he came out.

He shielded his face with an arm, made his way to their table.

"Empties!" he half-shouted, his voice heavily accented.

Kuura gathered up their glasses, Alixa's still half-full of a caramel-colored liquid she'd long ago abandoned, and passed them to him. "Have yeh got the door—?"

"Fine," he said, already moving away again. The door fought him as he returned inside. He won: it closed with a resounding *bang!* that the wind sucked away.

"Would anyone like another drink?" Kuura asked. "Huanatha?"

"I will purchase my own beverages," she said stiffly.

"Right, yes. Jasen, Alixa?"

"No," Alixa murmured.

"Jasen?

… Jasen? Would you like—"

"He's here."

And he was up on his feet, already marching out from under the awning, to the cliffside pathway.

Kuura and Alixa scrabbled up too. Huanatha, who had been sitting beside Jasen on the same bench, moved much more fluidly, her armor hardly whispering as she rose and pressed herself into a stride. Only when she stepped into the rain did it made a sound, as the raindrops pinged against it.

"You're sure?" Kuura asked.

Jasen nodded. "I'm sure." He had seen, against the blackened, stormy skies, two pulsing lights. Barely visible for the curtain of rain falling diagonally between them and separated by such a great distance, they were hardly pinpricks. Yet Jasen saw them, fixated on them now, blinking rapidly to shift the waters running down his face as he strode through the building storm. They'd just appeared on the clifftops that moment, so Baraghosa had either climbed from another direction—or he had somehow appeared there, at that instant. Neither seemed possible. There was no other pathway to the conduction fields, nor could a man vanish and reappear himself at will.

Baraghosa, though, was no ordinary man.

The five of them surged up the cliffside. It provided a small shelter from the storm: the winds had whipped in from the east, and so the cliffs themselves provided cover, at least from the rain. But the chill and howl were always present. Gooseflesh had been raised on Jasen's skin for hours now, surely had on all his companions' too. Had he not been so determined, the cold would have stopped him. He'd lift his hand to his mouth and breathe into his curled fingers, fighting to bring warmth to his digits. His entire body juddered with racking shivers. His teeth chattered, almost hard enough to chip their ends. The roar of the wind over the Aiger Cliffs felt like a heavy blanket, pressed over him, blocking his frozen ears and smothering him. None of it mattered. He had only one focus: scaling these cliffs so that he could confront Baraghosa once again, so that he could look into his face and watch as he ran him through with his sword, watch the life force drain out of him as his blood poured hot over Jasen's wrist, pooling between their feet, and Baraghosa died, and Terreas was avenged.

So he climbed—nay, ran—up the cliffside, his hand clasped upon the hilt of his sword.

Scourgey was at his heel. He spared her only a glance.

She was looking back at him, mouth open. The scent of death was hardly upon her now, whipped away by the winds that did manage to penetrate the alcove in which the city had been constructed.

Huanatha was behind, just half a step. "This Scourgey, she is with you," she said. "She will follow you till the very last."

Jasen nodded. "Good Scourgey."

"Are we sure about this?" Alixa called. She and Kuura were lagging behind, though how far exactly, Jasen could not be sure. Eight paces perhaps, or ten. From the way her breath caught, already they were hurrying to catch up.

A fire had been lit beneath Jasen's feet, though. They'd have to fight all the way to the conduction fields to keep pace with him.

"Baraghosa is atop these very cliffs now," Huanatha answered Alixa. "The time to defeat him is upon us—and defeat him we shall! For we have determination in our souls, a flame in our bellies, and justice in our hearts."

"I don't think …" Alixa began.

"Do not suggest to me you have lost heart, girl!"

"I have plenty of heart! It's just that my heart believes we should—"

"Leave Baraghosa unchecked? Let him have his way with the world, wreaking devastation on all the lands he touches?"

"I never said—"

"By letting him walk free, you are complicit in the very destruction he rained down upon you," Huanatha said fiercely. "Do you wish to enable a murderer?"

"*I just think the Emerald Fields are the best place for us,*" Alixa said. She spoke quickly, all her words blurring together in an effort to stop Huanatha from cutting over her.

"And the best place for Baraghosa's head is atop a pike! *Let it be ours!*"

"*Yeah, see, I didn't really sign up for a battle with a sorcerer! I left Terreas for some seed—*"

"A quest which has led you here, has it not? To this very moment?"

"*I AM NOT ON THIS HILL BECAUSE OF DESTINY!*" Alixa cried back—and though the roar of the wind fought to quiet her, she was louder, her face screwed up as she forced every bit of volume from her lungs. "*I AM ON THIS HILL BECAUSE I AM STUPID ENOUGH TO BE LED PLACES I WOULD RATHER NOT GO!*"

A sneer broke into Huanatha's voice. "You do not wish to cut off the sorcerer's head? Have you no shame?"

"I believe what Alixa is trying to say," said Kuura swiftly, "is that she is worried about the outcome of our battle. We are but four—"

"Four people with vengeance in our hearts!"

"Yes, yes, b-but just the four of us, against a sorcerer …"

"You have a fine axe in your hand," Huanatha growled. "The girl has a pair of daggers. Jasen has a sword—and I wield Tanukke, Blade of the Victorious!" She withdrew it from the small loop which affixed it to her waist. Brandishing it skyward, she loosed a battle cry: "*Your blood will wet this blade, Baraghosa!*"

"We are unpracticed," Alixa huffed. The trek kept her breathing hard, pumping her legs to keep up with Jasen and Scourgey as they led the charge. "We are not fighters, any of us."

"*I* am a warrior, girl."

"Fine—any of us except you."

"Alixa is correct," said Kuura, probably nodding his head along madly. "We have not gone to battle before. Skirmishes, yes, but—against a man of magic, who could spirit us over the cliffside with just a wave of his hand?"

"I have seen Baraghosa do no such thing," said Huanatha.

"He has brought storms upon us, storms that are not like any other this world has ever seen," said Kuura.

As if to underscore his words, the first bolt of lightning split the air. It flashed, blinding them for the barest fraction of an instant. Coming down practically above them, it forked, jagged tips of electricity licking the conduction rods.

Jasen pictured Baraghosa within them.

He hoped the sorcerer had been struck down by the blast. But he did not believe that he would be; and in any event, if Baraghosa were to be felled this night, then it must be Jasen to do it. Not inclement weather, nor any of the others by his side now. Scourgey herself could not leap up and tear out his throat.

Jasen—and Jasen alone—had to kill Baraghosa.

Could he stop any of the others from landing the killing blow?

Kuura and Alixa, he did not have to worry about. But Huanatha—

she was as determined as Jasen was. Fueled as he was, her own desire for vengeance would surely propel her at Baraghosa with Tanukke drawn as he surged in for his own killing strike.

There was no choice for it: he would have to be faster.

The cliffside fell away. Then they were climbing the pathway around the thick spire, like a tall, pointed shell, with its crystal extrusions. The lightning was coming quicker now. Striking directly above them, every white-hot arc that rent the air crashed against the conduction rods. They were no longer sheltered from the wind, and it whipped all noise from them, even as the thunderous explosions boomed. The very earth rocked, as if every strike of lightning did not just hit the conduction rods but was channeled through them, so that it felt as if the explosions were going off under them or beside them in the cliffs themselves. If two strikes should come down at once, surely it would blow this spire of twisted cliffside apart.

Up, up they went...

Rain sluiced down, violent and powerful. Kuura and Alixa shielded their faces from it. Backs bent, they could not see farther than the ground five feet ahead of them.

But Huanatha set her face, striding through it unperturbed. And Jasen cast his glare heavenward, pummeling droplets be damned. He stared up, watching as Baraghosa's lights bobbed, knowing that in another two turns ... now just one turn of this pathway ... he and Jasen would see eye to eye again. Despite the furious winds, those lights simply bobbed lazily in the air a hundred feet up or more, like a kite riding a breeze.

Jasen had hated them all his life, hated what they heralded.

That paled in comparison to his hatred now. Jasen realized that what he had known then was only a dislike—an intense one, to be sure, but a dislike nonetheless. Only with Terreas's destruction, and the death of his father, did Jasen know true hate. It burned through him, consuming every fiber of his being. It ate at his thoughts, a black fog that descended and directed all thoughts to itself, pushing him in one direction only. It could not be banished; at best it slunk back to the edges of his mind, where it twisted upon itself in dark waves, hating him, hating him, *hating him.*

It bayed for blood, like the scourge out in the rye fields, watching Terreas, waiting for an imbecile to climb the boundary and stumble out into their midst.

Jasen would satisfy that hatred if it cost him his life.

The pathway twisted around, taking the city out of sight. It rose, a thinning line, the last twenty feet to the field of conduction rods laid out atop it.

A crack of lightning split the air. It exploded on the rods, leaving a brilliant streak of white light burnt across Jasen's vision. The stench of gunpowder, but a hundred times more intense, filled the air, then was whisked away.

And still Baraghosa's lights danced their lazy dance.

Ten feet away.

Jasen's chest burned, his legs. His whole body seemed to be on fire inside. He'd pushed it, and dimly he knew that: his breathing was ragged, and half the wet on his face was not rain but sweat.

No matter. He was here now.

And he *was* here: the last of the path fell away, and the conduction rods came into view, a whole field of them. The air crackled with electricity, a palpable charge that tugged at every hair on Jasen's body. Some of the conduction rods—those that had been struck, surely—glowed.

Another bolt of lightning exploded. Jasen heard the sound before his brain processed it. Just two rows away, toward the cliff edge, its end split into tendril-like jags that licked across three conduction rods.

He was blinded for a second—

He blinked through it.

And there he saw him: body too long, and somehow bone dry even in the wailing storm, clothes untouched by wet and the wind. His back was to them. But Jasen recognized him, recognized too the hands, lifting something gleaming between fingers that had grown an inch longer than they ought have.

Baraghosa.

Jasen squeezed his grip on his blade's hilt.

Finally, he was here. The time had come—to kill him.

20

Lightning cleaved the air apart. Forks boomed against the tips of the conduction rods, tongues of electricity licking them for only a fraction of a second, but long enough to rend the air with bone-rattling explosions. The world went almost white in those moments.

Baraghosa stood untouched amidst it all, the inclement weather appearing to bend around him, as if even the rain dared not touch the sorcerer.

Jasen should storm for him now, strike while his back was turned. The ferocity of the unloading heavens, with the deluge of rain and near-constant lightning, would mask the sound of his approach. Baraghosa would not know until too late, when he felt the sting of a blade through his back, saw it pass out of his stomach, bloodied, growing longer by the inch as Jasen shoved deeper with it—

But now he saw him—now he saw this man who had wrought such utter devastation on his home, destroying near every part of Jasen's life in one cataclysmic event—Jasen could not kill him in shadow.

Baraghosa had to know why he was dying.

He had to see Jasen's face as it happened.

Another flash of lightning, blinding.

After those explosions, a wake of silence seemed to follow.

Into it, Jasen bellowed, "*BARAGHOSA!*"

The sorcerer turned, eyes searching—

Jasen's rage grew hotter still, scalding in its intensity. His muscles seemed to seize. Wind and rain and thunder forgotten, comrades behind him lost too, it was just him and the sorcerer now—an old man with his sallow face, and Jasen, hand locked tight on the hilt of his sword, so hard that none could pry his fingers open to part him from it.

Baraghosa saw him—saw all of them—and a look of confusion

bloomed across his features. Yet it was only momentary; and as he found Jasen again, at the fore, an amused sort of understanding replaced it.

The anger roiled in Jasen's chest.

"I see how it is," said Baraghosa easily.

Damn him. Damn him to the fires in the inferno he had unleashed over Terreas.

Jasen said through gritted teeth, "I've come to kill you."

Lightning rent the air again. It crackled, suffused with static, lifting the hairs on the back of Jasen's neck, on his arms. Deeper, it penetrated, right to his very muscles. Like pouring grease onto a fire, it energized him in ways the rage and adrenaline alone could not. And when the moment came, it would power him, power his thrusts, his stabs, and grant him the strength to push the blade through where muscle and sinew and bone would threaten not to yield, that it might keep this man held together as Jasen fought to split him in two.

"All of you?" Baraghosa asked. He waved a hand across them, over-elaborate in his sweep.

"You have wronged many," Huanatha growled. "Now your treachery comes back to you."

He laughed—and somehow, though it was a quiet sound, little more than a breathy *hah* that might be whispered to oneself while reading a faintly amusing story, it was loud enough that Jasen heard it over the storm.

Like the way he spoke in the meeting hall in Terreas, he realized: quiet, yet audible to all.

Jasen saw a glimpse of it: the hall, in the light of dawn, peaceful and serene with its cloying candles, burned down low in holders. Then it was buried in a mound of slag as the mountain was torn open, and the sky was suddenly full of ash, so much more choking than any overly pungent candle.

He clenched his teeth, ground them.

"You're a murderer," he said—but lightning struck again, behind Baraghosa this time. It forked, arcing across five conduction rods at once.

The boom came immediately. It was deafening.

Baraghosa said, "You'll have to speak up; I'm afraid I did not quite catch that."

Taunting. After everything he had done, he was *taunting* Jasen. Jasen seethed for a long, long moment. The black hatred churning inside him had reached its boiling point. It could go nowhere else: overspilled into all of him, it had but one last direction to move:

outward.

He opened his mouth.

"*ARGH!!*" he screamed—

And he flung himself across the space, raising his sword from its sheath.

If the others came with him, he did not know. Perhaps they did; or perhaps they knew that this was Jasen's fight first and foremost, whatever grievances with Baraghosa they had themselves and held back.

Whichever it was, Jasen did not care. Fire burned in his chest, fire for revenge, for atonement—and he would cut the sorcerer down, now, here, on these clifftops as the heavens unleashed their lightning in a terrifying tumult.

Baraghosa stared as Jasen sprinted through the conduction fields, screaming at him, screaming a battle cry that would be the last Baraghosa ever heard—

Then, at almost the last moment, when there were only ten or twelve feet between them—

Baraghosa lazily reached into his long, flowing jacket, a deep midnight blue almost the color of the sea at twilight.

From it he withdrew a small cane. Half the size of a man's walking stick, one easy pull on the gilded orb handle extended it to full size—

If he believed that a piece of wood would stop Jasen, he had another thing coming.

Jasen drew his sword back, preparing to thrust—Baraghosa's face was close now, closer than Jasen had ever seen it, sallow and waxy and looking as if it had been compressed at the cheekbones and grown slightly too long in the other direction to compensate—

He was smiling, very slightly.

When Jasen's blade pierced his stomach, that smile would be gone.

He flew, the last steps closing, Baraghosa hardly moving ...

Then the sorcerer slammed the cane against the earth.

It was as if he had tossed a rock into a pool of water—or that perhaps a rock had fallen from the very top of a mountain and landed in a pond at its base. A shockwave went out from it, invisible—it slammed Jasen hard in the chest.

His cry cut off as he was tossed backward, off his feet—

Then he crashed sidelong into a conduction rod. There was a second crash, bewildering—he could not figure this one out, could not figure anything out at all for a few moments—

Then his eyes opened. The world was topsy-turvy. A conduction rod pointed up directly overhead into the brackish mire that was the sky.

The second impact had been the fall, he realized dimly.

Alixa appeared. "Jasen!" she cried. Scourgey followed her a moment later. She whined—

Lightning boomed across the conduction field, throwing the world into bright relief. Alixa and Scourgey were shadows for just a mite of a moment.

"Are you hurt—?" she was saying, though her words seemed to come from very far, as if he'd sunk his head into a pail of water.

He pushed up. Alixa tried to hold him down; so too did Scourgey, it seemed, as she pressed low to him—yet he muscled past her, moved Alixa aside with a hand to the shoulder.

"You can't!" she said—

But he was already past.

Somehow, the sword had not loosened itself from his grip. How that had happened, he couldn't be sure; the crash was a blur, one he could not sort through, for it seemed to be an instantaneous thing even though he knew it was not.

Later, perhaps, he would thank the ancestors that he had not fallen and impaled himself upon it.

Baraghosa merely watched.

Jasen strode for him. Twenty feet, he'd been separated from the sorcerer.

This time he would not allow himself to be bested.

"You killed my family," Jasen growled.

"Is that so?" He sounded almost bored.

His words made Jasen's anger well up again. He broke into a run, crying out again, raising the sword—

This time Baraghosa sidestepped at the last moment. Jasen cut out with the blade, cleaving the air the same way the lightning strikes were ripping it in two—but Baraghosa was not touched.

Instead, he jabbed out with his cane again just as Jasen pivoted—

This blast caught him side-on. He stumbled back, forced six feet away before his legs could not keep up with his staggering lurch anymore and he fell.

Baraghosa ambled toward him—

Midway, he jabbed out with his cane, sideways and behind him. "Stay back, girl," he warned—Alixa jerked backward as though she'd walked into an invisible wall. Another thrust with the cane on his other side—"And you, old man."

"Leave the boy alone!" Kuura cried.

Jasen pushed back onto his feet.

He tasted blood now. It was in his mouth, but didn't come from his lip. A cut on his face, maybe? He didn't know. Wouldn't reach for it to feel—though the rain did not make sourcing the wound possible anyway. No, he just gripped tight his blade, adjusting his feet to shoulder width.

Distantly, he was aware that he was shaking—and not from cold.

Baraghosa strolled easily to him, watching Jasen through beady eyes. They were off-white, yellow with age, the irises discolored and faded.

An arm's length away from Jasen, he stopped.

Close enough to strike again.

Jasen held firm, waiting for the right moment.

"The boy from Luukessia," Baraghosa murmured. "Have you really crossed the sea to battle me?"

Jasen set his jaw. "Yes."

A moment—and though the downpour carried on, for that long second as Baraghosa considered this, it felt as if all the world had gone silent.

Then Baraghosa said, "Very well."

Jasen lunged, swinging—

Baraghosa lifted his cane. He jabbed it out at Jasen's chest—

It did not touch him, but an explosion of force hit him, square.

He cried out as the sheer power of it flung him back. This one felt was as if a wave comprised of half the sea had ploughed into him. He flew backward like a cannonball, conduction rods hurtling past in a blur—

Then he crashed against a rod, almost at its very top. His arms and legs snapped backward—he screamed, at least inside—

The sword flew from his grip.

Then he was falling—

He landed on his feet, but his legs hadn't the strength to hold him and sagged immediately, as if they had no bone in them at all. White hot pain tore through him again, another pulse of it that overrode his senses, threatened to blind his vision and mute his hearing.

He was down.

He swam there—

A boom of lightning brought him up again. He lifted his head—it was so heavy all of a sudden—to see Alixa charging a long way off, a dagger in each hand—

"*No,*" he tried to say. But he could not.

She stabbed out, a mad, frenzied look of fear in her eyes. Behind her, Scourgey lunged too, leaping skyward—

A simple flick of Baraghosa's cane sent them flying. Scourgey pirouetted backward, a tangle of limbs, landing somewhere out of sight—

Alixa also flew backward, arms and legs flailing like a ragdoll's. Baraghosa's blast had hit her more on one side, and she spun through the air like a top—

A conduction rod stopped her. She fell in a heap at its base and did not move.

From here, so very far, it looked as though Baraghosa *had* simply tossed a doll aside.

Kuura surged in on Baraghosa's opposite side. He hefted the axe in one hand, bringing it around, all three pronged blades on one side sailing for Baraghosa's head while it was turned—

But Baraghosa darted clear, ducking expertly. The axe swung overhead—then Baraghosa slammed his cane into Kuura's massive chest. Kuura roared, flying up and backward in a lazy arc …

"*Kuura!*" Jasen wished to cry … yet still his vocal cords did not work. He sucked in breaths that hurt. They were shallow, so very shallow. Had his ribcage been crushed onto his lungs? Surely they had. That or Baraghosa had pinned him with an invisible boulder, half the size of the mountain he had torn apart over Terreas.

None of him could move, he realized. He half-lay, half-squatted where he had fallen. Prone, he could do little more than breathe and keep his head up to watch the battle—and even that was difficult. His whole body was agonized. The pain was complete, coming at him from every direction, burning through all his nerve endings at once.

This was dying. It must be.

Huanatha pressed in while Kuura clambered to his feet. She had been watching the battle intently, watching Baraghosa, taking stock of his movements, the way he worked his feet, the twist of his body as he contorted so easily to avoid the blows that he had been threatened with. Now, she had the measure of him—or perhaps time was running short, and with Jasen and Alixa out of the fight, and Kuura struggling to stand, she knew that the time to strike was nearly past.

She drew Tanukke high overhead, then she crouched low and sprang forward, on her toes. She hurtled through the conduction rods, closing the distance between them, itself only fifteen feet perhaps as she had prowled inward while Baraghosa did away with the children.

Lightning struck at the same moment she did.

Jasen blinked. The image seemed to be paused, Tanukke raised high but swinging down over Huanatha's head in a killing blow, and

Baraghosa beneath it—

The afterimage faded though, and Jasen realized: Huanatha had missed. How Baraghosa had done it, he did not know: but now the sorcerer was weaving on feet just as quick as Huanatha's as she pressed in again, this time bringing Tanukke to bear from the left. The blade swung in a wide arc with a speed unlike any Jasen had ever imagined—

Baraghosa dodged nimbly.

Kuura came at him from the back. He lifted the axe—

A backward twist from Baraghosa, a strike with his cane—Kuura wheezed as if punched as he swung around and backward, like he'd been backhanded across the face. He staggered.

Huanatha thrust forward with Tanukke.

Baraghosa parried the thrust with his cane. Blade and walking stick connected. But where the wood should have been cut right through, it held. Baraghosa met the force of Huanatha's strike for a moment, the two of them frozen in a tableau. Then he swung, up and overhead. Huanatha was forced backward.

Kuura came in again.

"I tire of you, old man," said Baraghosa, voice still somehow audible despite the storm thrashing around them, and the distance between them. He barely spared a glance for Kuura this time, simply striking out with his cane under his arm and behind him.

Kuura was flung backward as another blast of invisible force slammed his chest. He rolled in the air, spinning exactly once. Then—

CRASH!

He collided with a conduction rod at the same moment another bolt of dazzling white lightning came down from the heavens.

Jasen's breath caught. The strike—surely it had not hit …?

But Kuura was rising seconds later. A trick of positioning only; the *Lady Vizola's* first mate had not been struck, nor had the conduction rod which had arrested his flight. One behind, then—though perhaps close. Too close.

Jasen needed to rise. This fight was his. In his blind pursuit, he'd allowed people to be drawn in who should not have been. Kuura, whose head bled from a gash as he readied himself for another, increasingly unsteady approach to Baraghosa; Huanatha, who flung herself at Baraghosa, Tanukke carving through the air yet missing once again as he wove away from her on spry feet; and Alixa, who cowered at the bottom of a conduction rod, alive but moving little more than Jasen.

Then Scourgey reappeared in his line of vision—Scourgey, who now sprinted again across the battleground that was the conduction field. She cut past a staggering Kuura, past a forest of lightning rods—

Another strike illuminated her from the rear, a black, leaping thing—

She flew, forepaws extended, claws out, her teeth bared for his throat—

Baraghosa slapped the cane at her without even looking. And away she went, careening somewhere in the opposite direction with a howling whine, like a dog that had been kicked in the chest.

No, Jasen thought. He reached out—

Pointless. He could not stop her. Could not stop Baraghosa.

Baraghosa had been able to dispose of him without so much as touching him.

Kuura came in again, from the rear. He hobbled now but he still moved, still clutched his three-pronged battleaxe. Intense eyes watched as Huanatha and Baraghosa danced, her leading with strikes, him fending them off but granted no time to strike out himself. They pivoted, a series of strikes and quick dodges that cut a jagged line through the conduction rods—

Huanatha was guiding Baraghosa toward Kuura, though. Jasen saw it now. His hope lifted in his chest as the gap between them shrunk. Fifteen feet ... twelve ... eight ...

Now six. Kuura clenched his teeth, baring them the way Scourgey had, a grimace as wide as any of his smiles—

He leapt, when Baraghosa was barely three feet shy of him. Swung—

At the same moment, Huanatha brought Tanukke around, low—

Baraghosa just sidestepped. It seemed impossible, that he could avoid two strikes coming from two directions at once ... but somehow he did, with unnatural grace.

Then he thrust out with the cane again.

Kuura bellowed as he was flung away from the battle once more. Jasen watched him go, spinning high this time. He sailed past a conduction rod, one of the horizontal bars at the top catching his arm and arresting his flight. He seemed to gasp, before falling into a heap maybe another ten feet on from it.

This time he did not rise.

Jasen's stomach twisted. Another one down—another failure.

Only Huanatha remained.

The last of their hope resting upon her shoulders, she pressed in with even greater fervor. Her strikes came faster, her whole body was a blur as she wove, swung, withdrew, thrust forward again. Baraghosa blocked and sidestepped, blocked again. Huanatha gave him no time to blast her with his cane, or strike out to claim his own advantage in the fight.

Jasen watched from a thousand miles distant.

He had failed in his fight. But Baraghosa could still be bested. Jasen would not be the one to defeat him ... but Huanatha could. She could avenge Terreas, avenge Jasen's father, where he himself had failed.

So he prayed:

Ancestors. He closed his eyes. Breathing was hard. *Give her strength. Aid in her fight.*

Just thinking, reaching out to them with his mind, cost him more energy than he had. He fell into a darkness where there was only him, his heavy breaths, drawn in like a death rattle, and the feel of the rain hammering down upon him.

Lightning ripped open the hole he had fallen into.

He opened eyes with heavy lids.

Huanatha and Baraghosa still raged in battle. She swung high, Tanukke cutting through the air, glinting pure white as an explosive bolt from the sky brought full daylight upon them momentarily. Baraghosa met the blade with his cane. He thrust her back—she danced on her feet, adjusting—and then she came back in, low.

"*You took my kingdom!*" she roared, a thousand miles away.

Baraghosa's arm snapped around. He caught Tanukke with his cane just in time—

"*Usurped my throne!*"

Huanatha pressed. She whirled around, bringing Tanukke over her head again, and down—

Baraghosa barely caught it.

Jasen's heart sped. The fog of pain threatening to overload him ebbed away, a surge of renewed hope flooding through his chest instead.

The sword and cane held there for a long moment. Huanatha pressed down—and Baraghosa gripped tight, arms shaking as he held the warrior woman back.

"*You will pay for the dissent you sowed among my people,*" Huanatha growled.

Baraghosa said calmly, "I simply showed them the truth."

Huanatha gritted her teeth. "*You bastard sorcerer.*"

Lightning flashed, casting them in a silhouette.

Huanatha suddenly thrust forward. Jasen's heart leapt into his throat—Tanukke would split Baraghosa in half down the center of his face!—but the sorcerer had sidestepped, using the brief flash of light as cover. His cane vanished, Tanukke fell through empty air.

Huanatha stumbled after it.

Too late, she recovered, twisting—

Baraghosa's cane swung through the air and smacked her hard in the cheek.

Huanatha cried, a sound that was lost to the thunderous heavens. She staggered, as though the hit had not just been the whack of a rod of polished wood, but the hammer of a god slamming against her cheekbone. Given all his magic powers, it might have been close.

And now the advantage was Baraghosa's. Matching Huanatha's backward floundering, he thrust with his cane. This time he did not connect, but Jasen saw the blasts those thrusts imparted all the same. Huanatha shouted, falling backward again and again. Past the conduction rods—Tanukke fell from her hand as her arm slammed one. She tried to scrabble to her feet—but Baraghosa was there, ready, and another blast pushed her down and away again—

Closer to the edge.

No!

She struggled—

Baraghosa slammed the end of his cane against the earth. An invisible wave plowed into her, and she was thrown back—she yelled, arms whirling—

She hit the earth on her feet, just inches from the edge of the cliff.

The momentum was too much. Ankles planted, her upper body tilted over, over—

Then it stopped. Hanging suspended over the edge, almost flat, it appeared as though she had slumped against an invisible net, keeping her from tumbling over the precipice.

Baraghosa stalked to her.

Jasen's stomach clenched.

He was toying with her.

Lightning struck again.

A wake of silence followed.

"Kill me then," Huanatha growled.

Baraghosa appraised her. Then:

"No."

And he raised his hand. Huanatha lifted with it—and just as he mimed tossing a ball, so too was she tossed, end over end, back into the middle of the field of conduction rods. She flew, a tangle of limbs and shining blue armor—and crashed headlong into Kuura.

She did not get up.

No.

No, no, no!

Defeated, all of them.

And Baraghosa had barely broken a sweat in doing it.

He smiled faintly, peering around the masses lying in heaps where he had flung them all. Shaking his head very slightly, he tutted.

Then he reached into his jacket and withdrew a glass flask. Stoppered by a cork on a piece of metal, its chamber was wide at the bottom but thin-necked.

It was also empty.

He strode deeper into the field of conduction rods, moving still as if the winds did not touch him, nor the floods of cascading rain.

He looked skyward.

His lips moved. This time, the sound did not carry in its unnatural way. But Jasen saw it, saw that he spoke what surely was an incantation, and his stomach filled with dread.

A blast of lightning like no other rent the sky. It exploded, a cataclysm to rival a quake that ripped an island apart and consigned it to the bottom of the seas. Every conduction rod was licked by those jagged, blinding forks. The noise was terrifying, as if the very world had ended all around them. Jasen screamed out, wishing he could plug his ears, or cut out his eyes to stop from being blinded even though his lids were together, screwed up as tight as he could make them.

The air hummed with electricity. The conduction rods whined, all that power unloaded into them.

And then—

Jasen opened his eyes. For long seconds he was blind, his whole vision replaced with a curtain of pure white.

Then it peeled away as a hole first opened in it and then widened to reveal Baraghosa, holding his flask high … and pure energy, channels of searing white, streaking out of the conduction rods, through the air, and into the flask he held aloft. The power poured in, filling it … and when the white glow in the air faded and the last of the power had filled the flask, he capped it with the cork, pressing down the metal loop to hold it in place.

He looked at it in his hand. It shone fiercely, as if he had ripped off a part of the sun and bottled it.

The shadows it threw over his face were stark.

His thin lips lifted at the corners, just a fraction. Just the barest trace of happiness—and it frightened Jasen terribly.

Then he stowed the bottle in his jacket once more. Taking a final look around, he seemed to remember where he was, remember that four bodies and a beaten scourge lay around his feet where he had discarded them just moments ago.

He set into an easy, long-legged stride.

His dancing lights, high in the sky, followed along behind him.

No, Jasen thought. Desperately, he tried to push himself up. Just the strength to rise to his feet, to cut Baraghosa off—to throw himself at the sorcerer's back and take the both of them off the cliff, if that was the only way to defeat him.

Yet he did not have it. Only agonizing pain answered him, racking his body with tremors.

Jasen fought against it. He gritted his teeth—though they were so very far away now ... He pushed—both arms trembled.

Baraghosa had reached the path back down to the city.

He descended without pausing.

Just before his face disappeared out of sight, he said, "Adieu."

Then he was gone.

But not gone yet—he would take the path down, to the Aiger Cliffs, to the docks, and to his boat. There was time yet to catch him up—time yet to stop him before he unleashed the power he had stolen from here ... Jasen still had hope! He still had a chance—!

Somehow, he rolled over—

A pure, screaming pain overtook him. He felt it for a second that felt like a lifetime, roaring through his body, overloading his every sense—

And then his body shut down.

21

Jasen woke, slowly at first. He felt something upon him, but he could not place it: just knew that it was touching his face, from all angles, an ongoing rush of motion—and as his awareness grew, he realized it stung.

His eyes opened—

He slammed them closed.

Raindrops danced across his face. One had landed with particular force in his eye, as rude an awakening as any.

He slammed his eyes closed again.

His stomach dropped as it all came back to him: the march up the cliffside to do battle with Baraghosa; the way Jasen had run first, and then the others joined him, flying at the sorcerer with hate in their hearts—at least in his and Huanatha's case, and surely Alixa's too, though she had come more warily, her foray into the battle short-lived.

Jasen had flung himself so tremendously hard at Baraghosa, sure of the justice he would bring the sorcerer to … and he had been dispensed with using barely a flick of the wrist. Alixa too, and Scourgey, and Kuura.

Huanatha had been his last hope … and though she had proven a worthy adversary for Baraghosa, she too had been bested, almost thrown from the cliffside.

Baraghosa had sucked the power from the conduction rods—and as the air came alive with the diffusing electricity, Jasen's body had finally given out after being pushed so far.

He had passed out.

And now he was returning to the Aiger Cliffs, his senses coming back to him after a dizzying moment of confusion as he tried to orient himself in the world. The sky moved as he twisted—and he realized now, too, that he was in the arms of someone, cradled like a parent carried a babe or a sickly child.

He blinked.

Kuura looked down at him. "Rest."

"Wh—" Jasen's voice was strained. It hardly came. The noise he did make was more wheeze than word.

He tried again. "We lost?" His throat felt like an old rope with little give.

Kuura said again, "Rest, Jasen."

"Pl-please." He tried to force himself up. Kuura's hold was too strong, though—and Jasen was much too weak. Whatever strength he had in him had fled.

Alixa's words came back: *Just a boy with a pilfered dagger.* It was true.

He was a boy, just a boy—and a failure.

"No," said Kuura, as Jasen struggled harder still. "Do not—Jasen, please, hold still. Your head—it is imperative you *rest*."

"*Let go of me!*" And he raked out with a hand, using the only weapon he had: his fingers and nails. They sliced Kuura's neck, down to his chest—

Kuura hissed and dropped Jasen.

"Kuura of Nunahk!"

"He scratched me!"

Alixa rushed to Jasen's side as he righted himself. Scourgey followed, whining sadly. She was limping and her head was down.

The world continued to sway as Jasen clambered to his feet; the sky in particular felt as if it had come half-loose from where it was moored to the earth. The ground shifted as Jasen rose, and the sky wobbled precariously, taking a couple of seconds to catch up. It was nauseating.

He took in his cousin. Daggers still at her hips—so she had not lost her weapons, as he had. Another stab of shame at that.

She was cut. Scratches marred her face. But given the way Baraghosa had flung her aside, a network of bruises would blot her ribs for months—assuming she had not broken anything.

"Are you okay?" he asked, groping for her hands.

"I'm fine," she said. "Are you? I—I wasn't sure if you'd wake … Kuura tried, by the conduction rods, but you just …" She shook her head, left the sentence unfinished.

"I'm okay," he said.

He was not. He did not know the extent of his injuries. Adrenaline had fought back the worst of it during his failed battle with Baraghosa. The drunken sway that made his surrounding tilt and pivot came from within his mind, and the fog that did it also dampened the aches and pains his body held. But they would come, he knew—and soon. He felt the start of it now: a jarring discomfort that had taken root around his bones. Maybe within them—until he had his full senses back about him, he could not know how far it penetrated. He hoped the damage he had incurred from Baraghosa was not enough to have broken him right down at the core. He'd seen men in Terreas whose injuries had been so thorough as to permanently afflict them. Rare though they were, they always drew the eye: like Wyllam Havers, who'd taken a fall before Jasen was born and still walked bowed forward. On the worst days, he couldn't get out, and Jasen had overheard plenty of Terreas's people lamenting what a rotten shame it was.

But then, why would it matter if Jasen was irreparably damaged? He had lost against Baraghosa. One thing he had set out to do. Alixa's warnings had fallen on deaf ears and so too had Kuura's, as the collision drew nearer.

Yet they had been right: Jasen could not battle a sorcerer. A legendary warrior like Huanatha had been able to clash on even footing with him—for a time. Then she had lost, like Jasen—perhaps like innumerable men and women who felt wronged by Baraghosa as he stalked foreign lands, bending people to his whims and sowing discord behind him.

Jasen had failed ... and there was no Terreas left for him to retreat to, where people would remark about what a shame it was that *he* had been damaged so greatly he carried it with him, for all to see, for the rest of his days.

He deserved to bear that failure. If he found he could only hobble his whole life, stooped so low his nose left a track in the dirt—he deserved that, a hundred times over.

"Don't look so bitter," said Alixa. "We're alive." She sounded sad though.

"And the rest of you?" Jasen asked, turning to Kuura and Huanatha.

"Alive, as far as I c'n tell," said Kuura.

A improvised bandage of cloth from his over-large tunic with its many folds (one less now), was tight around his forehead, angled almost jauntily so it covered his left ear. The deep blue was a shade darker where Jasen remembered, as a flash only, Kuura's head had collided with a conduction rod.

Another flash: Baraghosa swiping his cane—and Alixa tumbling in the direction he swung, as though she were a puppet on strings only he could pull. Her shriek, as she spun in the air—and then the hard *thud* of her body on a conduction rod.

He felt sick.

Another gash had been torn in Kuura's arm, apparently, for he was bandaged there too.

Huanatha's injuries were few. A few cuts and scrapes here and there. The worst she had fared was the physical slap of Baraghosa's cane when the scales tipped in his favor. It had left her cheek with a red welt. Already, though, it was fading. By the time she reached her apartment again, it might be gone.

Kuura still carried his axe—as did Huanatha with her own weapon, Tanukke tucked into the loop at her hip.

Another wave of guilt crashed over Jasen.

"I'm sorry," he said to Huanatha. "About your sword."

"You are forgiven," she said, and no more.

Maybe she meant it. For some, this was how disagreements went. In truth, it was how it had gone in Jasen's family. A mistake; an apology. There was no self-flagellation needed for the apology to mean anything, or to be accepted.

Here, as they climbed down the cliffside from this lost fight, however, Jasen wished he could flog himself. It would not bring the blade back from wherever it had fallen. But it might assuage his guilt.

So much of that now. So, so much.

"Where are we going now?" he asked. Still, he sounded worn, as though he had grown old before his time.

"Back to the *Lady Vizola*," said Kuura.

"No," said Jasen quickly.

"Jasen—" Alixa began.

He pushed her hands away as she grabbed for him and stepped back—away from all three of them.

Only Scourgey he allowed to follow—but she came only one step, then stopped there sadly. She held up her left forepaw like a dog begging a treat from its master ... or like a wounded creature, unable to put weight on it.

"I'm not going," he said. "I can't."

"You are injured," said Kuura. "We all are. We must go back to the ship. Medleigh will see to us—to your wounds. He will evaluate if you, or the rest of us, have any broken bones. He will set them, and heal them, better than I or Huanatha can do between ourselves."

"We gave it our best go," said Alixa. "But Baraghosa—he beat us. We lost."

Lost. Yes, they had, well and truly. Jasen knew this—and though he'd fight, as his instinct told him, fight against the rest of them even if they banded together to take him down this cliffside, a person latched to each limb and Scourgey carrying the last—what was the point of it? He had given it his all. They all had.

And Baraghosa had defeated them. He would again, and again, and again.

And there was nothing Jasen could do about it.

"I'm sorry," said Alixa, reaching for him.

This time, he let her.

Scourgey nearer too. Whining sadly once more, she pressed her nose against Jasen's wrist. He cast a look at her, thankful for the touch. It was a small comfort only, though, and he could not help thinking of one thing as he stood there, overcome with despair.

If only Longwell had been here.

If only he had not abandoned them.

Jasen hated Baraghosa, intensely. Never would he believe he could hate a man with half the fierceness that he despised Baraghosa.

Yet he could. For at this moment, he hated Longwell too. It was not the same hatred: not as harsh, or all-consuming. But he did hate him—hated him for leaving, hated him for giving him hope.

Would their battle have been different?

Perhaps.

But it did not matter because it was only a hypothetical question that even his ancestors could not answer.

Nor would he ask them. He'd failed to avenge the most recent among their number—the closest, his most beloved.

Jasen could never face his ancestors again.

The storm had mostly died down. The blasts that had racked the conduction fields had stilled the moment Baraghosa absorbed their energy into that glass, stoppered bottle. The bruised sky was turning a pale blue now the lightning had ceased. The rains were easing, though they still came down with some force. The wind had died off too, the howl giving way to a lower whistle as it swept over the Aiger Cliffs, huffing harder and softer like the very land itself were breathing. Only now and again did it gust with any real force, blowing the spattering rain diagonally. That was when the rain bit hardest. It needled Jasen's skin—even more painful for the bruises he was covered with—like wasp stings made of ice.

So down the cliffside they went. It was slow going. All Jasen's bones ached—the pain was blossoming now, stronger by the second—and every step of the way, he wondered: why keep going? What was the point? He had nowhere to go. He'd longed to see the whole world—but the whole world, to him, had been Terreas. It was gone now, and no city in any land would ever tempt his longing again. None of those places were home. The closest he had to that had been a ship's cabin, for a few days, where he built himself up to this.

He had failed.

Why carry on?

Some survival instinct inside him kept pushing though. He hated that too, hated it like he hated Baraghosa and Longwell. Why could it have not just died when Baraghosa flung him so like a rag doll against the conduction rods?

But he was weary—too weary. He could only hate it for so long before his energy gave out, and he was only walking, tugged like a puppet on strings … then his energy for even that gave out. He fell onto his face, a quiet, undramatic fall. The noise as he landed was like him: slight.

Alixa fussed. Scourgey did too, pressing her nose against him. She whined, a long, high-pitched bay, like a hound.

She smelled of death.

Then Kuura was there, sweeping past Alixa and the scourge. He eased Jasen up in strong arms with big hands—and again, he cradled him, as he had most of the way down the cliffsides. Like a babe, Jasen lay there in his arms, breathing because he had to, watching a gradually lightening sky.

Holes had been pocked in the clouds now. The sun came through one. As its rays hit the slowing fall of rain, now little more than drizzle, it cast a short-lived rainbow across his gaze.

The sky out to sea was the color of a peach.

Evening.

How was this the same day?

How had so much happened? So many hopes been brought to life—then crushed?

Hard to think.

Hard to think of anything at all. A fog had descended, like the mists that fell at the base of the mountains overlooking Terreas.

Everything was clouded.

So difficult to think. So hard not to just … close his eyes.

He thought of the waves, lapping at the beach. For so long, he'd pictured them, never comprehending just how much *water* there could be, how far it stretched—like the sky curved around on itself somewhere distant, beyond the horizon, condensed into a blanket of purest, bluest fluid.

He wished to drift away upon it—away from the beaches of

Terreas, away and past the horizon, and out of the world entirely.

And he did drift, for a time, upon it. Kuura's arms were the lapping waves on which he bobbed, softly, softly. He was carried beneath clear skies, out to a place a thousand miles from here, where he was alone ... where he might atone.

But when he opened his eyes again, the fog had cleared, and he realized that he did not ride the ocean waves to some eternal, peaceful abyss; instead, he saw skies filled with puffs of dark, dispersing cloud. Drizzle still came down, a fine, spitty spray that was hardly wet at all.

They were moving through the Aiger Cliffs toward the dock, and the *Lady Vizola* ... and failure.

22

Somehow, the docks were still alive with people, even as evening began to make its slow transition to night.

Vendors had moved their stalls back to the docks. Lamps had been lit. They floated like fireflies as Jasen bobbed up and down in Kuura's arms—or had the world gone runny again, unshackled from its moorings? The sun lay behind the ships. Still an hour or more from setting, it stained the sky progressively more orange. In the places between boats, it danced on seawaters growing more placid. And where it was blotted from sight, turning the boats into half-silhouettes cut out against a red-orange wash building softly into a looming twilight, it was as if the world had become a beautiful painting.

Kuura was large enough to cut a path alone. Huanatha, though shorter, was imposing enough that she did the same.

Between them, they made simple work of navigating the increasing dock traffic and reaching the *Lady Vizola*.

Jasen could pick out its sails, shorter than the boat alongside it.

Kuura stopped. Looking down at Jasen, he said, "Can yeh walk?"

"I think so," he croaked.

"Are yeh sure? Don't be forcin' yourself to do somethin' yeh're not up to."

"Let the boy try, Kuura of Nunahk," said Huanatha.

Reluctantly, Kuura leaned down, setting Jasen very carefully upon his feet. He released him only partway, keeping one hand around Jasen's hip as he took tentative steps.

Ancestors, it hurt so much. His muscles wanted to seize, locking back in the position they had been when he lay in Kuura's arms. But he pressed against them, forcing his legs to straighten and then bend, walking alone.

When Kuura warily released him, Jasen thought he would fall—

But Scourgey was there. She pressed in close to Jasen on the right—his weaker side, it seemed, for without Kuura's support he was sure to topple in that direction. Stinking of rot, she looked up at him sadly, lovingly, and nuzzled her nose against his bare arm. He was bruised there, too, and the slight pressure almost elicited a hiss of pain from Jasen. Somehow Scourgey sensed it, and she softened her touch.

"She is still with you," said Huanatha softly, "just as she promised."

Jasen nodded. He lifted a wan smile at Scourgey—then caught Alixa watching.

He turned away.

"Come," said Kuura. "Shipmaster Burund will have missed us."

There was something in his voice, something Jasen could not fathom.

He could not focus on it. They came back into motion, him leaning on Scourgey. Was it possible to walk on broken legs? He didn't think so, but the pain was so great that he knew he'd incurred serious damage.

But he pushed onward, Scourgey there to help him.

The *Lady Vizola* came into view around the boat ahead of her.

A steep gangplank, wide enough for two men to cross side by side, had been thrown down so Burund's people could take cargo off and on board. Steep was better than climbing the ladder, though; putting one foot in front of the other was difficult enough.

Men were upon the deck.

At sight of Kuura, they shouted.

Jasen picked out Burund's name.

Then, when he had reached the bottom of the gangplank, Burund appeared at the edge of the deck. He looked down, expression contorted in a mask of concern and—something else Jasen could not discern, moreso with the sunlight fading behind the shipmaster and his dark skin blurring his features.

His eyes, though, Jasen saw. They flicked to him first of all. Flashed. Then they flitted to Alixa, Huanatha—another momentary flash there, but a different sort—and then they landed upon Kuura.

"I apologize for my tarrying, Shipmaster," Kuura called. "Today I—"

Burund ignored him. He turned, barked something to men lingering nearby, watching. Jasen believed he was dismissing them, but then the pair rushed down the gangplank and ushered Jasen up, steadying him against their sides after a dirty look at Scourgey.

He clambered up—so much hurt—and then, stepping over the edge, fell again.

"Jasen!"

Alixa was behind him in an instant. Forcing her way through the legs of the two sailors, she clutched her cousin. Rolling him onto his side, fearful eyes raked over him.

"I'm okay," he wheezed.

"You are not." She touched his face—

Jasen winced, clenched his teeth.

She withdrew her hand as though he had snapped for it with his teeth.

"You're burning up," she said.

Was he? But it had been so wretchedly cold out, after the storm came in.

Kuura was upon the deck too, Huanatha with him.

"Jasen must be seen by Medleigh," he said, looming over the boy.

Jasen tried to push them off—with his hands, or words.

No energy though.

He was back on the sea. Back to drifting.

Or maybe sinking.

He thrust out with his arms in it, fighting to keep afloat.

"I'm ..." he began, in a strangled whisper.

"Medleigh is coming," said Burund. He was crouched now by Jasen's head, though Jasen did not remember seeing him move. "What happened to him?" Then, his voice suddenly strained: "What happened to all of you? You have been gone all day. Do not tell me the words that have made their way to my ears are true."

"What is it you have heard?" Alixa asked.

"That a man, a warrior woman, and two children with a strange beast searched for Baraghosa. That they were last seen climbing the clifftops, heading directly into the storm."

Kuura did not answer.

Burund turned hard eyes upon him. "Is this true, Kuura?"

Kuura screwed up his face. But he confessed: "Aye, Shipmaster. It is true."

One of the sailors aboard said something.

Burund said, "And you found him." His gaze fell over Jasen again, lying almost prone upon the deck. The wood was wet—soothing, almost, against his face. "Did you not?"

"Aye, Shipmaster," said Kuura softly. "We did find Baraghosa, yes."

Burund pursed his lips. He said nothing—but there was a roiling anger bubbling beneath him, and his face, so often hard to read, showed it: in the set of his jaw, the way his eyebrows pushed down, low on his forehead, and by the way a fire danced in his eyes. A deck door opened, and Medleigh appeared. He squatted down by Jasen and immediately began asking questions. Jasen could not understand, but it did not take a translator to know that he asked what had happened, where he was hurt, perhaps how he felt. Burund snapped answers to these, only occasionally looking for Kuura. He added more, talking at length over some things.

Huanatha spoke too, once or twice.

Jasen let it wash over him. He let Medleigh prod. Then he lay back, listening to Alixa's murmurings—that it was going to be okay, he would be all right, he would feel better soon. And then Medleigh was back with a wooden flask. He lifted Jasen's head, gripping his neck with the firm, calloused fingers of a man who worked hard when he was not treating his rare patients aboard the *Lady Vizola*. He pressed the flask to Jasen's lips and gave a two-syllable instruction Jasen took to mean *Drink*.

He obeyed.

It was unpleasant—foul, even, tasting of dead plant matter and spices that were overpowered by something similar to cinnamon, but much more bitter, and the texture was thick and milky. Had Jasen the strength, he would have gagged. But he had none so he swallowed it.

Then he lay down.

Hot. He felt it now. But though the thick, bitter fluid was unpleasant, he felt it going to work almost as soon as all of it had hit his stomach. Cool waves radiated throughout him, starting very softly—but strengthening.

He opened his eyes. His lids were less heavy than they had been, when those imagined waves in his mind threatened to carry him not off but under.

"What was that?" he asked.

"A salve," said Burund. "It is to ease your pains."

"Is he going to be okay?" Alixa asked anxiously.

Burund and Medleigh exchanged words.

"He will heal," said Burund. "But it will take time."

"Have I," Jasen began, but then his voice gave out. He cleared his throat. It was still thick with fluid, congealed to it. "Have I broken any bones?"

"Not that Medleigh believes," said Burund. "He will take a closer look when you can stand."

"I can," said Jasen, believing it—but Alixa set him straight:

"Jasen, you *cannot* stand. A second ago you could barely keep your eyes open! Just rest, *please*."

"Listen to your cousin," said Burund. "She has a wise head upon her shoulders."

Alixa held his hand. "I told you," she said softly.

She was not unkind.

And they were right, both of them. Jasen should have listened.

Now look what he had done to himself. What he had done to all of them.

All of Terreas, destroyed because of him … and now these comrades, who he had led into a battle half of them did not wish to participate in, had been broken in their own ways for his bullheadedness.

On top of it all, he came back again and again to the same thing: he had failed. Not *they*, but *he*. His quest to kill Baraghosa was his alone. Yet he'd led a band of people onto the cliffside when he should have stood on his own against the sorcerer.

He'd almost gotten all of them killed.

He closed his eyes.

"Don't cry," Alixa whispered. "It's okay."

It was not. Not anywhere close. Nor would it be, ever. Atonement would never come.

He could never face his ancestors again.

I'm sorry, he thought to them, at the same time wishing he could cast his face away so they could not see. *I am so, so sorry.*

All he had ever wanted was to do right by the long chain of them; to see Terreas avenged …

And he'd failed.

Burund had risen. He and Huanatha were speaking. She had drawn eyes when she boarded, the stares of men who knew this woman once had been royalty, even if now she found herself exiled. A crowd had come up from below, and they watched with awe.

Burund must have felt it too. He spoke to her as he would an equal—as he had conversed with Jasen and Alixa in their short time aboard the *Lady Vizola*. Yet he also stood back, his hands clasped behind his back. Where Kuura had fallen to one knee, totally deferential, Burund spoke to her as an equal.

"… his power cannot be left unchecked," Huanatha was saying. "I implore you to reconsider."

"I, too, have seen Baraghosa's power first-hand," said Burund. "Just days ago, he rent the sea with a storm like no other."

"So you know that he must be stopped."

"Many would agree with you."

"Not you?"

"I am not the man to stop him. Nor are these children."

"You have men at your command," Huanatha said. "They were besieged by this storm too, were they not? All would carry arms and wage a war against Baraghosa if you ordered it."

"Your days as queen have affected your understanding of men," said Burund. "A man under your command may go willingly to war if you order it. But I am simply the shipmaster of a cargo ship. We are traders, not warmongers."

"No?" Huanatha's nostrils flared. She marched away and encircled Kuura with an arm. "And what of Kuura of Nunahk?" she demanded, thrusting him forward. He winced, not wishing to go. "This man is one of yours. He took up an axe and climbed the Aiger Cliffs at my sides that he might slay Baraghosa! You are telling me the rest of your men are not cut from the same cloth?"

Burund regarded Kuura flatly, lips pursed.

When he spoke, his voice was dangerously low. "He is not cut of the same cloth as my men."

Jasen's heart skipped at that. He raised his head, pushing up—

Kuura had stood to one side, near enough that Shipmaster Burund could address or summon him, but far enough from them that he was separated by an invisible barrier. Now he'd been pushed to the fore, he looked pained. There was no hint that a too-wide grin had ever touched his face. He looked only sad and fearful, looking down at the wet deck of the *Lady Vizola* rather than his shipmaster.

"Tell him," Huanatha said in Kuura's ear. "Tell him how the fires filled you as you lifted the axe. Tell him of the honor you felt, walking into battle this night."

Kuura did not speak.

Huanatha glared at Burund. "You silence him with your face."

"I do no such thing."

"He is afraid to speak—"

"He is afraid," Burund roared suddenly, throwing his arms into the air and jabbing them out at Kuura, "because he has *failed!*"

Jasen stared, mouth open.

"He is afraid because he had one task only: to care for these children. They were his to watch over, his sacred honor dependent upon it. I sent him to the Aiger Cliffs today with that very purpose. And now he presents himself to me, strung up in a bandage like a man who should be pitied—and the children are hurt. Worse, he marched with them to do battle with a warlock, who could have snapped their necks with but a click of his finger. *That* is why *Kuura of Nunahk*—" he said this mockingly, voice rising high, "—is afraid. He knows he has failed his people. He has failed me. And he has failed himself." He leveled a dark stare at Kuura. "Now he must face the consequences of his failure."

Alixa shot Jasen a fearful glance. "Shipmaster, what—"

Burund said only one word to Kuura:

"Leave."

Kuura flinched, as though Burund had lifted a hand to strike him.

"No," said Alixa—

Jasen did too: "*No!*" He pushed himself onto unsteady feet. Wobbled.

"Jasen," Burund began, lifting a hand to still him—

Scourgey braced Jasen. He lurched forward with her.

"Please, no," he said—and he threw himself in between the shipmaster and his first mate. "Don't exile him."

"He had a simple task—"

"And I dissuaded him from it!" Jasen cried. "Me! I was the person so intent upon finding Baraghosa. All Kuura could do was follow."

"A man can choose not to follow."

"I made him," said Jasen. A note of panic rose in him now. Like bile, it bubbled up through his throat. All these people, broken—and now Kuura was to be cast from the ship? He could not ruin another life—not like this. "Please," he begged—and he clutched for Burund's tunic, holding it in limp hands. "Please, reconsider—"

"No," said Burund with flat finality.

"Please—"

"No," Alixa moaned.

"Kuura," said Burund. "You are relieved of your post."

"You would exile a man who acted honorably, with justice in his heart?" Huanatha hissed. "You are no captain."

Burund ignored her. Glaring at Kuura, he continued to him only: "Go below decks and collect your belongings. You are banished from my ship."

"Nooo …" Alixa was crying.

Jasen gripped harder. "Please—"

Burund stepped back. A slight shake, and he was loosed from Jasen's weak hold.

Kuura still had not looked up.

"Go," Burund said.

And Kuura went, with only a nod, eyes downcast—through the door, and to his cabin for the final time. Silence followed in his wake. The men on the deck watched in stunned silence. Even the docks below seemed to have quieted under the setting sun.

"You are a vile captain," said Huanatha, "with no goodness about you."

"I am a man of honor," said Burund.

Huanatha scoffed—

"And I will stand by my duties."

"Shipmaster—" Alixa began.

"Do not ask me again to reconsider," he said curtly. "I will not do so."

Jasen sagged. Another life wrecked—not ended, like those in Terreas, but torn to tatters and thrown into wind.

He had done this.

"We are not done speaking of this," said Huanatha acidly.

"That is unfortunate," said Burund. "I was planning to offer you passage to Coricuanthi with us."

Huanatha's lips thinned.

"Is that where we're going now?" Alixa asked.

"We will," said Burund. "From there, I will see you both have safe passage to your Emerald Fields."

"Not with you?"

"No. There is another shipmaster I trust. He makes regular journeys there." He lifted an eyebrow. "You do still wish to travel there, do you not?"

Alixa nodded fiercely. "Yes." She clasped her hands together as though she were praying. "Please."

"Has Longwell returned?" Jasen asked, hoping even though he wished not to see him, in case the mere sight of him, his betrayal, broke him in different ways than Baraghosa could have tonight.

"No," said Burund, and Jasen drooped with disappointment.

So that was that. The Aiger Cliffs had come, as promised. So too had Baraghosa, and Jasen's clash with him. The battle over almost as soon as it started, Jasen had come not even an inch closer to the vengeance he sought. He had lost, well and truly—lost a sword that was not his, too—and his friends had taken a beating for it. Worse, Kuura was to be cast out from the life he had known, left on strange shores far from home.

It was all Jasen's fault.

Again, he wondered: if Longwell had not abandoned him, would things be any different?

It did not matter either way. In a short time, they would be on their way to the Emerald Fields ... and Baraghosa would be behind him—

Like the people he had doomed to a fiery death in the shadow of the mountain.

23

Jasen watched on the *Lady Vizola's* deck, from afar, as Huanatha spoke with Shipmaster Burund. She was animated, all wild gesticulations.

Burund waited respectfully, yet his bearing was stiff. He had not said anything in some time.

Alixa sat at Jasen's side. She petted Scourgey, who lay slumped morosely over Alixa's lap.

"The Emerald Fields," she kept whispering. "We're really going there."

Jasen rubbed a knuckle against the deck, hard. It hurt, so much more than it should've for all the pain Baraghosa had left him in. But it was only a fraction of what he deserved, though, for failing his ancestors, for failing his friends—and now, on top of it all, for failing Kuura—Kuura, who this very moment was below deck, gathering up all the possessions he had upon this boat he rode to pay the way for a family he loved but so rarely saw, and preparing to be exiled.

"Other Luukessians," Alixa murmured. "Oh, how I long to see their faces ... I wonder if any of them will look familiar? Kin of our kin—"

He could not take her cheer any longer. "Kuura is banished," said Jasen flatly.

That stirred her.

"Perhaps Shipmaster Burund—"

"He will not reconsider."

"Huanatha appears to be making her case. Maybe he will—"

"He won't," said Jasen.

Alixa quieted.

The bustle of the docks drifted over them. Full darkness was not long from falling. Yet somehow, still there were people milling about, going to and from their ships and into the city—or perhaps up the cliffside pathway, beyond the towering rocks and arches and into towns and cities on the other side—a whole world, waiting just past the cliffs, at the end of the road.

Hard to think that there was a time when Jasen would have done anything for the opportunity to see it, where now he did not wish to see anyplace that was not home.

Harder to think that it had only been a few weeks ago.

How things had changed.

"I am sorry for Kuura," said Alixa after a time. "I am, truly. But … he is only banished from the *Lady Vizola*. There's nothing to say he cannot pay for passage back to his village."

"And how do you know how banishment works for his people?" Jasen countered. "Huanatha was exiled from her tribe, and left the entire land behind."

"Why did Shipmaster Burund offer her passage back to Coricuanthi then?"

Now it was Jasen who had no answer.

They were quiet again, for longer this time.

Jasen imagined Kuura now, in his cabin. Jasen had not seen it, but he could paint a picture of it well enough. The same size as the one he and Alixa had shared, Kuura's would be decked out with the trinkets of a life lived on the sea: talismans from far-off place, perhaps, where he had consulted with a shaman. A tapestry might hang on the wall, or a map, like in Burund's office. Or perhaps Kuura's possessions would be homely. Yes, that seemed more accurate. He might have a family tree, sketched out on canvas, linking him and his own ancestors through the generations back in Nunahk. Maybe a thin piece of log cut from a stump, inscribed with a message done in black ink, or burned in. There would be books from his village, stories once handed down by campfires, then committed to text by hand, arduous in process but enduring. Writings, too, from his family: letters from his wife, his children, about how they loved him and missed him and thanked him for all he did, traveling so far away, treasuring the moments they had together.

He saw Kuura collecting up these things, looking them over before he stowed them in a knapsack to sling over his shoulder, one that would hold everything he had in life, or at least everything he had that was not an ocean away. He saw Kuura bite his lip, fighting to keep a tear from trickling down his face, thinking—about how it had been him who failed.

It was an awful kinship that Jasen and Kuura shared.

He wished he could walk down the stairs into the ship now, to apologize … but what good would it do? There was nothing Jasen could do to change things. His words were just that: words. They would not undo the damage Jasen had caused.

He closed his eyes and rested his head on his knees.

"I destroy everything," he whispered.

"You don't," said Alixa.

Jasen didn't respond. He didn't believe her. Just words, again.

"This whole thing," Alixa said, and her words came slow, as if she was picking them with great care, "came about because you wanted to fix something. That was the case with the grain from Wayforth. And it's why we came here, and found Huanatha, and went up to the clifftops."

"Both were failures," Jasen muttered. "What's your point?"

"The grain …" Alixa shook her head, left the thought unfinished. "What if the ancestors are guiding you, not to fix things, but to—to bring us here?"

Jasen looked around with a skeptical eye. "To a boat docked by the Aiger Cliffs?"

"To bring us to the Emerald Fields—"

Jasen groaned, so Alixa spoke louder:

"—so that we might be with our countrymen."

"The ancestors are not whispering to me to find grain and look for Baraghosa so I can go live in some long grass with people I have never known. Those were *my* ideas."

"But what if the ancestors are guiding them? Guiding both of us?"

"They are not."

"But they might be," Alixa insisted. "They look out for us, all of them. Perhaps they knew Baraghosa would tear apart the mountain. And so they sent us to go for grain, that we might be saved."

"And left the rest of Terreas to die?"

But Alixa had found a kernel of something that she could not drop. "Maybe that is why they sent me too—because they knew that I would hear of Emerald Fields and try to steer us that way."

"You agreed to come with me," said Jasen, "not for any reason other than our kinship."

"That's what I *thought*," said Alixa. "Well, that and helping to save Terreas and heal its rifts. But what if the ancestors were speaking to me without my hearing? What if they sent me out with you, knowing that we would be saved from the mountain burying Terreas in ash, and would find ourselves on the *Lady Vizola*—and then, in turn, rescue Samwen Longwell, who would tell us of the Emerald Fields …"

"It's a pretty convoluted plan, is it not?"

"... and then I could convince you that we should go there!"

"You have not convinced me," said Jasen.

"But the Emerald Fields," she began, voice rising with exasperation. Then she paused, returning to her previous thread. "I have not convinced you of it, but now that we have lost our home, the Emerald Fields are the only place for us. You have battled Baraghosa—valiantly," she added quickly, before he could protest that too, "—but we have lost. Without me, you might try to fight again." *To lose again* was left unsaid. "But I am here—and so I am guiding you to the Emerald Fields, like our ancestors want!"

She looked victorious at having explained all this. Her eyes glittered with determination, the setting sun and its very last streak of orange reflected in her dark brown eyes.

Jasen shook his head. "You may feel that way, but...I don't believe it."

She hardly sagged. "You must, though." She gripped him by the wrist. "Think of it, Jasen: our countrymen are out there right now, waiting for us. We are not the last of the Luukessians! For all our lives, we believed we had been almost entirely extinguished, save for Terreas. Yet we have learned that our brethren live on. We *have* to join them, Jasen. We *must*. It is what the ancestors want!"

"You realize," said Jasen, "that you can turn all this on its head?"

Alixa frowned. "What do you mean?"

"You believe the ancestors led us out of Terreas, to get to the Emerald Fields ... but what if they led us out so that I would live on to fight Baraghosa?"

"Jasen—"

"No, just listen. It's just as likely that our ancestors guided us here so that I might defeat Baraghosa."

"And what purpose am *I* here?"

Jasen shrugged. "I don't know. This was your idea."

"But why would they want—?"

"Revenge."

Alixa paused. "Revenge." She repeated it, both a question and not one.

"Baraghosa killed them," said Jasen, "or at least some of them. Why would they *not* want revenge?"

"But ... in the Emerald Fields ... we would be safe ..."

"Do you think the dead do not hold grudges?" Jasen asked.

Alixa fell into silence. Her expression was troubled. Uncurling her fingers from Jasen's wrists, she slumped back against the wooden wall of the rear deck, her lips coming together in a tight pout. Scourgey moved to place her head upon Alixa's lap, pausing to look up at her expectantly for five or six seconds. She garnered no response though, and lay down again.

The docks were noisy still. Growing louder, by the sound of it. Strange, that the city was so active for so long … but then, he supposed, the Aiger Cliffs were a port, and boats did not only arrive during the daylight. They could come at all hours—and the city would accommodate them, the most dedicated vendors still manning food stalls. Jasen smelled one now, though only at a distance. Game of some sort was turned on a spit above a coalfire.

If he had not had all his interest in the world beaten out of him, the scent of it might have enticed him.

He closed his eyes, listening to the conversation. A lot of voices out there—they drowned out the discussion between Huanatha and Burund. Jasen would have liked to hear their conversation, but in any event, they'd switched into their native language some time ago. Last Jasen had heard, Burund remained immovable. Huanatha might talk at him for a thousand years, and his view on the matter would still not change.

The door from the deck swung open.

Jasen opened his eyes.

Kuura stepped out. A knapsack made of brownish-green canvas hung off one shoulder. He had removed the improvised bandage about his head now, revealing a great gash almost six inches long, running from the middle of his forehead and down to the outer corner of his left eye. The one on his arm remained.

He glanced backward, catching Jasen's eye.

Jasen tensed, expecting an outburst—it was he who was responsible, after all—instead, Kuura smiled. It was not one of his wide grins, with all his teeth on display for the whole world to see. This was tinged with sadness and a hurt that filled his eyes.

Jasen opened his mouth—

At the same moment, Huanatha cried out, "Kuura of Nunahk!" She strode toward him immediately, peeling off from Shipmaster Burund. Looking harried, he followed quickly, opening his mouth too, to say—what, Jasen did not know. A protest, probably.

Whatever it was ended up lost to a hubbub on the dock beside the *Lady Vizola*.

It drew all their attention.

"Samwen?" said Burund.

Jasen thrust himself up at the name, all his pain forgotten. He went to the edge of the *Lady Vizola*—at a lurch, for his body still remembered his injuries even if his mind did not—and saw there, a crowd parting around him: a warrior in dark blue armor, a great lance raised overhead.

Jasen's eyes blazed.

Longwell had returned.

24

Once Longwell had clambered aboard, he made clear he wished to speak—with all of them. He'd not say a word more of what the matter might be concerning, so Shipmaster Burund ushered them all into his office—Jasen, Alixa, Huanatha, Longwell, himself ... and, begrudgingly, when Longwell demanded it, Kuura.

The space was very cramped. Kuura was sizable in a stocky kind of way; Burund was imposing not just in height but in the way he carried himself. Huanatha must surely be the tallest woman Jasen had ever laid eyes on. And Longwell, in his suit of armor, and carrying around that enormous lance, which he refused to be parted from and instead had to awkwardly maneuver through the door and into the cabin— between them all, the room looked very small indeed.

That Scourgey had crept in after Longwell, and now watched him intently crouched at Alixa's ankles, did not help matters.

Burund had not taken up his seat behind his desk. This, he offered to Huanatha. She scowled back at him, leery-eyed, but did not respond. The chair was unfilled.

"I have accommodated your request," said Burund to Longwell. "What is it that you wish to discuss?"

"First," said Longwell, "I must apologize."

Burund hesitated. "I do not believe there is anything for which you owe me an apology, Samwen."

"The apology I must make is to these youths," said Longwell. He turned to Jasen and Alixa—Jasen in particular. Stooping in that suit of armor, so bulky and seemingly inflexible, unlike Huanatha's, he bowed low to Jasen, dropping to a knee.

"I am most sorry," he said. His head, too, he sunk, so that although his eyes were closed, he was looking through the floor.

Jasen could only imagine how odd it must look: this hulking man, holding a weapon that could run through an entire army, bent in complete supplication to a bloodied, bruised teenager.

Longwell continued, "We discussed Baraghosa—our mutual desire for revenge in battle. I saw hope burn in your eyes, and I knew that you wished to take arms up with me, to slay him. I knew that. Yet the moment we touched down at the dock, I left you."

Jasen peered at him sadly. Hours ago, clutching Scourgey and making their way down the cliffside in the wake of defeat at Baraghosa's hands, he had been certain that he hated this man. Yet now, faced with him … Jasen felt no hate at all. Perhaps he had lost the energy to feel anything but failure and shame.

Still, it was true: Longwell had left them.

So Jasen asked, "Why?"

"I heard tell that Baraghosa had made his way to a city a quarter-day's journey from here." Bitterly, he added, "The rumor was incorrect."

"He was here," said Jasen.

Longwell's head snapped up. He stared at Jasen, wide-eyed. "Here? In the city?"

"On the cliffs," said Jasen, "this evening. We fought him."

Longwell's eyes grew wider still. "You?" At Jasen's nod, he glanced to Alixa. "And you with him?"

Alixa cast her glance down. "I tried."

"Yes," said Longwell, quietly. "I see now." He turned upon his heel. Gaze raking over Kuura and Huanatha, he took in their wounds. The glance he gave Burund was brief: though Huanatha's injuries were minor, she still bore signs of the clash with Baraghosa. Burund was in as good condition as he had been this morning—Longwell clearly concluded he had not ventured to the clifftops with them.

Scourgey made a whimpering sort of noise, edged forward.

Longwell looked down at her.

Scourgey lifted a paw.

She was cut too.

Longwell stared at it. "Even your scourge—?"

Alixa nodded. "We all tried."

"And did you defeat him?" Longwell demanded.

"No," said Alixa. "We lost."

Jasen nodded. His head hung too, now. "Badly," he whispered.

Longwell turned inward. "I would not have thought … that the two of you would have the courage … the others, yes, but …"

Children? Jasen almost put in.

"They should not have gone to face him," said Burund.

Huanatha bared her teeth the way a wolf did. "You have no sense, *Captain*."

"The children—"

"Did a great thing," Huanatha cut across.

Burund's lips thinned. "They are only children."

"And yet the strength in their hearts that carried them to that peak—"

"They are not children," said Longwell suddenly. And he rose, turning a steely gaze upon Shipmaster Burund and Huanatha. "These two—these brave two—they are Luukessians. They have a will forged from the finest steels—yes, they do, *of course they do*," he said, glancing to them yet speaking to himself. "And it is that will that drives them, to do the brave things they have done.

"Like me."

Alixa stared. "What do you mean …?"

Longwell nodded. "I am the same as you. I, too, am of Luukessia."

Alixa practically exploded. She whirled, gripping Jasen tight by the shoulders. Dragging him in—he bit off a yelp as she pulled him, and he almost toppled, but her grip was firm and she held him aloft even as his legs threatened to fail—she cried, "*We are not the last Luukessians! Not even on this BOAT!*"

Something else had rattled Jasen, something other than Alixa's shaking, which made his bones feel as though they were on the verge of falling apart. Disentangling himself from her grip, he twisted back to Longwell and said, "Did you say we're—the same as you?"

"You just heard that!" Alixa cried. Genuine glee lifted her voice, for the first time in long days—as if, after a long, long night, she was finally seeing the sun again.

Longwell nodded. "Yes, I did say that," he said. "I come from the Kingdom of Galbadien, the fallen land south of your Syloreas. I have seen the mountains of your country with my own eyes, fought alternatively against and at the side of your last, great king, Briyce Unger. We bled together, he and I—and I have been shoulder to shoulder with many of your kith and kin.

"You are Luukessian, like I." Longwell's eyes burned with intensity. "I see in you the courage I have come to expect of every Sylorean, every Luukessian. So too are you brave and courageous."

"Like you," said Jasen.

A slight smile lifted Longwell's features, one side of his mouth only. "Well … it is an arrogant thing to say, but …"

"These two…their bravery knows no bounds," said Huanatha. Despite saying it to Longwell, she shot a pointed look at Burund.

"They ought to be applauded—they, and any who chose to fight with them."

"I applaud your bravery too," said Longwell.

Huanatha swore, made a cutting motion with her hand. "I am not looking for praise. I speak of him." She gestured at Kuura, who for this whole time had stood in silence, his head hung in disgrace.

"Yes …" said Longwell, taking him in. "In fighting with you all, Kuura has shown himself to be cut from the finest cloth—the same cloth as our Luukessians—and," he added, at the first sign of Huanatha's lips parting, "the same as your Muratam—Queen Huanatha."

She scowled. "Do not call me that. I am queen no longer—and it is Baraghosa's doing."

"Hmm. So he despoiled your lands too." For half a second, Longwell considered. Then, he said with finality, as though the matter was settled and he was simply summing it up: "Baraghosa must be stopped—and he must certainly be stopped now, or as soon as we can manage it."

"*Yes,*" said Huanatha.

"The question now is this," said Longwell—and he turned back to Jasen and Alixa. "Will you fight again—with me?"

Jasen stared. For long moments, he could not speak. He, who had come so close to the edge of utterly breaking in his battle with Baraghosa? He, who could not hold onto a sword, and had barely the strength, let alone training, to wield it in any fashion?

How could he possibly fight alongside a man—a *warrior*—like Longwell?

Longwell sensed his trepidation. He stooped again. Resting a hand upon Jasen's shoulder, he looked him in the eye and said very earnestly, "You have shown great courage, of a sort that puts you among the greatest of Luukessians. You may have lost this day—yet you have earned a place alongside me, to battle again—and this time to see victory."

Jasen's breath caught in his chest. Could it really be true?

"So," said Longwell. "What say the two of you?"

Jasen hesitated. His answer should be his alone. Yet he had come all this way with Alixa, dragged her into something she didn't want to do but which she had done anyway. She had taken her own beating at Baraghosa's hands tonight. Jasen owed it to her to ask, this one last time, if she would be willing to take the battle to Baraghosa once more.

He glanced at her, fully expecting a "no."

"We will fight," she said.

Jasen stared. "We will?"

Alixa nodded. Resolutely, she said, "Baraghosa must be stopped, by any means necessary."

"Alixa," Jasen said. "Are you sure? I thought you said—"

"I know what I said," she snapped. "A person may change his or her mind." To Longwell: "We are with you." Then, to Jasen, quickly: "At least—you are with us, are you not?"

Another hesitation. Could he engage with Baraghosa again, after having failed so miserably here? Could he face the man who had destroyed his village, murdered the last remnants of his family, except for this girl beside him, knowing all the while that even if he harbored all the hate in the world in his heart, it would not do a lick of good in stopping the sorcerer?

Could he fight on?

Scourgey put her head under his hand. She lifted it up—forward.

"She stands alongside you still," said Huanatha, "as she said she would."

Jasen stared into her black eyes. After a long moment, he croaked, "Why?"

"For the same reason as we do," said Huanatha. "For your courage—your bravery—your desire to deliver justice even when doing so seems impossibly hard, or dangerous."

"You are with me too?" asked Longwell.

"Yes," Huanatha confirmed. She might have unsheathed Tanukke to brandish the blade high, but with all their bodies pressed so close in this tight space, she would have risked cutting Burund in two. "I will fight Baraghosa by your side, Samwen of Luukessia."

"I appreciate your company in this battle, Huanatha." To Jasen, Longwell said, "Well?"

He thought, his mind racing over the options. There were two: he could face Baraghosa a second time, or turn his back on this fight, as Alixa had been trying to convince him all this time, and venture out, alone, cast out as Shilara had been.

Where would he go?

Not to the Emerald Fields. He could not face his ancestors after backing down from such a fight; he surely could not slip in among other Luukessians, keeping the secret of his failure from them. No, Jasen would need to travel elsewhere, find another land where he could make his home, make his bed, and then lie in it, alone at night with his shame.

Two possibilities.

But looking them over now he was presented both, he realized there was only one option, at least for him.

"I will fight with you," he said. "Whatever comes of it."

Longwell grinned. He squeezed Jasen's shoulder. It shot him through with pain—but he grinned back, hope flaring in his chest once more, overriding the aches that had settled deep into his bones.

"And you," said Longwell, rising now and addressing Kuura. "Baraghosa has marked you most greatly of all, at least on the outside. Will you overcome that pain to battle alongside us?"

Kuura kept his eyes downturned. He bit his lip—glanced to Jasen, and then Shipmaster Burund.

"Why do you look away from me?" asked Longwell.

"His captain has banished him," Huanatha growled.

"Banished?" Longwell's face evinced confusion. "Whyever for?"

"Kuura of Nunahk—" Huanatha began.

"—led children into danger," Burund cut in, finally making his mind known.

"Baraghosa is a menace," said Huanatha hotly.

"Jasen and Alixa were Kuura's quarry," Burund countered. "He was tasked with protecting them, as his honor required. He failed in that task."

"Failed?" said Longwell, his frown deepening. "These children are alive. They are bloodied and bruised—as is the way of a battle. Yet they live on. So too does their spirit—you see it before you now, Shipmaster. They wish to fight another day. Do you truly believe Kuura did not do his best to protect them?"

"Kuura of Nunahk threw himself into battle like few men I have seen," said Huanatha. "He is a protector, and a warrior of his own right. That he should be banished for this …" She cursed, throwing up a hand in a gesture Jasen did not understand, other than it must surely be offensive in Coricuanthi culture.

"Kuura had one task," said Burund.

"And he still may act upon it," said Longwell. "Reconsider this matter, Shipmaster. He is a good man. And we need all hands we can get in our battle with Baraghosa."

Burund pursed his lips. He fell into a silence that stretched out interminably.

"You saw the storm," said Alixa softly. "You know what Baraghosa is capable of."

"We saw the volcano too," said Kuura. His eyes were lifted now. He looked at Burund, met his eye imploringly. "We have heard many tales of him, of the power he wields. And now he has more of it."

"More?" asked Longwell, head snapping around.

Kuura nodded. "The council granted him permission to drain the conduction rods after the storm tonight. He has made off with a flask of it."

"For what purpose?"

"Misdeeds," said Huanatha. "The sins of a wretch born of shadows."

"The storm tonight was a terrifying sight," Burund murmured. He looked out of the window, a troubled expression crossing his face, eyes far away. Jasen followed his gaze—but he was looking back in time too, surely, as full dark had fallen outside now, the rock spires invisible against the night sky.

"Think of what he might do with that power," Huanatha pushed.

Burund considered. Again, the seconds dragged. The waiting was awful: now that Jasen had set his mind upon catching up with the sorcerer again, every moment they were not moving was a moment wasted. The greater time and distance separating them, the nearer Baraghosa came to unleashing the power he had stolen tonight for whatever dark purpose he had collected it.

Longwell broke the silence. "I need a decision," he said curtly. "If Kuura is to be banished, then so be it. We will leave your ship, and make our own way. If you are willing to reconsider …"

"You are asking if I will take you upon this vessel," Burund finished.

"To the isle where Baraghosa makes his home," Longwell confirmed with a nod. "Yes."

Burund looked agonized. He pressed a hand to his forehead. Index and middle fingers on one temple, thumb on the other, he rubbed in hard circles. Finally, he said: "I will do this thing."

Jasen's heart leapt.

"I am not happy about it," said Burund—and he strode around them, to a map upon the wall. Removing it from the nails that held it in place, via hanging loops on each corner, he brought it over to his desk. Laying it out before them, he bowed over it, fingers tracing enormous lands, finding—Chaarland. "But I will take you there."

All heads bowed forward, Alixa's closest of all.

"I don't see it," she said, squinting.

"I hear tell the isle is not marked on maps," said Longwell. To Burund: "But you know where it is?"

"Of course I know where it is," Burund agreed. He pointed to an apparently empty patch of sea, midway between Chaarland and Coricuanthi. "How else would I know, as all sailors do, to sail around its cursed waters?"

25

The journey began the next morning, in the early hours, delayed only to visit Huanatha's apartment and gather new weapons: another sword for Jasen, with a black and white marbled blade that appeared to be cut and polished stone rather than any metal. It was heavy, and three inches shorter than his last, halfway between both sword and dagger. Alixa's daggers were also swapped out for a shorter set. Closer to her hands, Huanatha said she would achieve greater dexterity than with the first pair.

Alixa muttered, "I did not achieve *anything* with them." Huanatha reassured her, in her usual fiery way.

Huanatha considered her collection of spears and lances, wondering if she should bring anything back for Longwell that would fare better than his weapon—"an impressive spear, to be sure, but not hewn of Muratam steel." In the end she did not select anything: time was wasting, and Longwell had heard her offer of new weaponry but chosen to remain aboard the *Lady Vizola*. "It would only go unappreciated," she said, resigned—though for the next few days, she watched Longwell with a sullen expression and tight lips, as if his decision not to select one of her weapons was a personal insult.

And so, in the early hours of the morning, a long time before dawn came, the *Lady Vizola* departed the Aiger Cliffs. The winds were light, seeming to have mostly died off in the night. Progress felt terribly slow to Jasen, watching first from the deck and then through the window of his cabin as the city receded, the glimmers of firelight shrinking into a great distance.

Eventually—long after Alixa had drifted into slumber—Jasen slept too.

The days accumulated.

Every one, Jasen asked Burund of their progress.

"We will not arrive yet for many days," Burund answered—every time.

"How long?" asked Jasen.

Burund said, that second morning on the seas, "It will take us more than a week, but less than two, to reach the isle of Baraghosa."

Between eight and thirteen days. Jasen asked for more specificity. Burund either could not, or would not, give it. "A watched pot does not boil," he said with a crooked smile at Jasen's impatience one morning, and on another said, "The sea is not a tame thing. Our journey depends upon her temperament." Fortunately, she had a pleasant enough temperament. There were no storms. The winds were high, as they had been in the Aiger Cliffs, and they filled the *Lady Vizola's* sails with salty breath.

They should be making good time.

Yet Jasen could not help fearing, day after day, that somehow Baraghosa would be swifter than they. The sorcerer had had a lead of only six or eight hours, and his boat had been small, Stanislaus had said. Lighter in weight—yet it also meant perhaps only one sail, and a small one at that, for the wind to carry it.

He asked Burund about it: whether Baraghosa could be caught, or if he would only slip farther and farther away. Burund answered diplomatically, "I have not seen his boat, so it is not possible for me to draw conclusions." Jasen wished to press him for answers—but what use was it? He would only spin himself in circles, and no answer Burund could give would be satisfactory.

To help keep himself from ruminating, he busied himself.

Huanatha spent most of every day upon the *Lady Vizola's* top deck. An imposing woman, famed among the Coricuanthians, she forced a wide berth around herself simply by her presence. This, she made use of. From before the sun crested the horizon to past sundown, she drilled over and over with Tanukke. She leapt and lunged and struck and parried invisible targets, repetitive motions she spent hours each day ensuring were perfect in ways Jasen would never discern. Her armor flashed in the sun, iridescent blue plates glinting, a sudden bright flare of light the first indication that she had moved before the brain processed her swiftness.

First, Jasen watched.

On the third day, Huanatha said, "You will learn more by doing than you ever will by watching."

Jasen hesitated. "Uhm."

Huanatha practiced another strike, a forward thrust, as though spearing a man through the shoulder and immediately retracting the blade. She held Tanukke poised in the air afterward, horizontal, as if it had just exited through the wound she had made. Narrowed eyes glared down the length of the blade. She scowled. To Jasen, it appeared perfect; to Huanatha, some error had been made, inexcusable.

"Gather your sword," Huanatha told Jasen after a long quiet. "Bring it here."

He scrabbled up, rushing for the door into the ship.

"And your cousin, too," Huanatha called.

Alixa was in the hold with Scourgey. Few animals remained. How many had drowned in Baraghosa's storm versus how many had been sold in Aiger Cliffs, neither she nor Jasen knew. Jasen did not expect she *wished* to know. Hopefully it was not as many as were missing now though. The hold was practically bare. One of the birds remained in its cage, above a spot mostly cleared of scat since the hold had been half-flooded. It clambered about the metal bars restlessly, chittering to itself madly. The sow remained, but her piglets were gone. One cow remained too. But apart from these and Scourgey, the *Lady Vizola* was empty of non-human life.

Alixa was softly speaking to the restless bird. She held out a broken piece of hardtack, almost to the edge of the cage. The bird would need to poke its beak out to grab it. Rattling about its living space, it showed little interest.

Scourgey saw Jasen before Alixa did. She lumbered up on a paw that she still limped on very slightly, and approached him.

Alixa looked round. "Oh, it's you."

"Huanatha wants for us to practice with our weapons."

"Oh. Right. Yes, I suppose that makes sense. Now?"

"I think so," said Jasen. "She told me to fetch you."

"Okay." To the bird: "I'll be back later. You sure you don't want this?"

She reached up with the hardtack, pressing it through the bars.

The bird leapt across and bit her finger hard. Alixa hissed, withdrawing her hand but dropping the hardtack.

The bird disregarded it immediately, and went back to stalking along the bars, chittering and clanking its beak.

"Are you okay?" Jasen asked.

"Stupid bird." Alixa slunk past.

Him with his sword, and Alixa with her daggers, they joined Huanatha upon the deck, in the wide space below the mainsail. There they began their lessons. Moving between them with ease, Huanatha showed them how to hold their weapons, how to grip strongly but not too tightly so they could move fluidly.

They did not get this, at first.

"But you will not," Huanatha said when Jasen pointed it out, perhaps an hour into their first lesson together. "It takes a warrior a lifetime to master it. Why do you think I still practice my strikes?" Once she deemed them competent at holding their weapons, Huanatha instructed them in how to swing and how to strike.

For two days, they drilled on these. Huanatha continued her drilling too, demonstrating for Jasen and Alixa with Tanukke, giving them time off so they could process it all, so their muscles could rest, and so she too could continue to lunge at invisible foes in preparation for their meeting with Baraghosa.

On the third day, Huanatha conjured invisible enemies for them. She spoke of their movements, and Jasen and Alixa were to strike out at them using the techniques she had taught them.

She was not soft on them. Over and over, she informed Jasen and Alixa that they had been killed, run through with an assailant's sword, gored by the swing of a mace, their heads cleaved from their shoulders.

Were this training occurring in Terreas, it would have been terribly disheartening.

Aboard the *Lady Vizola*, their second clash with Baraghosa nearing by the second, Jasen refused to let defeat drag him down. He returned to his starting position, braced himself, let her words wash over him again—and he tried once more.

Kuura had stayed mostly out of the way, during the first week of their journey. Jasen saw him at mealtimes. Otherwise, though, he remained in his cabin.

Jasen had asked Huanatha if he should seek out Kuura, that he might practice with them.

"He will not join us," she said flatly.

"Why?" Jasen asked.

Huanatha's nostrils flared. "He is held in disgrace by a man who he respects. So now he buries his head in the ground, like a lummocbird."

Jasen bit his lip. "Maybe if I …"

"Leave him," said Huanatha—although she did not sound happy to be doing so. "He will come around on his own, when his *shame* has eased."

For the next hour, she muttered to herself, glowering all the while. Her thrusts were over-strong, and for the first time Jasen saw what he perceived to be a clumsy Huanatha, some of her precision sapped.

Her scowl grew steadily darker, until eventually she gave up with a great huff and stalked back into the ship, leaving Jasen and Alixa to train alone.

Kuura was not the only person Jasen saw little of. Longwell's appearances were infrequent. Whenever he did show his face, Jasen saw him speaking with Burund intensely. They would retire to Burund's office.

"What are they talking about?" Jasen asked.

"They discuss approach plans," said Huanatha, distracted by her thrusts and parries.

"Approach?" asked Alixa. "To the isle of Baraghosa, you mean?"

Huanatha struck—and nodded.

"What's to go over?" Alixa asked. "Surely you just sail right up to it."

"The waters are cursed," said Jasen. "That's what Burund said."

Alixa's face fell. "Oh."

On the eighth day Jasen began to see more of Kuura, Longwell and Burund again. They had seemingly come to some conclusion about the approach to the isle of Baraghosa, and so Longwell too joined them upon the deck, practicing with his lance. His fighting style was different from Huanatha's. The exiled queen could contort in unbelievable directions, her whole body twisting like a serpent's. Longwell was bulky, immoveable like a rock, yet when he clasped his lance and swung it, Jasen believed that he and Huanatha could battle for days and neither gain an upper hand. His every stab was precise and powerful—and blindingly fast. If Huanatha could run a man through, Longwell, it seemed, could blast him swiftly from half the world away with a single blow.

On the ninth day, Kuura appeared at the door into the ship. He had with him the axe he had taken from Huanatha's apartment before setting off.

Huanatha lowered Tanukke when she saw him. "Kuura of Nunahk. You have come."

He hefted the axe. "I wondered if I might learn with you."

Huanatha smiled at that. "I would be most honored if you would."

Kuura grinned, that too-wide show of all the teeth he possessed, and fell in with them, following Huanatha's instructions, practicing swings that she guided him through with much more swiftness than Jasen and Alixa. He had carried a weapon before, and he breezed through the lessons on poise. When not practicing, he talked and joked with them just like normal.

On the tenth day, the mist rolled in.

"We are getting nearer," said Burund to Jasen that morning. Jasen had found him atop the deck, just after dawn's first light—though, in the murky fog, the sun was barely a pinprick as it lifted above the horizon.

A wave rocked the *Lady Vizola*. It was only a gentle one, eliciting only a quiet creaking. Certainly the boat was not threatened by waves like this one.

Still, between the fog and its strange chill, when the mornings were usually so warm, it was unnerving. Even more so knowing that Baraghosa was not very distant—and that Jasen would have to face him again.

"Why are you taking us to his isle?" Jasen asked.

Burund regarded Jasen for a long moment, silent. Then, clasping his hands behind his back and turning out to the sea once more, he said, "I have watched you practicing with your sword upon the deck."

Jasen blinked. "You have?" He racked his brains, trying to think of a time when he had been aware of Burund's eyes upon him.

"Nothing on the *Lady Vizola* escapes my attention," Burund answered, and Jasen realized, stupidly, that of course he had been watching from his office, during his conversations with Longwell; there was a window in the wall. "On other occasions too, though, I have kept an eye on you and Alixa." He looked sideways at Jasen. "You are determined."

Jasen nodded. "Yes." At Burund's words, he felt it almost steeling inside him: that sense of duty, solidifying in his chest.

Burund assessed him. Maybe he saw it on Jasen's face. "I have children of my own, back at home," he said. "Two; the age of you and Alixa. You remind me of them."

"Oh …?"

"Not physically," said Burund. "Their skin is not pale as milk, like yours." He crooked up one corner of his lips, and Jasen belatedly realized he was making a joke, but by that time the shipmaster had gone on.

"Perhaps because of that, or perhaps because of other things, I have a fondness for the two of you that stretches beyond my honor. And so, although my honor and fondness says that I must deliver you out of the hands of danger, I know you well enough to know that you will persevere in finding Baraghosa." He paused. Looking sidelong to Jasen again, he said, "Am I correct in this?"

Jasen nodded again. "Yes."

"Then I wish to see that you are delivered safely. I can entrust many hands in doing this, but none moreso than my own."

"So you're endangering yourself, and everyone on this ship," Jasen said slowly.

"To take you to Baraghosa," Burund finished. "That is correct."

Jasen did not know what to say. The best he could manage was, "Thank you." It sounded poor, coming from his lips.

"You are most welcome, Jasen."

The sea churned. Waters broke against the *Lady Vizola's* hull.

How Burund could navigate in this fog, Jasen did not know. Compasses and sextants and an experienced nose for it, probably.

He asked, "Are these waters really cursed?"

"I have heard it said so," said Burund. He rolled his shoulders in a lazy shrug. "Ships stray too close to the shore and never return. Stories, perhaps."

Perhaps.

They would only know by sailing on, deeper into the murk.

By midday, it was so thick that it was nigh impossible to see one end of the *Lady Vizola* from the other.

By the afternoon, the fore and aft decks could not be seen from each other's respective doors.

Visibility almost nonexistent, practice had to be cut short. There was no telling who might shamble out of the mists at the precise moment Huanatha or Longwell struck.

Jasen was not sure how to feel about the respite. His body was tiring again. Days of this had built him up. This time, he felt he had acquired information that might actually be useful in stopping Baraghosa. It was imperative he continue to practice—especially as, now the isle drew nearer, his antsiness had started once again to grow. Sitting still was harder than it had ever been.

He was sweating, though, and so he sat, knees clasped to his chest. His fingers were laced, but he fidgeted.

Kuura laid his axe down beside him. "I will be glad of the day I do not have to wield this thing again."

Huanatha swore in her own language.

Kuura barked a laugh. "What? I long to be rid of it!"

"You fight like a warrior," Huanatha answered. "It is a disservice to your strength that you wish to put down your weapon when you might fight for great justice for the rest of your days." She stabbed at the heart of an imagined man lunging for her. "That is the highest honor a man or woman can achieve."

"I am no warrior," Kuura chuckled.

Huanatha leveled her blade at him. "Then why are you here?"

Kuura's smile faded. Looking down into the folded fabric of his shirt, he said, "I have been with Shipmaster Burund for a long time—a very long time. He took a chance on me, many decades ago, and I … I failed him. I will not fail him again."

Huanatha sneered. "As I thought." And she went back to her strikes and swings with Tanukke. "Your sense of honor is faulty, Kuura of Nunahk."

He did not say anything. In the absence of a reply from him, Alixa said, "Why are you here, Huanatha? To be queen again?"

"Baraghosa has taken much from me, crown included," Huanatha spat. "He has sown discord in my country, among the people I love most in this world." She swiped Tanukke through the air, teeth gritted—this time, her invisible foe was not a generic target, but Baraghosa himself. "My war with Baraghosa is personal. And this time, when we do battle … things will be different." Another strike.

"Different how?" Alixa asked.

"One—" she struck again, in emphasis, "—we are prepared. Two—" another blow with Tanukke, "—I have seen the way he fights, through watching you all do battle with him, and myself.

"And three," she finished, swinging Tanukke from low, into an arc that brought it up and over her head, as if she had cleaved a man in two from between his legs to the top of his skull. "Though Baraghosa has great power, so too do we." And she looked to Longwell, who rested against the mast, one hand on his spear.

The mists on the eleventh day were no worse. Nor were the waves, breaking on the side of the ship. If anything, they softened as afternoon drew into evening—though it was difficult to say for sure, as the darkness of the fog made discerning daylight hours troublesome. The fog did seem to be shifting when the light was fading. With barely any light left at that time, though, Jasen could not ascertain if this was the case for very long.

He slept fitfully, worried that they'd overshot the isle of Baraghosa, if indeed the mist was clearing.

Then, on the twelfth day, they saw it.

26

Luukessia and Chaarland had been enormous lands, rendered small to Jasen only by a combination of his proximity to the sea and, in Luukessia's case, a lifetime of inaccessibility. Both lands were grand things though, and he had come to understand that as both slipped out of sight, spread across the entire horizon as the *Lady Vizola* sailed in or away.

The isle of Baraghosa, on the other hand, was so minuscule it could fit into the port at the Aiger Cliffs with room to spare.

It rose between the tenuous mists that clutched the surface of the sea. A jagged crag of a rock, it appeared to have been hewn from the night itself. No green adorned it, not anywhere that Jasen could see; it was black like coal, or like the eyes of a scourge.

The island rose like a mountain. The base of it flared out, like the jagged petals of an onyx flower.

A crude dock was constructed where one of those jags reached out for the water.

Tethered to it was a small black boat.

So Baraghosa had arrived here first—as expected. But that he was still here—that was what caused Jasen's stomach to tighten into a knot.

And there was only one place upon the island that Baraghosa could have gone.

Inland some way, two, perhaps three miles of semi-treacherous climbing, was a spire. Not quite as dark as the island's small mountain, it rose like a pencil stood on its end. Heavy stones bore small, slitted holes for windows, through which Jasen supposed an archer could make a stand against an oncoming wave of enemies. There appeared to be seven floors in all, though perhaps there were more; from so far away still, it was a challenge to pick out the windows as it was, let alone accurately count them.

The top of the spire was a squat point. The building was thicker beneath it, by just a fraction. Squinting, Jasen thought he could *just* make out a stone barricade running around it. A walkway of some sort, he presumed.

The island bore nothing else.

So that spire—that was where they would find Baraghosa.

Burund watched. Jasen and Alixa were on the top deck with him, joined by Scourgey, who watched from beside Jasen's hip. Her bulk leaned gently into him. He'd given her one idle pat on the head, but no more.

Huanatha, Kuura, and Longwell looked out too, on the other side of Burund. A handful of crew joined them. They arrayed upon the deck, talking in low murmurs which Jasen could not understand.

The gist, though, he could make out:

this was a cursed place—and they were both frightened and awestruck to have come here.

"You have your sorcerer," said Burund grimly.

"Unless he has fled," Alixa murmured.

"He won't have," said Jasen. To Burund, he said, "Thank you—for bringing us. For endangering yourselves."

Burund nodded. "We are fortunate not to have incurred his wrath." With a sidelong look, he added, "I trust that you will slay him between yourselves, and ensure a safe passage from this place too."

"We will have his head," Huanatha growled. "I will part it from his shoulders myself. Tanukke will be stained red with his blood."

Longwell said, more calmly, "We will see to it that Baraghosa does not set even a foot beyond his tower ever again."

If Burund had his doubts, he did not let on. Instead, he said, "I will wait at the dock. But do not tarry. When the evening slips to night, I will have no choice but to raise the anchor and to leave this place behind." He finished, "We will not be back."

A full day to slay Baraghosa.

It would, Jasen hoped, be many hours more than they needed.

The *Lady Vizola* crept in toward the dock. The island became only more frightful as it neared. The rock was madly twisted. It looked as though a giant had upheaved a mountain and wrung it in his fists for hundreds of years, contorting it in every direction—or, where the rock flared out into dagger-sharp jags, as though magma had been poured into the water from a great height, and cooled into rock as it sprayed and rebounded.

The dock was tiny. Baraghosa's boat took up most of it, so the *Lady*

Vizola had to dock edge-on to the wooden jetty.

"He is not visited often," Kuura remarked as the ladder was thrown down.

"Nor shall he be again," said Huanatha.

They descended, the five of them. Scourgey leapt off the boat as Jasen was clambering down the ladder. The heavy thump seemed to fill the air with a momentarily more pungent blast of that deathly scent that hung around her ... although, today, Jasen barely acknowledged it. Another smell lingered in the air, like something hot and sweet and sticky had been cooked to the point of burning, and then long, long past it.

Burund looked down at them from the deck when they had all disembarked. "Good luck," he said.

"We need no luck, Burund," said Huanatha. And she turned, stalking down the dock and inland with no further farewell.

Kuura hesitated a moment, apparently caught between following Huanatha and bidding his shipmaster a (temporary, if all went to plan) goodbye. His shame won out; rather than addressing Burund directly, he lifted his axe and nodded at the ground, then turned and made his way down the dock.

"Till our return," said Longwell.

Jasen and Alixa were left.

Jasen searched for words. Something about this felt very ... final. But it would not be, he reminded himself. The five of them would defeat Baraghosa, and Burund would be waiting for them, atop the *Lady Vizola*, just a few short hours from now. Maybe as little as two! The spire would take forty, fifty minutes to reach at most. With their practice this past week, their experience in battling Baraghosa once, and Longwell at their sides, the sorcerer's defeat would not be hard won.

Steeling himself in the certainty that they would be back, that he would see Burund again, he nodded. "See you," he said, lifting a hand.

When he was halfway down the dock, Burund called a last warning.

"Remember: I will wait until nightfall. I will not wait past that."

The rock was sheer. Up close, Jasen's impression that a giant had twisted it into its malformed shape only grew. It twisted chaotically in all directions. A rough path rose up to the spire. In some places, it was smooth and their passage was simple. In others, the rock contorted dangerously, so they had to pick their steps carefully. It twisted and turned as it wound around, so if Jasen looked backward, only half the time during that first mile could he see the dock and the *Lady Vizola*.

After a sudden turn, hard right, the ship was blotted from sight. No matter how often Jasen looked back, the landscape did not permit it to reappear.

The spire loomed. Rising skyward like a specter, it became bigger as they gradually grew nearer.

As they did, Jasen picked out Baraghosa's lights. They drifted around the roof of the structure, dancing lazily on a breeze softer than the sea winds blustering against his back.

As he watched those lights, the foreboding sense of dread in his stomach grew. It grew in all of their stomachs, he thought, as few words passed between them.

And then they were at its foot.

A heavy door made of dark wooden beams bolted together with dark steel bands stood ajar.

Longwell moved for it—

"Stop!" said Huanatha.

He paused.

"A trap has been laid," she said.

Longwell squinted.

So too did Kuura. "How do we pass it?"

Huanatha closed her eyes. "Give me a moment." She frowned, her look of concentration deepening over the course of a long moment.

When she opened her eyes, she said, "I will trigger it. Wait here."

She approached tentatively.

Jasen watched with his breath held as Huanatha reached the door. Planting one hand upon its surface, she gripped Tanukke's with the other, poised to draw it from the loop at her hip at a moment's notice.

She pushed, and the door opened in a slow yawn ...

When it would go no farther, there was silence but for the wind.

They waited.

After maybe ten seconds, Longwell grew impatient. "Time is wasting. We must—"

A gaunt, skeletal figure suddenly lurched from the darkness. Its face was long. Its eyes had clouded. Recessed into dark holes, they stared accusingly.

Its mouth hung open, jaw much too low.

Jasen shrieked—

It howled.

Longwell grappled to bring his spear around—

Huanatha was faster. "Begone, spirit," she hissed—and Tanukke swung through the air, carving upward in a fluid swipe.

The spirit was cleaved apart—and then it vanished in a sulfurous puff.

Kuura stared. "Any ... more?"

"No." Huanatha stowed Tanukke. "We are safe of Baraghosa's traps now."

Alixa asked, "How did you ...?"

"As I have said before," said Huanatha, "I am a shaman."

Longwell pursed his lips. "Magic again," he muttered. He brushed past and into the yawning door. "Can't get away from it, no matter how far I go."

Jasen braced for another ghostly vision. But none came, and so the rest of them followed suit.

Stairs led up immediately to their left. These followed the outer wall, and by the look of the room immediately before them, ran alongside vast chambers that spanned the full width of each floor. Wide open except for a pair of columns rising to east and west, this bottom one was empty.

"He is above," said Huanatha.

"Do your spirits tell you that, too?" Alixa murmured.

"They tell much," said Huanatha, but no more.

"Ancestors, she's like Vaste." Longwell huffed, drawing a strange look from Huanatha. He passed, clambering up the stairs. "Hurry your footsteps. I have a debt to settle."

"So too do I, dragoon," Huanatha said.

"And me," Jasen muttered.

They climbed.

Their footsteps echoed in the silence. Any hope of surprising Baraghosa vanished as the five of them, plus Scourgey, clambered up flight after flight. If not their footfalls, Baraghosa would surely hear the heavy clunking of Longwell's armor. Jasen tried to tell himself that the element of surprise did not matter; not with another great warrior on their team, and more experience now for all of them. But his fears would not be assuaged.

Worse: that fatigue started once more to creep in. It was an old, familiar thing now—and as Jasen clambered up the fifth flight of steps, his tunic gripping to his back where he was sweating, he dimly puzzled at why he should be so exhausted so easily, now.

At the bottom of the sixth flight, purple mist rolled down the steps.

"Found you," murmured Longwell. And without a backward look, he began mounting the steps two at a time.

Jasen swallowed against the lump in his throat.

This was it. The time had come.

Alixa reached out for him, caught his wrist. She squeezed it—to be comforting, perhaps. He was not sure; when he glanced over, she would not look at him. Instead she glared at the top of the stairs, where the purple fog was thicker. Her free hand frittered at her own belt for a dagger. A moment later, she had loosed him and was reaching for the other.

Huanatha followed Longwell—then Kuura.

Now Alixa.

Jasen and Scourgey were left.

Scourgey reached under his hand, like a dog forcing its master to pet it upon the snout.

She is with you, he thought of Huanatha saying.

It steeled him.

Gripping the hilt of his sword, he climbed, and Scourgey ascended with him, padding along at his side, all the way to the top and into the chamber.

Dense purple fog filled the chamber. It seemed to pour from a pewter pot, no larger than a tea kettle, that rested on a pedestal in the chamber's center. A bright, pulsing glow came from it. With each pulse, it breathed out another cloud of purple mist.

And in front of it, his back to them—stood Baraghosa. One hand raised, the cane in it, he was murmuring words Jasen could not pick out.

"Baraghosa," Longwell commanded. Leading the charge, he lifted his lance, tipping its pronged end forward. "Turn and look at me as I kill you."

The sorcerer pivoted.

"Oh." He looked upon them with only the faintest interest. "Visitors."

27

Longwell stalked in, his lance raised. "We shall be the last you ever see."

"Mm?" said Baraghosa. He barely glanced at Longwell as the dragoon crept around him to take up position on the other side of the room. So too did he ignore Huanatha and Kuura, stalking into their own places.

He had eyes only for Alixa … and Jasen.

"Hello again," Baraghosa greeted him. "Jasen, was it?"

"Don't you dare speak to him, you monster," Alixa growled. She covered Jasen's body with her own—though, half a head shorter, she did not offer much in the way of protection.

Baraghosa squinted at her. "That is not a very nice word for a child to bandy about."

"These are no children," Huanatha spat.

Baraghosa assessed quietly, in the purple mist enveloping him. Finally, he said, "No. Perhaps not."

"You are a monster," said Alixa. "A murderer." She tightened her grip upon her daggers. "You would have murdered him if you had the chance. Just like every person you took from Terreas."

"Terreas?" Baraghosa said distantly, as though recalling a place he might or might not have ever heard of—not a place he had buried under the rubble of a torn-apart mountain.

"*You know Terreas!*" Alixa shouted. "*Pityr! You took him from us LAST YEAR for seed!*"

"Pityr," Baraghosa repeated.

"*YES! PITYR!*" Brandishing her daggers, Alixa took a step forward. "*YOU TOOK HIM FROM ALL OF US. WHAT HAPPENED TO HIM?*"

Baraghosa stared at her, blankly, before answering. "He died."

It was so simple, and had been so obviously true ... and yet it landed like a pile of bricks upon Jasen's chest. It hit Alixa just as hard too, for she sagged backward as if struck. She made a choking sound.

Tears glazed her eyes. "You ... you ..."

"Yes, your friend is dead," said Baraghosa plainly. "I assume that is why *you* are here." To Jasen: "And you? What brings *you* back to face me again?"

"You destroyed Terreas," Jasen said.

For all the rage he had had over these past weeks, his voice came out strangely flat.

But then, his rage had changed, had it not? That first night, on the clifftops, it had come explosively. Now it had settled into something colder. Still strong, but he could control himself now, the way he could control the swings of his blade. And control them he would—when the time was right. Not a moment sooner.

"Terreas," Baraghosa said dimly.

"Clear your ears out, phantom," Longwell commanded. "You know of it. You know *much*, don't you?"

Baraghosa ignored him. "I am listening, child. Go on."

Jasen swallowed. Clenched his teeth. Maybe there *was* still a boiling edge to his rage. He fought to temper it, hold it back.

"You destroyed Terreas," he repeated—slow, not only so the sorcerer comprehended it, but so his anger and his hatred did not spill out of him when he still needed to keep it at bay. "You tore open the mountain because we did not accept your deal, and buried our village."

"You're a *MURDERER!*" Alixa shrieked.

Her voice rebounded accusingly in the space.

Baraghosa blinked. "Terreas is gone?"

"Don't play games, magician," said Huanatha. "You know this."

"I did not," said Baraghosa. And he turned back to Jasen, looking—almost *earnest* as his eyebrows came down and he frowned at him. "You have come for me, left your lands, crossed the seas, because of *that?*"

"I know you did it," Jasen said through clenched teeth.

"I did not," Baraghosa answered.

Alixa: "*LIAR!*"

Scourgey growled from her ankles.

"I did not," Baraghosa repeated. "Power over volcanoes ... I have no such thing ... not at the present moment, anyway ..." He shook his head, as if coming back to himself. "Terreas. Gone. A shame, but no great loss there, I suppose—"

Alixa howled with rage. She lurched forward—

Jasen grabbed her by the wrist, pulled her back.

"THAT'S MY FAMILY!"

But again, Baraghosa shook his head.

"You are a vile man," said Kuura. "A vile, despicable man."

Baraghosa said something in Kuura's native language—

Kuura's mouth fell.

Huanatha spat something back.

Baraghosa only smiled.

"And you," he said, turning to face Longwell. "You have joined this band of misfits. To what end?"

Longwell answered, "You destroyed my boat."

"You tried to follow me."

"You should not have tried to escape Reikonos," Longwell rumbled back.

"Reikonos …" Baraghosa sighed. "I did no wrong there."

"You were held to account—" Longwell started.

"For my father's sins."

Baraghosa's eyes glittered. His face parted in a grin—a ghastly, terrifying grin, the sort found only in the darkest of nightmares. "Now, though … I plan to commit sins of my own," he said, waving at the pedestal just beside him. "Right now, in fact."

Baraghosa lifted his cane—Jasen gripped the handle of his sword— and he slammed it into the bricks at his feet.

A concussive blast of energy ripped through the air, and slammed Jasen in the chest just as he took his first step into battle.

28

Jasen was rattled by the blast. He shook his head to clear the cobwebs—

Already, Huanatha had pressed in. She sailed forward, Tanukke swinging—

Kuura followed suit a moment later.

If they had been in perfect time, Jasen believed Baraghosa might have been felled that moment. But the slight pause between them gave the sorcerer a fraction of an instant to deflect the attacks one by one.

He flung up his cane, whirling toward Huanatha. Tanukke and cane met, clanging as though steel rung against steel.

He thrust up, forcing her backward—

Then he spun to Kuura. Instead of meeting the axe, he thrust out with the cane—and a blast of power spat from its end. Hitting Kuura hard in the chest, he yelled as it tossed him backward, end over end.

Huanatha was already coming back in. She swiped, low—

Baraghosa stepped over the blade as if he were a child jumping a length of rope. Then he hit the cane against the stone underfoot, between himself and Huanatha. A wave of invisible energy rolled at her, hitting her feet. She staggered back, almost toppling—

And then Longwell surged in.

Every moment Jasen had imagined Longwell flying into the fight with Baraghosa—and he had done so, every night upon the sea between the Aiger Cliffs and this cursed isle—he had pictured the same swipes and thrusts that he had watched Longwell perform upon the *Lady Vizola's* deck. They were precise, powerful blows—

But those practiced blows that were nothing compared to this. Longwell moved as a literal *blur*. He sped forward in an instant, like a man flung by a cannon. His lance cut through the air—

Baraghosa sidestepped, barely in time.

A harried look crossed his face, the slightest flare of his temper.

Hope exploded in Jasen's chest.

Longwell turned—

Baraghosa struck out with his cane.

A blast hit Longwell, knocking him back—

But he hardly stumbled. Where Huanatha and Kuura and Jasen and Alixa and Scourgey had all been tossed easily aside by Baraghosa's attacks, Longwell endured it.

He gripped his lance and pushed forward again.

Baraghosa dodged.

Huanatha flew in again, swinging high with Tanukke.

Baraghosa lifted his cane to meet the strike—and he did—but the movement was spastic, sudden, without precision.

We can do this, Jasen thought. *We can beat him…!*

Longwell thrust out with his lance—

Baraghosa deflected with a blow of power from the end of his cane. The lance's tip was thrust out of its path—

Kuura blundered in. He had the axe raised high. A war cry came from his lips—

Baraghosa blasted him away again—

Already Huanatha was sailing in again.

He met her blade—

She cut in low instantly. Baraghosa dodged back, jerking a foot out of the way—

She swept in again.

He twisted out of the way of Tanukke's razor-sharp edge.

He thrust out his cane. A blast of energy hit Huanatha side-on. She was punched backward by one shoulder—

Now Scourgey leapt into the gap between them. Carving a hole through the fog behind her, she sailed, a perfect black silhouette against the pulsing light in the middle of the room—

Baraghosa smacked at her with his cane. But with so little time to force her away from him, instead of blasting Scourgey with an invisible shot of energy, the cane made contact. It must have lost some of Baraghosa's power, for although Scourgey was pushed out of the air, she landed only a few feet away.

Scrabbling quickly to her feet, she bared her fangs—

"Damned scourge," Baraghosa murmured. He thrust out with the cane, and

Scourgey jerked backward as though she had been kicked in the face. She howled—

"*NO!*" Alixa roared. And she flew into battle, her daggers raised—

Baraghosa twisted toward her. His eyes widened momentarily.

The cane lifted—

Then Longwell was flying back toward him. "*YOUR DAYS OF HARMING CHILDREN ARE DONE!*"

Baraghosa sidestepped, to be met by Huanatha again, on one side, Tanukke cleaving through the air—

He dodged that too—

Then Kuura came in again, swinging for Baraghosa's guts with his axe—

"Meddlesome man," Baraghosa muttered. He jabbed out with the cane twice. The first blow knocked Kuura backward, stalling his momentum.

The second hit him like an uppercut to the jaw. He yelled, arcing high overhead—

"*CRUEL SORCERER!*" Alixa cried.

She thrust out with her daggers—

Baraghosa turned to her. The cane lifted again—

This time it was Jasen who surged in. Drawing his sword high, he sprinted hard at Baraghosa. He was aiming not for the sorcerer's head, or neck, or heart, but instead his hand, with its horribly knobbled knuckles and fingers which were far too long. He would slice it off, parting him from that damned cane—

Huanatha swung in again too.

Baraghosa's eyes flared. A moment of panic registered upon his face—

Then he slammed his cane to the brick underfoot.

A pulse of power exploded from it, rebounding outward. Jasen was thrown backward. Alixa sailed too, shrieking—

He crash-landed near the steps,

blinking back stars—

"*Do not touch that!*"

Whose voice was that?

For a second, Jasen was sure that it was his father's.

But that was only where something had rattled loose inside of him. He rose to find that it was Longwell who had shouted. At the chamber's edge, he was pushing into motion once more, becoming a blur as the lance stretched out for Baraghosa—

—who was reaching for the pewter pot within the center of the chamber.

He gritted his teeth. Braced.

Then he stepped sideways.

Longwell had pre-empted him, though. He changed course at the last moment—and Baraghosa gasped, eyes and mouth wide, like the specter he had summoned to defend his spire in case of intrusion—

He thrust out with his cane. That movement, too, was a blur—

It crashed into Longwell's back.

There was an almighty *CRACK!*, as though lightning had struck within the chamber.

Longwell sailed clear across the room—

He slammed headlong into the western column—and fell, slumped so that he was half-sitting.

He did not move.

"Longwell!" Jasen cried.

He rose—

Baraghosa rounded on him. "Cease this, boy." He jabbed at him with the cane, and

Jasen sailed backward, slamming the wall.

Alixa sprinted for him, daggers raised again. "*NOT MY COUSIN!*"

Baraghosa gritted his teeth. He lifted the cane—and as though she were suspended on strings, Alixa was lifted too. Her body went rigid, as though ropes bound it—

"Leave her alone!" Kuura boomed.

He sailed in again—

But Baraghosa said, "You are too old and too tired for this." He swung his cane around to meet Kuura's axe. It caught in the point between its two heads—

Then he smiled, the grin of a monster. Kuura's eyes went wide—

Then Baraghosa pushed.

A blast of energy threw Kuura back. He spun, end on end through the air, over Jasen's head—then slammed against the wall and fell down upon the stairs.

Like Longwell, he did not move.

Alixa still hung. Utterly petrified, her face was a mask of terror. Her knuckles had gone white, clutching her daggers by the handles. But none of her fear could slip past her lips; an invisible binding seemed to cover her mouth, too.

"Meddlesome, all of you," said Baraghosa. He glanced sidelong at the pewter pot. The pulses of light were farther apart now. It still coughed intermittent bursts of purple vapor, but the mist had mostly dissipated from the chamber. With Baraghosa's focus elsewhere, the spell upon the pedestal was no longer belching enough cloud to rejuvenate the fading fog.

"Leave her alone," Jasen said. He approached slowly, sword raised.

"*No.*" And with another thrust of his cane, Jasen was done away with; he careened backward, landed in a heap. Pain erupted through him—pain, and a wave of exhaustion that did not pass.

"Do you know," said Baraghosa to Alixa, "how easy it would be to destroy any of you? It would be very simple—very simple indeed. Why, just like … pulling a string."

He lifted a finger … and Alixa's left arm rose with it, exactly as though he controlled it. It rose and rose, until her fist was level with her face—and then it twisted, so the dagger she held there was pointed down … then angled … and then her arm descended, under Baraghosa's control, so the tip of the blade rested against her stomach.

She stared in horror, still unable to move.

"I could do it, you know," said Baraghosa. "Easily."

"No," said Huanatha. "You could not."

And she struck out with Tanukke, from behind him, where she had snuck—

Baraghosa roared as the blade cut through his dark jacket, carving a gash into his shoulder. He threw out a hand, a true spasm this time. Alixa was loosed—she was thrust upward, and slammed the ceiling, then the floor—

Jasen cried, "*ALIXA!*" He sprinted for her—but he was tired, so tired, and his steps were heavy—

He fell at her side.

Blood spilled from her head.

He reached out—

Baraghosa's cane hit the ground. An explosive wave of energy carried through the room again. It hit Jasen hard in the face, forcing him back.

Huanatha's attack had drawn blood—but only that. He stared at the wound grimly in the moment's pause he had been granted by the impact of his cane.

Huanatha spat at him, from her place on the floor, "Another thousand of those is still less than you deserve."

Baraghosa turned to her. He drew in a long breath.

They stared at each other, hate burning in both their eyes.

Then Huanatha shoved onto her feet. She roared, a battle cry that would have made Kuura proud, and flung herself at him, Tanukke raised—

Baraghosa clenched his teeth, baring all of them. He drew up his cane—

Tanukke swung through the air—

Baraghosa met it with a blow like no other. Steel rang, a high-pitched clang that threatened to burst Jasen's eardrums—

Then Tanukke's blade exploded. Fragments showered in all directions.

Huanatha gasped, the shower of fragments slashing her face with dozens of small cuts, little drips of dark crimson rolling down from her cheeks and forehead. She seemed not to notice. "What—?"

"Begone, shaman," Baraghosa growled.

And he hit her in the chest with his cane.

The enormous force of it flung her backward. She made a strangled sort of noise, armor crumpling into her breast—

And then she hit the wall, and all was still.

Jasen panted, dazed.

They were down, all of them—Longwell, by the column; Kuura, his form slumped over the steps; Huanatha, her armor splintered and Tanukke shattered; Alixa, face-down on the stone, scarlet seeping about her head.

All five, and Scourgey too ... bested by Baraghosa.

Again.

All that remained of them was Jasen—Jasen, who was exhausted beyond belief, who could barely stand, after only the slightest exertion.

But he *could* stand, if he forced himself. Still there were energy reserves upon which he could draw. He could still raise his sword—could still drive it through Baraghosa's heart.

So he pushed himself up, from his cousin's side. His body shook under the strain ...

Yet he rose.

The sorcerer looked down upon the body of Scourgey. She lay there in a crumpled heap. Dead? Jasen did not know. He hoped not—hoped none of them had died in this mad quest—but Huanatha's words rung out in his mind: Scourgey was with him until the last. She had known the choice she was making, in her strangely intelligent way. They all had known what they were walking into.

And he most of all.

He lurched toward the pedestal in the chamber's center. The purple mist breathing out of it had mostly dissipated now. Only a faint cloud was left, drifting by the ceiling. The liquid inside glowed with yellow light, as if part of the sun had been poured into the vessel. But even that, too, seemed dimmer somehow. Had they interrupted the spell long enough for it to wear off?

Or perhaps, a distant part of Jasen thought cynically, his vision was only failing.

Whether the spell remained at full strength, or it was dissipating—it was imperative Jasen stop Baraghosa.

So he took painful, tired steps. So little strength left in him ... but he moved, closing the gap between him and the pedestal, Baraghosa's power, waiting to be tapped ...

He was four feet from it when Baraghosa tapped his cane on the brick. The *click* sound that came from it was stark in the silence, now the battle was almost done.

"This," the sorcerer said slowly, "is all that remains to stop me." He turned, away from Scourgey—and those dull, dark eyes of his fell upon Jasen's face. "One dying boy?"

Jasen froze.

The question was wrought on his face, for Baraghosa nodded. "You heard me. You are dying. An illness grows within you. You won't last the year."

Dying? Illness?

Jasen stared. His mouth had gone dry.

Somehow, he croaked, "It's not true."

"Oh, but it is." Baraghosa began to amble toward him. He used his cane as a cane now, not a weapon. *Click ... click ...* The quiet between his steps was terrifically long—yet it filled with the sound of Jasen's heart, suddenly beating in a frenzy.

"It's why I chose you as my sacrifice, you see," said Baraghosa. "I sensed it within you ... the way your pet does." He waved a hand, backward, to Scourgey's limp form. "It ... clings to you, like a bad scent. To the scourge, perhaps it is. Bad meat. Unpalatable. Not worth pursuing. Perhaps that sense they have gave them other insight as well—perhaps the volcano brewing beneath Terreas was why they avoided it for all those long years. I didn't sense that one. But this I see clearly, the pall hanging over you ... it's death."

He was close now—close enough that Jasen could lunge, could stab out with his blade, and could slice those too-long fingers from his hands as Baraghosa gestured.

Yet he was frozen. Horror had overridden him. All he could do was stand. And stare.

"It lingers around you," said Baraghosa, "twisting ... spiraling." His fingers traced a contortion of darkness Jasen could not see. "You appear to be embraced by thorns. It grows over you now. Why, in just the few weeks since I set eyes upon you, when my trade was denied, it has grown incredibly fast. Around your chest—" He pointed, fingertip swirling. "Its tendrils snake ever nearer to your heart ... to your brain … I could show you, if you like."

"No." Another croak—one Jasen hardly heard.

"No?" Baraghosa nodded distractedly. "Of course … so few wish to see, after all. To look death in the eye … but you'll see it soon enough. Here the whisper of its footsteps in your waking mind."

Dying. Ill.

It could not be true.

And yet … all his fatigue these past weeks; the way he had struggled, when others had not.

When had it first manifested itself?

He recalled that climb up the pathway to the clifftops, how he had needed to pause to catch his breath, how he had toppled when the stress grew too much.

But that was not the first, was it? As if remembering a part of some other lifetime Jasen recalled that he had almost succumbed to exhaustion on the road between Wayforth and Terreas too. How had he justified it then? Poor sleep? Stress? Too little food?

Had there been earlier signs of this darkness growing within him?

He racked his brain for them—

And then the pewter pot behind him coughed. Pink fog spewed over its edge, one thick spurt of it that rolled over pedestal and onto the ground. It spread out, already thinning.

It brought Jasen back to the room. For, at this moment, this was all that mattered. Not death. Not illness. Not when he might have seen, how this might have been prevented.

The only important thing in the entire world was stopping Baraghosa.

Jasen steeled. Gripping his sword tightly, he turned back to the sorcerer.

His teeth clenched, bared.

Baraghosa lifted an eyebrow. "Why do you look at me as if I am a monster?"

"You're a murderer," said Jasen. "A monster. A stealer of children."

Baraghosa nodded. "I confess, I have done monstrous things, yes," he said, more to himself than to Jasen. "But I have made decisions to limit death. For example … all your friends here are alive." He swept a hand around the chamber, and the still—unconscious, if he was to be believed—bodies littered throughout it. "I have taken no lives in my action against you, even when my own was threatened. Twice now you have assailed me with your blades … and twice I have let you walk away, bruised but little worse for wear, when in return you would have bled me dry."

His gaze lingered on Jasen's sword ... and then fell, once more, upon Jasen's face.

Jasen took a breath.

"You believe me a monster," Baraghosa lamented—

And suddenly, in a flash, he was beside Jasen, the distance between them crossed in a blink. He gripped Jasen by the shoulders, tighter than a man of his frame should ever be able to grip. And his long face leered down into Jasen's, almost gaunt, ghastly and terrible, eyes dark and flat and so awful upon him—

"But I am not what you think," he whispered.

And before Jasen could gather his wits to raise his sword, Baraghosa shoved him aside—

He fell, feet tangling—he pivoted, rolling an ankle—

Baraghosa reached for the pewter pot.

Jasen's knees slammed the stone. Jarring pain shot through him.

At the same moment, the light in the chamber's center flared. As bright as a thousand suns, all brought to within kissing distance of the isle's shores, it was so blinding that it overloaded his sight and seemed then to spill over every other sense he possessed. His entire body screamed against it—

And then, as quickly as it had flared, it faded.

Jasen blinked. His senses came back, one by one.

He was on the stone floor.

His sword was gone.

Click ... click ...

And as his eyes finally were able to see again, that vibrant, multicolored after-image fading, he saw—

Baraghosa's back, retreating through the door, then down the steps of the spire ... and out of sight.

29

So he was dying.

He could not process it. Death—a chasm that he would slip into, in less than a year's time, never to return from.

It should have frozen him.

Somehow—perhaps in the same way Terreas's people had continued living their normal lives, even growing their population in the small niche they had been permitted to exist in—it only spurred him on. Expand his life and efforts to fill the space allotted. He had to keep moving, had to.

He was alive. All of them were.

And they must move—after Baraghosa, again. He had gone; the *click* of his cane had faded as Jasen lay here and tried to process this. Now there was only silence.

How long had he lain here?

He did not know. Too long, surely. If he were to put his face to one of the slitted windows, he would see neither of Baraghosa's trailing lights ... and if he could see the dock from here, he was sure that it would only be the *Lady Vizola* out there.

He hoped the ship was left untouched in Baraghosa's parting.

The part of him that had believed Baraghosa had destroyed Terreas, had killed his family ... that part was certain that Baraghosa *would* throw fire and fury at the *Lady Vizola*, for he was a spiteful, murdering beast.

Yet another voice had woken within him. And its murmurings ... Jasen was not sure what to make of them.

But he did have to move. This, he knew. So, slowly, he rose. His body ached. A deep fatigue had settled into his bones—like the thorns Baraghosa had mentioned, their roots pushing down, down into him, impossible to loosen.

Truly impossible, though?

This thought, he swept aside too. Healers were for another day. The only matter now was rising to his feet and pursuing Baraghosa once more. Now his spellcasting was complete, he was more dangerous than ever, and they could not allow this second failure to dissuade them.

He rose on shaky legs. Gathered up his blade—his grip was weak—and stowed it.

He surveyed his comrades.

Who to rouse first?

His heart said to go to Alixa, as he had when Baraghosa had tossed her so easily aside. Her or Scourgey. But he could do nothing for them—and in the aftermath of their first encounter with Baraghosa, atop the Aiger Cliffs, it had been Huanatha who had fashioned bandages for their wounds. So, mumbling an apology to Alixa and asking the ancestors to forgive him for bypassing his only remaining kin, he went instead to the blue-armored warrior.

The plating had been crumpled in around her chest. To Jasen, it did not look far enough to break ribs, but the armor did not appear to have done much to protect her right arm. The blast that had broken Tanukke a moment before hurling Huanatha backward had forced her arm around at an unnatural angle. Now it hung limp at her side, pointing the wrong way.

Jasen reached out—

Huanatha gasped as his fingers made the barest of contacts. Shuffling backward and away from him, she said, "Do not touch it!"

"S-sorry," he wheezed.

Huanatha looked down at her arm. She winced—trying to move it, apparently, but it would not go. In spite of her cry to Jasen, she reached out with her free hand and cradled it.

She muttered something in her native language.

Jasen began, "Are you—?"

"Arm is broken," said Huanatha. Lines crossed her face. After a moment: "Goddess, this hurts."

"Is your chest …?"

Huanatha looked down at the impact point. It was driven in at least an inch. A spiderweb of lines ran throughout the buckled plates.

Frowning, she said, "It did the job it was supposed to. Need new armor though." A pause. She took a long breath. It rattled in her throat. "Constricted. Need this off. Help, will you?"

"Okay," said Jasen, nodding. "What do I …?"

"There are buckles." Huanatha eased over, and gestured toward a point along the side of her ribs where the plates all converged. "Reach under, and release them. Then lift it off."

Jasen obeyed. His fingers ferreted about, grasping at the underside of the armor. Confines were tight though—the armor was form-fitted, and gave him little maneuverability.

"I think I've—" he said, finding something—then losing it.

He bit off a curse.

Someone wheezed—a laugh.

It was Kuura. He lifted his head from the steps where he lay—and then coughed.

"Ooh, that is painful." He looked up. Eyes widening at the sight of Jasen fumbling under Huanatha's armor, he said, "Am I interrupting something?"

"Cease your jesting," Huanatha growled. "My armor is damaged."

"So is your sword."

That was Longwell. He'd roused too. Beneath the column, he still half-sat in the position where Baraghosa had tossed him, looking almost casual rather than like a man defeated in battle. But his eyes had a distant look to them. His blinks took just a fraction too long. His pupils drifted. With effort, he forced his gaze upon Tanukke again—or at least the hilt, upon which only a jagged piece of metal remained. The rest of its fragments littered the chamber like the remnants of an exploded glass bottle.

"Tanukke, Blade of the Victorious." Huanatha considered what remained of it sadly. "She has served me well." Then, a moment later: "Baraghosa will pay for this," she growled.

"The sorcerer," said Longwell, as if remembering. "We lost?"

"His body does not lie before us," said Huanatha.

Longwell closed his eyes. "Damn."

Kuura climbed onto unsteady feet. He braced against the wall. Then, moving for Jasen and Huanatha, he said, "Let me help with that."

He squatted at Jasen's side. Carefully, with large hands, he braced Huanatha by her ribcage and the upper portion of her back. She grunted, sucking in haggard breaths as Jasen fought to find the buckle, whilst at the same time assessing Kuura's injuries. He looked the best of them; no bloodied cuts or scrapes, and nothing bent out of shape.

Alixa moaned.

Jasen's head snapped around, Huanatha immediately forgotten.

"Go, boy," said Longwell, pushing himself up too now. "I'll assist with the armor."

216

Jasen scurried off to her—although in his state, a "scurry" was at best a quick stagger, not only chasing Alixa but also his center of gravity, which was determined to stay a half-step ahead of him.

He landed hard at Alixa's side.

"Alixa," he murmured, hands on her. He rolled her over—

She groaned. "Ow, ow, ow …" Her face screwed up. It was very white—whiter still, perhaps, for the blood smeared down her face and which still oozed from her forehead. How much she had lost, Jasen did not know. The puddle was small … but it had leaked into gaps in the brickwork. Perhaps a half-pint of it was gone. Not enough to endanger her—but gruesome nonetheless.

"It's okay," said Jasen.

"It hurts …" Alixa raised a hand to her head—

Jasen caught it. "Don't."

She looked at him with wide eyes near panic. Then her eyes shifted around—and found the blood pooled under her.

Now she seemed to grey.

"It's okay," said Jasen. "You're okay. It's just a little cut. Huanatha can—she can patch it up."

She closed her eyes, breathing heavily. But she nodded … and though she gripped Jasen by the forearm, so tight that she could stab crescents into his skin even through his clothes, she allowed him to sit her up, and then begin to wipe away the blood upon her face.

When Huanatha had been stripped of her armor, she joined Alixa's side and shooed Jasen out of the way.

"The wound is not so very deep," she said. "For now, I can bandage it. We will have to return to the ship for it to be stitched, though."

"Stitched?" Alixa asked, voice rising.

"She doesn't like blood," said Jasen.

Alixa said, "I don't like the thought of a *needle* being—"

Huanatha cut her off before she became too shrill. "No one does. In life, though, sometimes we must endure things we do not wish to. Kuura? A bandage, if you please."

Kuura ripped off a strip of his tunic. Grinning, he said, "My taste in fashion has done us well, yes?"

As Alixa let Huanatha bandage her head—quite roughly; her bedside manner left a little to be desired—she said, "How is Scourgey?"

"I believe she will walk again," said Kuura from beside her. He ran a gentle hand down the scourge's shoulders. She whimpered softly. Lying almost in the same position she had landed, she looked as though her body had given out, and she was only inches from dying. Perhaps, Jasen thought with a stab of guilt, she was. "I would like to look at her more closely aboard the *Lady Vizola*."

"Is this where we are going?" asked Longwell.

"For now," said Huanatha.

"And Baraghosa?"

Huanatha turned a hard eye to Jasen. "What happened to him?"

"He got away," Jasen said simply. It was the truth, but the omission of their final conversation made him feel as though he were telling a lie.

"He accomplished his spellcasting?" Longwell asked. He strode for the pewter pot in the center of the chamber. His body moved stiffly.

"Yes," said Jasen.

Longwell looked sourly into the pot. Empty—no light, no purple fog, nothing. "Gone," he muttered.

"To what end?" asked Kuura.

The question was posed to no one—yet Jasen felt as if he must provide the answer. "I don't know," he said.

"What he has done has left traces," said Huanatha. "It will take some time, but I believe ..." She closed her eyes. "We might yet track him."

"Then we track him," said Longwell instantly.

Kuura said, "First, we should report to Shipmaster Burund."

Right. The *Lady Vizola*. They had injuries to patch up before leaving off ... though, Jasen thought, Burund might not wish to chase Baraghosa a second time over these seas.

30

The rain came down.

"I will follow him," said Longwell. "Whether any of you joins me, I will follow." Grinding a fist into his open palm, he muttered, "This debt will not be left unpaid."

They were on the way back to the dock.

Every step, Jasen's heart lurched. They could not see the *Lady Vizola* from here; the rock rose in jagged waves that blocked it, and much of the surrounding sea, from view.

What Jasen could see were dark stormclouds.

"We will follow," said Huanatha, determination in her voice. "All of us."

Kuura was more balanced: "You cannot speak for all—"

Huanatha rounded on him, nostrils flaring. "Backing out now, are you, Kuura of Nunahk?" Before he could answer, she made a cutting motion with her hand. Teeth bared like a wolf's, she said, "I believed you a fine warrior, dedicated to doing what is right. You are hurt the least of us—and you wish to fall out of this fight?"

"I am saying no such thing," said Kuura quickly. If he had not been carrying Scourgey upon his shoulders, he might have thrown up his hands in surrender. "I just mean, yeh cannot speak for everyone. The children—"

"Are just as determined and dedicated to honor!"

"Let them have their own say," said Longwell, words measured.

So Huanatha rounded on them now, too. "Well?" she demanded.

Jasen opened his mouth—

Yet Alixa was first to answer.

"We cannot let him go now," she said. "I cannot." Shaking her head, she added, "Baraghosa killed our countrymen. He must pay for that."

Longwell nodded.

Huanatha looked satisfied at Alixa's answer. Still, a slight moue remained as she turned to Jasen. "And you?"

For once, the answer was not immediate. That little voice that had made itself known in the chamber, after Baraghosa's departure—it came back, whispering doubt. For though he was certain that the sorcerer was a cruel man who must be stopped—and he was; he had confessed that he planned sins of his own—the pushing force behind Jasen had changed somewhat. Because, in spite of himself, Jasen believed him when he said he had not had a hand in the destruction of Terreas.

Just as he believed it when Baraghosa told him that he was dying.

Yet Huanatha was fierce, and her wrath not a sort Jasen wished to incur. So he said plainly, "I will follow him." She nodded, her lips tight, and resumed their route down the treacherous path to the dock.

It was slick, and grew only slicker as they neared.

Every crag Jasen believed was the last, the one that would peel away and reveal the waters around the isle of Baraghosa to them—and the *Lady Vizola*, which he prayed desperately was still there, that Burund had not turned away at the sight of Baraghosa descending to the dock, finally extricating himself from this awful chase he had become a part of …

A bolt of lightning split the air.

A bolt of vibrant purple lightning.

Jasen stopped, stared—

"The ship!" cried Longwell.

And suddenly they were running. Kuura led the charge, then Huanatha and Longwell were passing him, he faster than her despite all the armor and the enormous lance he carried. Jasen beat feet to keep up, pushing himself as another peal split the air and the rain hammered down harder still. He threw a hand out as he passed by Alixa, catching her wrist. She was wrenched along in his wake, down the path they had picked out through the wretched, twisted onyx rock, and around a sudden fork, to see—

A pure white blast exploding upon the sea. There, the sea swelled, rising terribly high—

A wave surged to the shore.

It towered high above the *Lady Vizola*—Jasen realized that there was nothing they could do. Yet he roared anyway, crying out as if his voice could carry the full mile down to the dock, could warn them in time—

The water broke across the *Lady Vizola*.

For a fraction of a second, the boat held her place.

But the wave was too great. The boat was shunted, first into the dock—then the dock splintered, coming apart like a matchstick in a man's fingers—and the wood and boat flowed with it into the rock, that jagged, sharp rock—

"NO—!"

The *Lady Vizola* smashed into it.

Her hull broke apart—and then vanished almost immediately under the water.

Jasen stilled. He stared in horror as the sea churned. Another bolt of lightning ripped from the sky. This streak was bright green. It exploded on the sea, whirling the waters into a terrifying frenzy once more. The sound came a couple of seconds later—a world-ending *BOOM!* he had hoped never to hear again.

A burning scent came with it, overwhelming the salt in the air, cloying in Jasen's throat.

As the rain pelted down, he turned back to the dark spire looming above them.

Gooseflesh rose on his skin.

"No," he whispered, the word so terribly distant in his ears.

No one would come for them.

Here, on this forsaken island, trapped walled off by the rest of the world by strange fogs, and whispers of curses that kept even the most foolhardy away...

They were trapped.

Jasen and Alixa Will Return in

A HOME
IN THE HILLS
Ashes of Luukessia
Volume Three

Coming Mid to Late 2018!

Author's Note

Thanks for reading! If you want to know immediately when future books become available, take sixty seconds and sign up for my NEW RELEASE EMAIL ALERTS by visiting my website. I don't sell your information and I only send out emails when I have a new book out. The reason you should sign up for this is because I don't always set release dates, and even if you're following me on Facebook (robertJcrane (Author)) or Twitter (@robertJcrane), it's easy to miss my book announcements because...well, because social media is an imprecise thing.

Come join the discussion on my website:
http://www.robertjcrane.com!

Cheers,
Robert J. Crane

ACKNOWLEDGMENTS

Editorial/Literary Janitorial duties performed by Sarah Barbour and Nick Bowman. Final proofing was handled by the Jeff Bryan. Any errors you see in the text, however, are the result of me rejecting changes.

The cover was once more designed with exceeding skill by Karri Klawiter of artbykarri.com.

Thanks again to my co-author, an amazing life-saver who makes my life easier in pretty much every way in which his life intersects mine.

The formatting was provided by nickbowman-editing.com.

Once more, thanks to my parents, my in-laws, my kids and my wife, for helping me keep things together.

Other Works by Robert J. Crane

The Girl in the Box
and
Out of the Box
Contemporary Urban Fantasy

Alone: The Girl in the Box, Book 1
Untouched: The Girl in the Box, Book 2
Soulless: The Girl in the Box, Book 3
Family: The Girl in the Box, Book 4
Omega: The Girl in the Box, Book 5
Broken: The Girl in the Box, Book 6
Enemies: The Girl in the Box, Book 7
Legacy: The Girl in the Box, Book 8
Destiny: The Girl in the Box, Book 9
Power: The Girl in the Box, Book 10

Limitless: Out of the Box, Book 1
In the Wind: Out of the Box, Book 2
Ruthless: Out of the Box, Book 3
Grounded: Out of the Box, Book 4
Tormented: Out of the Box, Book 5
Vengeful: Out of the Box, Book 6
Sea Change: Out of the Box, Book 7
Painkiller: Out of the Box, Book 8
Masks: Out of the Box, Book 9
Prisoners: Out of the Box, Book 10
Unyielding: Out of the Box, Book 11
Hollow: Out of the Box, Book 12
Toxicity: Out of the Box, Book 13
Small Things: Out of the Box, Book 14
Hunters: Out of the Box, Book 15
Badder: Out of the Box, Book 16
Apex: Out of the Box, Book 18
Time: Out of the Box, Book 19
Driven: Out of the Box, Book 20* *(Coming June 1, 2018!)*
Remember: Out of the Box, Book 21* *(Coming August 2018!)*
Hero: Out of the Box, Book 22* *(Coming October 2018!)*
Walk Through Fire: Out of the Box, Book 23* *(Coming December 2018!)*

World of Sanctuary
Epic Fantasy

Defender: The Sanctuary Series, Volume One
Avenger: The Sanctuary Series, Volume Two
Champion: The Sanctuary Series, Volume Three
Crusader: The Sanctuary Series, Volume Four
Sanctuary Tales, Volume One - A Short Story Collection
Thy Father's Shadow: The Sanctuary Series, Volume 4.5
Master: The Sanctuary Series, Volume Five
Fated in Darkness: The Sanctuary Series, Volume 5.5
Warlord: The Sanctuary Series, Volume Six
Heretic: The Sanctuary Series, Volume Seven
Legend: The Sanctuary Series, Volume Eight
Ghosts of Sanctuary: The Sanctuary Series, Volume Nine
Call of the Hero: The Sanctuary Series, Volume Ten* *(Coming Late 2018!)*

A Haven in Ash: Ashes of Luukessia, Volume One *(with Michael Winstone)*
A Respite From Storms: Ashes of Luukessia, Volume Two
A Home in the Hills: Ashes of Luukessia, Volume Three* *(with Michael Winstone—Coming Mid to Late 2018!)*

Southern Watch
Contemporary Urban Fantasy

Called: Southern Watch, Book 1
Depths: Southern Watch, Book 2
Corrupted: Southern Watch, Book 3
Unearthed: Southern Watch, Book 4
Legion: Southern Watch, Book 5
Starling: Southern Watch, Book 6
Forsaken: Southern Watch, Book 7* *(Coming 2018!)*
Hallowed: Southern Watch, Book 8* *(Coming Late 2018/Early 2019!)*

The Shattered Dome Series
(with Nicholas J. Ambrose)
Sci-Fi

Voiceless: The Shattered Dome, Book 1
Unspeakable: The Shattered Dome, Book 2* *(Coming 2018!)*

The Mira Brand Adventures
Contemporary Urban Fantasy

The World Beneath: The Mira Brand Adventures, Book 1
The Tide of Ages: The Mira Brand Adventures, Book 2
The City of Lies: The Mira Brand Adventures, Book 3
The King of the Skies: The Mira Brand Adventures, Book 4
The Best of Us: The Mira Brand Adventures, Book 5* *(Coming 2018!)*
We Aimless Few: The Mira Brand Adventures, Book 6* *(Coming 2018!)*

Liars and Vampires
(with Lauren Harper)
Contemporary Urban Fantasy

No One Will Believe You: Liars and Vampires, Book 1* *(Coming Early 2018!)*
Someone Should Save Her: Liars and Vampires, Book 2* *(Coming Early 2018!)*
You Can't Go Home Again: Liars and Vampires, Book 3* *(Coming Early 2018!)*
In The Dark: Liars and Vampires, Book 4* *(Coming 2018!)*
Her Lying Days Are Done: Liars and Vampires, Book 5* *(Coming 2018!)*

* Forthcoming, Subject to Change

Made in the USA
Las Vegas, NV
13 February 2021

17610289R10128